44

P9-DNZ-295

PENGUIN TWENTIETH-CENTURY CLASSICS

THE NIGGER OF THE 'NARCISSUS'

Joseph Conrad (originally Józef Teodor Konrad Nałęcz Korzeni-
owski) was born in the Ukraine in 1857 and grew up under Tsarist
autocracy. His parents, ardent Polish patriots, died when he was a
child, following their exile for anti-Russian activities, and he came
under the protection of his tradition-conscious uncle, Thaddeus
Bobrowski, who watched over him for the next twenty-five years.
In 1874 Bobrowski gave in to his nephew's passionate desire to go
to sea, and Conrad travelled to Marseilles, where he served in
French merchant vessels before joining a British ship in 1878 as an
apprentice. In 1886 he obtained British nationality and his Master's
certificate in the British Merchant Service. Eight years later he left
the sea to devote himself to writing, publishing his first novel,
Almayer's Folly, in 1895. The following year he married Jessie
George and eventually settled in Kent, where he produced within
fifteen years such modern classics as *Youth*, *Heart of Darkness*, *Lord
Jim*, *Typhoon*, *Nostromo*, *The Secret Agent* and *Under Western Eyes*.
He continued to write until his death in 1924. Today Conrad is
generally regarded as one of the greatest writers of fiction in
English – his third language. He once described himself as being
concerned 'with the ideal value of things, events and people'; in the
Preface to *The Nigger of the 'Narcissus'* he defined his task as 'by the
power of the written word . . . before all, to make you *see.*'

Cedric Watts is Professor of English at the University of Sussex. His
books on Conrad include *Conrad's 'Heart of Darkness': A Critical and
Contextual Discussion* (1977), *A Preface to Conrad* (1982), *The
Deceptive Text: An Introduction to Covert Plots* (1984) and *Joseph
Conrad: A Literary Life* (1989). He has also edited *Joseph Conrad's
Letters to R. B. Cunninghame Graham* (1969), *'Typhoon' and Other
Tales* (1986), *Lord Jim* for Penguin Twentieth-Century Classics
(1986) and *'Heart of Darkness' and Other Tales* (1990), and has
written the Penguin Critical Studies on *Nostromo*, *Measure for
Measure* and *Jude the Obscure*.

THE
NIGGER OF THE
'NARCISSUS'

JOSEPH CONRAD

EDITED, WITH AN INTRODUCTION AND NOTES, BY
CEDRIC WATTS

PENGUIN BOOKS

PENGUIN BOOKS

Published by the Penguin Group
Penguin Books Ltd, 80 Strand, London, WC2R 0RL, England
Penguin Putnam Inc., 375 Hudson Street, New York, New York 10014, USA
Penguin Books Australia Ltd, Ringwood, Victoria, Australia
Penguin Books Canada Ltd, 10 Alcorn Avenue, Toronto, Ontario, Canada M4V 3B2
Penguin Books India (P) Ltd, 11, Community Centre, Panchsheel Park, New Delhi – 110 017, India
Penguin Books (NZ) Ltd, Private Bag 102902, NSMC, Auckland, New Zealand
Penguin Books (South Africa) (Pty) Ltd, 5 Watkins Street, Denver Ext 4, Johannesburg 2094, South Africa

Penguin Books Ltd, Registered Offices: 80 Strand, London, WC2R 0RL, England

First published 1897
Published as *The Nigger of 'Narcissus'/Typhoon and Other Stories* in Penguin Books
by arrangement with the Trustees of the Joseph Conrad Estate and J. M. Dent & Sons Ltd 1963
Published in Penguin Classics with Introduction, Notes and other editorial matter 1988
Reprinted in Penguin Books 1989

15

Introduction, Notes and other editorial matter copyright © Cedric Watts, 1988
All rights reserved

Printed in Great Britain by Antony Rowe Ltd, Chippenham, Wiltshire
Filmset in Monophoto Photina

Except in the United States of America, this book is sold subject
to the condition that it shall not, by way of trade or otherwise, be lent,
re-sold, hired out, or otherwise circulated without the publisher's
prior consent in any form of binding or cover other than that in
which it is published and without a similar condition including this
condition being imposed on the subsequent purchaser

CONTENTS

ACKNOWLEDGEMENTS AND EDITORIAL NOTES

I renew my debt to Alan Sinfield for general encouragement and for help with the proofs. I am also grateful to the staffs of Hofstra University Library and Sussex University Library. Articles which proved to be particularly useful were: Kenneth W. Davis and Donald W. Rude: 'The Transmission of the Text of *The Nigger of the "Narcissus"*': *Conradiana* V (1973), pp. 20–45; Donald W. Rude: 'Joseph Conrad, *The Nigger of the "Narcissus"*': *Joseph Conrad Today* V (1979), pp. 132–6; and Jakob Lothe: 'Variations of Narrative in *The Nigger of the "Narcissus"*': *Conradiana* XVI (1984), pp. 215–24.

When quoting texts, I have endeavoured to preserve any errors or idiosyncrasies that they contain, except that in a few cases, in the interests of clarity, I have supplied the emendations which are enclosed in square brackets. In quotations, a row of three dots (. . .) represents an ellipsis already present in the material being quoted, whereas a row of five dots represents an omission that I have made.

Those rules apply to the editorial matter. The rules for *The Nigger of the 'Narcissus'* and Conrad's 'prefaces' are given in the section of this book entitled 'Notes on the Text'. For the reasons stated in that section, the typographical conventions of the present text of the novel attempt to duplicate those of the first British trade edition (Heinemann, 1897).

This Penguin volume was prepared between 1985 and 1987.

ROUTE OF THE NARCISSUS
(based on the route-map corrected by Conrad in 1915)

INTRODUCTION

I

When I first read *The Nigger of the 'Narcissus'* I enjoyed its richness and thematic density; nevertheless, I grumbled to my teacher about its politically reactionary features. During subsequent years we sustained, intermittently, our discussion of the novel. At our last meeting, in 1964, the teacher lay dying in a hospital at Reading; he could not lift his head from the pillow but continued to defend Conrad in quiet, clear tones; and when I stood up to leave, he said: 'Remember Singleton. "He steered with care."'

Conrad dedicated his novel to the brilliant critic Edward Garnett. If this Introduction had been worth a dedication, it would have been offered to a conscientious teacher, Douglas Brown, whose quiet tones for me are mingled with the different voices of the text.

II

Conrad's first two novels, *Almayer's Folly* and *An Outcast of the Islands*, were distinctively sombre and pessimistic but in some ways cumbrous and laboured. The third novel, *The Nigger of the 'Narcissus'*, marked a dramatic shift in his evolution as a writer: it is richly graphic, indeed cinematic; scene after scene is colourful and vivid, and the observer's camera is active, probing and mobile; we share a voyage with a diversity of voyagers. The tale is densely textured, variously eloquent; thematically layered; pressing again and again towards symbolism. It imprints on memory a sequence of starkly lit images: Wait stepping out of darkness into the light on the quarter-deck; the ship gliding as a white pyramid through glowing mist; the storm scattering rainbows over the drifting hull; Singleton drenched at the wheel, his beard tucked under his top button; Jimmy dying in a cabin that resembles a silver shrine; the crew separating in the sunshine that floods down on the stained walls of the Mint. Conrad claimed in the Preface that his aim was 'before all, to make you *see*':

> That – and no more, and it is everything. If I succeed, you shall find there according to your deserts: encouragement, consolation, fear, charm – all you demand; and, perhaps, also that glimpse of truth for which you have forgotten to ask.

'Also that glimpse of truth for which you have forgotten to ask': the concluding emphasis there is important. By '*see*', Conrad means 'gain insight' and not merely 'behold the spectacle'. It's tempting to call the method of *The Nigger* impressionistic, because of the richly visual emphasis, the strongly scenic presentation; and Conrad well knew that impressionism was, as *The Review of Reviews* reported in 1895, 'the "new thing" in fiction'.[1] Partly as a result of the interest aroused by the Impressionist painters, numerous writers of tales, essays and poems were producing works which purported to be 'impressions' and which concentrated on the moment-by-moment impact of events upon the observer's senses. But Conrad's response to literary impressionism was a guarded one: he felt that it tended to yield results which, though vivid, were superficial. One leading figure was Stephen Crane, the American writer whose life was to be tragically short. Conrad sometimes spoke of 'mere Crane-like impressionism', remarking 'He is *the only* impressionist and *only* an impressionist';[2] but his friendship with Crane was warmly affectionate, and there is no doubt that Conrad had studied closely his great novel of the American Civil War, *The Red Badge of Courage*, which had been published in England by Heinemann in 1895. 'Read the *Badge*,' said Conrad to Cunninghame Graham. 'It won't hurt you – or only very little. Crane-ibn-Crane el Yankee is all right. The man sees the outside of many things and the inside of some.'³ When *The Nigger* appeared, a reviewer in *The Daily Telegraph* suggested that the novel's technique had been modelled on that of *The Red Badge of Courage*; and Conrad himself stated later:

> Stephen Crane dealt in his book with the psychology of the mass – the army; while I – in mine – had been dealing with the same subject on a much smaller scale and in more specialized conditions – the crew of a merchant ship, brought to the test of what I may venture to call the moral problem of conduct.⁴

So, if we seek one cause of that rapid development in colourful descriptive exuberance between *An Outcast* and *The Nigger*, it may perhaps be Conrad's study of Crane's war-novel; certainly, as Conrad noted, there are strong thematic resemblances. Crane dealt with the chastening entry of a group into the chaos of battle, an initiation by confusing ordeal into maturity; Conrad dealt with his crew's encounter with the threat from without – the storm that threatens to sink the *Narcissus* – and the threat from within – the subversion of solidarity, the danger of mutiny, met and overcome.

Other influences may have been exerted by Rudyard Kipling and William Ernest Henley; and both these may have helped to push the text's political implications more to the right than we might expect in a work by the author who was soon to publish *Heart of Darkness* and *Nostromo*. Conrad distrusted Kipling's jingoism but admired his technical accomplishments. In *The Nigger*, however, he comes closer than elsewhere to endorsing themes of which Kipling was a famed popularizer: the importance of the solidarity of people working as a team in a patriotic cause; the value of a stoical ethic of labour and duty; and the merit of ordinary men who, by doing the dirty work, know more of reality than do the gentlemen in remote offices who presume to legislate for all.⁵

One of Kipling's warmest admirers was W. E. Henley, poet and editor; and, as Conrad had hoped, while *The Nigger* was still being written Henley agreed to publish it in his magazine, *The New Review*. There were good literary reasons for Conrad's ambition to be published by 'that remarkable man',⁶ for during 1896 and 1897 the *New Review*'s contributors included Stephen Crane, H. G. Wells, Henry James (*What Maisie Knew*), Arthur Morrison (*A Child of the Jago*), Arthur Symons, Paul Valéry and W. B. Yeats. The magazine also featured various political commentators who echoed Henley's patriotic, royalist and imperialistic opinions. For example, in articles entitled 'Imperialism', C. de Thierry asserted that the Royal Pageant and the Diamond Jubilee celebrations of 1897 proclaimed the triumph of the British Empire, because now 'the stormy Atlantic, the illimitable expanse of the Pacific, the lonely waste of the Southern Ocean, are bridged by the fleets of English ships'. He continued:

> Time was when the Prime Minister represented England in the eyes of the world. But since the ship of State has come to be guided by a captain, whose master is a shifting majority, and manned with officers and a crew who scout obedience, the Councils of Europe, which trembled at the name of a Chatham, a Pitt, or a Canning, have learned to ignore their successors . . . . . The Crown is a quantity in European affairs as certain as the British Cabinet is uncertain. To ripe judgment, sagacity, and decision, the Queen adds an unrivalled knowledge of political history since the beginning of her reign . . . . . All the dominant races have, unconsciously, raised themselves a monument in the sands of time, but none a monument as noble and inspiring as the English. A world-wide dominion, whose foundations are laid deep in the national character, is an achievement of which the gods themselves might be proud.[7]

Some parts of *The Nigger of the 'Narcissus'* harmonized well enough with de Thierry's notion that the 'ship of State' needed a sagacious master who was not 'a shifting majority' and with Henley's conviction that socialism tended 'to weaken the fibre of men and destroy their individuality';[8] the narrative may have been inflected by Conrad's sense of the *New Review*'s patriotic readership; and the rhetorical passage in Chapter V which extols England as 'A great ship! . . . . . A ship mother of fleets and nations! The great flagship of the race' seems to echo the proud sentiments of Henley's popular ode, '*Pro Rege Nostro*', which invokes England as the 'Mother of ships whose might. . . . . Is the fierce old Sea's delight'.[9]

Conrad needed little prompting to offer tributes to his adoptive country: after the oppression which he had experienced in the Russian-dominated part of Poland, life in England was in various ways intellectually and culturally congenial to him; though an exile, he had found sympathetic friends – among them Edward

Garnett, G. F. W. Hope and Edward Sanderson. Furthermore, his admiration for the traditions of the British Merchant Navy was not merely a romantic appreciation of the calling and dangers of the sea, or of the long historic saga of adventurous trading, but was solidly based on his many years of work on sailing-vessels and steamships which had made the ethos of co-operative labour tangibly real and valuable to him. One of the main sources of *The Nigger of the 'Narcissus'* was, obviously, recollection: in April 1884 Conrad had joined the real *Narcissus* at Bombay as second mate, and after a stormy passage past the Cape of Good Hope she had reached Dunkirk in France on 16 October. For partly patriotic thematic purposes, the novel changes the place of landfall from Dunkirk to London. The fictional James Wait may have been based on the 35-year-old Joseph Barron, an able seaman who died during the voyage; and biographers have suggested that Donkin was based on another seaman, Charles Dutton, who, on the outward voyage from Wales to India, had been consigned to jail at Cape Town. The fictional Belfast may well have been engendered by James Craig, a sailor whose home was Belfast, and Archie by Archibald MacLean, aged 23, from Scotland.[10] Conrad affirmed, however, 'I do not write history, but fiction, and I am therefore entitled to choose as I please what is most suitable in regard to characters and particulars to help me in the general impression I wish to produce.'[11] Just as thematic co-ordination and symbolic intent have established a landfall at London instead of Dunkirk, so they have generated the Wait–Donkin relationship; and the more one reflects on the implications of the changes, the more it may appear that the primary source-material of *The Nigger* is a cluster of Conradian preoccupations with political and psychological subversion rather than any simple memorializing impulse. Indeed, so purposeful is the co-ordination that the obtuseness of some of the early reviewers seems almost incredible. Conrad was understandably perplexed when the anonymous reviewer in *The Daily Mail*, 7 December 1897, declared:

The tale is no tale, but merely an account of the uneventful voyage of the *Narcissus* from Bombay to the Thames. One of the ship's crew is an intelligent negro named James Wait. He lies in his bunk most of the voyage, and at last he dies and is buried at sea. This is positively all the story in the book. There is no plot, no villainy, no heroism, and, apart from a storm and the death and burial, no incident. The only female in the book is the ship herself, which Mr. Conrad describes lovingly and with an intimate know-ledge of seamanship unrivalled even by Dana or Clark Russell.

The one surpassingly good quality of this masculine narrative is the distinctness of Mr. Conrad's characterisation of old Singleton . . . . . and the rest of them. Their talk and their swearing, especially the latter, is absolutely natural. One only regrets that they never do anything else than their mere commonplace duties, and that they are not connected with a story.[12]

Conrad had vigorously anticipated such objections to 'mere commonplace duties' in the famous coda to his novel, the 'Author's Note' or 'Preface', which emphasizes the significance of 'obscure lives' among 'the disregarded multitude'. The reviewer was looking for conventional plotting of the kind to be found in W. Clark Russell's maritime novels – tales of beautiful heroines rescued from drifting hulks by heroic young sailors.[13] Conrad's customary proce-dure, on the other hand, was to take some of the ingredients of popular fiction (the treasure-quest in a jungle, a mutiny on the high seas) and to ferment them in a philosophically experienced intelligence, shifting the main interest from an intrigue between characters to a struggle between problematic principles: the dynamics of the plot now stemmed from its thematics. One central struggle in *The Nigger* is between conservative co-operation and subversive sympathy. On one side lie the stern but salutary tradi-tions of the Merchant Navy: respect for the hierarchy, duty, work and the team spirit; on the other side are disrespect for the hier-archy, fear, sloth and a sympathy which the text defines as vica-rious egotism or oblique self-pity, all of which may lead to anarchy and destruction. An obvious (if therefore inadequate) political view of the text would see as its intended ethical heroes the captain, his loyal mates, Singleton and the more stalwart members of the crew; as its 'heroine' the ship herself (for she is given an active ethical role); and as ethical villains James Wait (disruptively ambiguous, false, self-pitying, lazy), Donkin (selfish, anarchic, scheming, thieving) and those members of the crew who support them against authority. Probably the most severe aspect of the tale's conser-vatism is summed up in this narratorial comment on the crew's attitude to Wait: 'The latent egoism of tenderness to suffering appeared in the developing anxiety not to see him die.'[14] Whereas so many novels of the eighteenth and nineteenth centuries commended 'tenderness to suffering', *The Nigger of the 'Narcissus'* stresses that 'latent egoism': the crew's sympathy with the dying Jimmy is partly a vicarious self-pity. Those who are apparently ruthless (like Singleton, telling Jimmy to get on with his dying and to make less fuss about it) are thus true altruists, because their unsentimental concern for work and duty sustains solidarity and helps to preserve the ship and her voyagers; while those who seem most sympathetic to Jimmy are neglecting their duties and weakening the hierarchic order on which the general good depends. The general political implications of the voyage are clearly indicated. Donkin, who foments subversion by exploiting Wait's plight, is presented as a hypocritical spokesman of socialism; notions of trade unionism are rebuffed ('strike, boys, strike!' is the rallying-cry of the abortive mutiny); and the narrative even goes to the extreme of assailing Samuel Plimsoll and his followers, whose benevolent campaigns against exploitative ship-owners actually saved the lives of many seamen – the text indicts a 'Plimsoll man' as an interfering sentimentalist.[15] Plimsoll had collaborated with J. Havelock Wilson, leader of the National Amalgamated Union of Sailors and Firemen, and Conrad would have known that in the 1890s the Union had suffered a series of defeats in its struggle against the employers' Shipping Federation.[16]

The Nigger of the 'Narcissus' is predominantly secular (Podmore's religious fanaticism is satirized, and the text suggests that the heavens are empty and that life's meaning is 'wrung out' by men and not pre-ordained); but, as has been suggested elsewhere,[17] the novel also holds a covert plot which is 'metaphysical' and which, by sufficiently endorsing the sense of a supernatural hostility between Wait and the ship herself, offers mystical reinforcement to the tale's conservative elements.

III

The Nigger of the 'Narcissus' is the first of Conrad's major works; but the reader may detect various flaws ranging from the relatively small to the relatively large. In this section I discuss some possible criticisms.

(i) Descriptive excess?

In later works, and particularly after 1910, Conrad moved gradually towards a descriptive style that was lighter, more 'transparent', less conspicuously intense and energetic. In *The Nigger* there is a relentless descriptive energy which at times strains Conrad's resources. Occasional lapses remind us that he had not totally mastered the English medium: sometimes a Gallicism or archaism will intrude ('inabordable' for 'repellent', 'rumour' for 'murmur', 'balancing' for 'swaying'); and sometimes, in his bold attempt to offer a variety of accents and idioms, the dialogue will lapse into specious colloquialisms, offering spellings which suggest dialect but make no evident difference to the sound: 'speshul' for 'special', 'masheens' for 'machines', 'wimmen' for 'women', 'giv'' for 'give' and 'ov' for 'of'. Some descriptive passages modulate into 'Conradese': those habits of rhythm, syntax and diction which Beerbohm noted so acutely in his Conradian parody.[18] One kind of Conradese is the predictable or automatic placing of adjectival triplets after the noun, as in: 'a voice mournful, immense, and faint', or 'A sun enormous, unclouded, and red'; another is a facile or excessive simile-hunting, often linked to the pathetic fallacy of the animated inanimate: the sun declines low 'as if bending down to look into their faces', stars are 'more pitiless than the eyes of a triumphant mob, and as unapproachable as the hearts of men', and windows are 'as troubled and dull as the eyes of over-fed brutes'.

Nevertheless, although the energetic, self-aware, consciously wrought style occasionally becomes too conspicuous, as though soliciting inclusion in a Victorian anthology of 'fine prose', the text is predominantly an astonishing testimony to the mastery of the English language achieved by this Polish-born writer: there is a splendidly contrastive diversity of eloquence, from the quarrels of the seamen to the tumult of the storm, with notation of the absurd, farcical or nightmarish as well as of the philosophical implications of scene and situation. And our 'Notes on the Text' in this edition show how Conrad continued, over the years, to worry at details, pruning here and rephrasing there.

One such revision was a reduction in the blatancy of Donkin's over-aspirated cockney accent ('I ham a Henglishman, I ham', etc.). Perhaps Conrad sensed that the relentlessly derogatory presentation of Donkin is a flaw which betrays the novel's political tenor. The characterization is memorably vivid, but with the vividness of caricature. Donkin is so fiercely depicted as mean, vicious and predatory, a gutter-snipe, vulture or kite, as to reduce the plausibility of his subversive power over the crew; the reader may suspect that seamen so gullible as to be led astray by this blatantly sordid and rapacious character are scarcely worthy of the warm tributes that the narrator pays to his 'good crowd' of 'brothers'. The political animus directed against Donkin seems to be partly self-defeating: if he is indeed a grave threat, he should not be depicted as so ludicrously and patently contemptible. There is a related defect in the presentation of several subsequent Conradian villains: Cornelius and Brown (in *Lord Jim*), Nikita (in *Under Western Eyes*) and Jones, Ricardo and Pedro (in *Victory*) seem to have intruded from the world of theatrical melodrama.

(ii) Inconsistency of narratorial identity?

The narrator of the tale has a peculiarly protean identity. Sometimes he uses the pronoun 'I', and identifies himself as one of the seamen. Sometimes his pronoun is 'we': his identity merges with that of the crew. At other times he establishes a distance between himself and them: the men are 'they', not 'we'. And often his identity is the amorphous intelligence of the traditional 'omniscient narrator', with the power to roam the skies or to penetrate walls and skulls, recording the innermost reflections now of Wait, now of Donkin, now of Singleton. The different forms of narratorial voice and identity could be listed under pronominal headings, thus:

1. 'I': Personal recollection by a crewman who was there, involved in the action, but who is eventually left alone after the completion of the voyage.

2. 'We': Personal recollection by a crewman who was there, involved in the action, and who tends to identify himself with those seamen who were capable of being deceived or confused.

3. 'They': (a) Personal recollection by a crewman who was there, involved in the action, but who is now recalling the actions of others as he saw them.

    (b) Personal recollection by a crewman seeking a detached perspective.

    (c) Detached account by a reflective, but not necessarily omniscient, narrator.

    (d) Detached reflections and observations of an omniscient narrator.

    (e) Omniscient voice in lyrical interludes.[19]

There are affinities between 2 and 3(a), and the transition from 3(a) to 3(b) is frequently blurred. Some critics (notably Marvin Mudrick) have been troubled by the apparent inconsistencies in narratorial identity, while others share Ian Watt's opinion that Conrad is 'at liberty to use his pretended narrator in whatever way will best serve his turn'.[20] The latter opinion has the ring of civilized common sense but neglects an interesting oddity of this novel. *The Nigger of the 'Narcissus'* does generate, locally, a greater sense of narratorial inconsistency than do other Conradian texts, particularly in its alternation between 'we' and 'they' as the pronoun for the crew. The apparent inconsistency stems from complementary but partly conflicting narrative intentions. One intention is to dramatize 'from inside', as though autobiographically, the labours, struggles and uncertainties of the ordinary seamen. Another intention is to offer a richly interpretative 'overview' of the voyage and its symbolic significance. In the former case, the narrator enacts restricted knowledge; in the latter, he enacts extensive knowledge. Subsequently, Conrad's most distinctive solution to the problem of their reconciliation was the use of Marlow as a narrating character; for Marlow could enact (as well as observe) limited awareness while also offering a sophisticated reflective commentary.

(iii) Thematic discords?

If there are tensions within the narratorial strategy of this novel, there are also marked tensions within its thematic structures. A benevolent reader might say that these constitute enlivening paradoxes which we can resolve as we read (e.g., by inferring a complex authorial personality which veers in judgement); a more inquisitorial reader might say that these constitute contradictions which reveal conflicting ideological allegiances within the text. There are certainly tensions between (a) rationalism and anti-rationalism, (b) the ship regarded as microcosm and the ship regarded as heterocosm, and (c) a prejudiced and an unprejudiced view of Wait's blackness.

The Nigger of the 'Narcissus' belongs to a venerable and continuing tradition of texts which are both rationalist and anti-rationalist. Such works are culturally sophisticated yet commend cultural primitivism: they commend a state of being which is far simpler than that of their authors or of their assumed readers. In particular, *The Nigger* advocates 'hard' rather than 'soft' primitivism.[21] The latter extols a life of hedonistic ease; the former suggests that a life of austere toil promotes human virtue, dignity and order, taming egotism and checking introspection. In the taxing discipline of the ship, and particularly during the battle against the storm, ordinary men attain a transfiguring solidarity, dignity and heroism; but when conditions become relatively easy, as during the sunny calm that follows the stormy phase, they become quarrelsome and contentious; and on land they dwindle and scatter. At sea, Singleton gains the status of patriarch, sage and Homeric stalwart; on land, he's a bleary-eyed, tobacco-stained old alcoholic who can't tell day from night. Yet the narrator who advocates unreflective toil also provides a searchingly reflective commentary on it, and we will often be reminded of Conrad's remarks to Cunninghame Graham: '[S]ystems could be built, and rules could be made – if we could only get rid of consciousness. What makes mankind tragic is not that they are the victims of nature, it is that they are conscious of it.'[22] An inquisitorial reader of *The Nigger of the 'Narcissus'* might therefore grumble: 'This novel is radically self-contradictory. On the one hand, it says: "Ignorance is bliss; unreflective toil is redemptive." On the other hand, it says: "Learn from me: share my pleasures of philosophical contemplation." So it subverts what it advocates.' A more lenient person might reply: 'Why melodramatize as self-contradiction a familiar and ancient mixture of attitudes which is still part of our everyday experience? Toil offers its pains and consolations, and so does reflection. An articulate, "hard primitivist" nostalgia is naturally a perennial feature of a civilization's culture; what matters is that Conrad gives some new vigour and cogency to a very old paradox.'

This lenient reader might add that the novel's commendation of the austere life is complicated (as is often the case in primitivist myths and legends) by a version of the ancient notion of a fall of man from innocence into experience, from simple integrity into knowledge and corruption. In Chapter I, the narrator postulates a broad contrast between an older generation of seamen and a newer generation. The older

had been strong, as those are strong who know neither doubts nor hopes. They had been impatient and enduring, turbulent and devoted, unruly and faithful . . . . . [T]hey had been men who knew toil, privation, violence, debauchery – but knew not fear, and had no desire of spite in their hearts. Men hard to manage, but easy to inspire; voiceless men – but men enough to scorn in their hearts the sentimental voices that bewailed the hardness of their fate . . . . . Their generation lived inarticulate and indispensable . . . . .

Those were 'the everlasting children of the mysterious sea', whereas their successors are 'the grown-up children of a discontented earth':

They are less naughty, but less innocent; less profane, but perhaps also less believing; and if they ha[ve] learned how to speak they have also learned how to whine.

There is a modicum of historical substance in this broad rhetorical distinction. The progress of education in Europe during the latter half of the nineteenth century, and particularly, in England, the Education Acts of 1870 and 1880, meant that younger seamen were indeed rather more likely to be critically articulate and informedly argumentative than their predecessors; and, in the 1880s, when Conrad sailed on the real *Narcissus*, left-wing ideas were being widely disseminated. However, the narrator's romantic phrasing, as when he claims that the older seamen 'were strong and mute; . . . . . effaced, bowed and enduring, like stone caryatides that hold up in the night the lighted halls of a resplendent and glorious edifice', tends to dissolve historic fact in nostalgic myth. In part, this myth is a maritime version of the biblical story of the fall from innocence, from a condition in which labour is obediently offered to a condition in which labour is experienced as punishment; and we may recall the Ovidian tale of descent from a harsh but sinless Bronze Age to a complex and corrupt Iron Age.[23] The hyperbolic image of the 'stone caryatides' suggests that those old seamen were sustaining the very edifice of civilization – that they were 'built into' the social and political order. *The Nigger of the 'Narcissus'* may imply an elegy for the age of sailing-ships, but it is also a valediction to the dream of a hierarchic society with the stability of a temple.

Sometimes the text invites us to think of the *Narcissus* as a microcosm, 'a small planet', whose lonely progress across the open seas resembles that of the earth, bearing life through the wastes of space. Sometimes the *Narcissus* is a microcosm in a more immediate, political sense: we are invited to see an analogy between the captain and officers, contending with mutinous forces among the men, and the authorities in the state, contending with working-class agitation. And at other times the *Narcissus* is a heterocosm: a contrasting (and better) world. The contrast is emphasized both at the beginning of the narrative, when the vessel leaves the clamour of harbour, is released from the grimy tugboat (the 'aquatic beetle') and asserts her own majestic beauty, and at the end, when the *Narcissus* sails up the Thames and is beset by the urban, industrial world, like a fair martyr sacrificed to a brutal mob. The prose becomes insistently emotive:

Brick walls rose high above the water – soulless walls, staring through hundreds of windows as troubled and dull as the eyes of over-fed brutes. At their base monstrous iron cranes crouched, with chains hanging from their long necks, balancing cruel-looking hooks over the decks of lifeless ships . . . . . The *Narcissus* came gently into her berth; the shadows of soulless walls fell upon her, the dust of all the continents leaped upon her deck, and a swarm of strange men, clambering up her sides, took possession of her in the name of the sordid earth. She had ceased to live.

The inquisitorial reader could argue, then, that although *The Nigger of the 'Narcissus'* solicits various allegorical interpretations, these interpretations cannot cohere. England is 'a great ship', the 'ship mother of fleets and nations'; yet England is an urbanized, industrialized foe to the beauty and community of the *Narcissus*; and, furthermore, the dirty commercial arena which seems so antithetical to the sailing-ship has actually brought the ship into being: cash profit on imported goods is the 'sordid inspiration' of the *Narcissus*'s 'pilgrimage'. (The text has an invisible centre, for the cargo is never specified or described: an instance of political mystification by means of reticence rather than eloquence.) The vessel is sometimes analogous to an England in which the authorities have to contend with class conflict; yet the vessel contains a small, atypical community, cosmopolitan and entirely male, in which everyone is known personally to everyone else, duties are clear and reciprocal, and all run the same risk of drowning.

A sympathetic reader could, of course, argue that the alleged 'incoherences' make the text more interesting and more revealing as a cultural document, for it clearly manifests the tensions between Romanticism and realism, between the Aesthetic outlook and the practical outlook, between Anglophile patriotism and a patrician distaste for the commerce of 'a nation of shopkeepers',[24] and between a faith in a hierarchic yet 'organic' community and a contrasting knowledge that such an ideal is the material for obsequies rather than for campaigns.

The most awkward problem for that sympathetic reader will almost certainly be provided by the text's treatment of Wait. The narrator commends 'brotherhood', but does that 'brotherhood' embrace James Wait? *The Nigger of the 'Narcissus'* presents obvious difficulties to readers who admire Conrad and dislike racism. The very title is an embarrassment these days; and it's a clearly inadequate defence to say that in the 1890s the term 'nigger' was used commonly and casually by the British, for that defence merely relegates Conrad to the world of common and casual prejudice. In April 1897, four months before the serialization of the novel commenced, R. B. Cunninghame Graham (soon to become a loyal friend of Conrad) had published a satiric article entitled ' "Bloody Niggers" ', which denounced the term and its implications:

'Niggers' who have no cannons, and cannot construct a reasonable torpedo, have no rights. 'Niggers' whose lot is placed outside our flag, whose lives are given over to a band of money-grubbing miscreants (chartered or not) have neither rights nor wrongs. Their land is ours, their cattle, fields, their houses, their poor utensils, arms, all that they have; their women, too, are ours to use as concubines, to beat, exchange, to barter for gunpowder or gin . . . . . Cretans, Armenians, Cubans, Macedonians, we commiserate, subscribe, and feel for . . . . . But 'niggers', 'bloody niggers', have no friends.[25]

Conrad read this article in the Marxist magazine *The Social-Democrat*, and remarked, 'very good, very telling'.[26]

The most forthright denunciation of *The Nigger of the 'Narcissus'* as a racist tract is probably that offered by the American critic Eugene B. Redmond. He says: 'Conrad makes James Wait a whipping-boy for his and Europe's insecurities and moral hang-ups . . . . . Through him, Conrad and the critical establishment practice racism under the banner of realism and symbolism.' Critics who treat Wait as a symbol 'avoid the awful "burden" of considering or accepting his humanity.'[27] Whether Wait is regarded symbolically or non-symbolically, the case against Conrad seems clear. Wait is a sinister symbol, for the plot enacts the double connotations of his name: he is a 'weight' – a burden – to the ship; and he makes it 'wait', delaying its progress, so that only after his death and burial at sea can favourable winds blow the ship rapidly to its destination. In his character, he is a slothful and cunning parasite.[28] From the time of his arrival he is ill, suffering from tuberculosis; but when the illness is relatively mild he exaggerates its extent so as to avoid work, and when the illness is relatively severe he lies to himself and to others, falsely claiming that he is ready and able to work. His duplicity divides and confuses the crew: their pity for him subverts their true allegiance to the ship and enables Donkin to foment the near-mutiny. The term 'nigger' is identified in the text as a pejorative (as when Wait says 'You wouldn't call me nigger if I wasn't half dead'), yet it is frequently

used by the narrator, most offensively in the description of Wait's
face: 'a face pathetic and brutal: the tragic, the mysterious, the
repulsive mask of a nigger's soul.' Old Singleton, the laconic sage,
reproaches the crew for their anxiety about 'such a thing': 'And a
black fellow, too, ... I have seen them die like flies.'

The extent to which *The Nigger of the 'Narcissus'* seems guilty
of racial prejudice may depend partly on the reader's race
(though anyone who, like Redmond, suggests that white critics
generally endorse such prejudice may appear to be practising
racism himself); it may depend partly on the reader's period (for
readers in the 1970s, for example, were more sensitive to such
matters than were those in the 1890s); and it certainly depends
on the reader's attentiveness or inattentiveness to the text. I believe that *The Nigger of the 'Narcissus'* is indeed tainted by racism,
but I also believe that this taint is not as extensive as Redmond
suggested and is greatly outweighed by various positive factors
whose tenor is anti-racist. The laconic Singleton may tell Wait
to get on with his dying and to make less fuss over that job, but
the narrator takes care to dramatize 'from within' the anguish
and loneliness of Wait in his death-throes. On the moral scale,
Donkin, a white man, is undoubtedly far worse than Wait, so
there is no suggestion that moral turpitude is a prerogative of
blacks.[29] In addition, what makes Wait subversive is not that he
is black but that he is confusingly duplicitous; and, in other
Conradian texts, whites are capable of similar duplicity and wield
similar apparently supernatural powers: examples include Kurtz
in *Heart of Darkness* and the corrupt sea-captain in *The Shadow-
Line*. The main psycho-political thesis of the novel – the thesis
that apparent solidarity based on 'sympathy' may frequently be
a false solidarity based on vicarious egotism – may be con-
troversial, but it is not a racist thesis; it is concerned with the
various ways in which people may come to terms with the fear
of death. Finally, if we accept that virtue should not be fugitive
and cloistered but should be tested against opposition, a for-
midable text whose range includes implications with which we
do not agree may have greater merit than a text which appears
to mirror our values.[30] The legendary Narcissus fell in love with
his own reflection and consequently pined to death. If we value

only those texts which consistently reflect our own principles and assumptions, we might as well convert every library into a hall of mirrors.

The Nigger of the 'Narcissus' offers most readers much to enjoy, much that challenges and much that troubles; its eloquence is sometimes forced and specious, often acute and illuminating. The text includes inconsistencies, willed intensities and intermittent recourses to stereotypes which suggest that Conrad's creative intelligence has not yet found the modes of co-ordination which were to result in his major achievements, *Heart of Darkness* and *Nostromo*. Nevertheless, at its best, *The Nigger of the 'Narcissus'* offers an exuberant linguistic exploration of experience which challenges some of the bases of conventional political understanding; it offers standards of articulate imagining compared with which most non-fictional political discourse seems insufficiently alive, insufficiently human, and therefore inadequately political. Read, reflect and decide. I think that the prestige of this vivid novel is now, partly for good reasons, in decline; but *The Nigger of the 'Narcissus'* has already outlived many judges, and it may well outlive many more.

1986

NOTES TO THE INTRODUCTION

1 *The Review of Reviews* XII (December 1895), p. 561.

2 *Joseph Conrad's Letters to R. B. Cunninghame Graham*, ed. C. T. Watts (London: Cambridge University Press, 1969), p. 130. *Letters from Conrad 1895 to 1924*, ed. Edward Garnett (London: Nonesuch Press, 1928), p. 107.

3 *Joseph Conrad's Letters to R. B. Cunninghame Graham*, p. 59.

4 In *The Daily Telegraph* (8 December 1897, p. 4), W. L. Courtney said: 'Mr Joseph Conrad has chosen Mr Stephen Crane for his example, and has determined to do for the sea and the sailor what his predecessor had done for war and warriors. The style, though a good deal better than Mr Crane's, has the same jerky and spasmodic quality; while a spirit of faithful and minute description – even to the verge of the wearisome – is common to both.' See *Conrad: The Critical Heritage*, ed.

Norman Sherry (London and Boston: Routledge & Kegan Paul, 1973),
p. 86. The Conrad quotation is from 'Stephen Crane' [1923] in *Last
Essays* (London: Dent, 1955), p. 95.

5 For Conrad's ambivalent attitude to Kipling, see *Joseph Conrad's Letters
to R. B. Cunninghame Graham*, pp. 45, 47–8, 126. Kipling sent Conrad
a cordial letter of praise after reading *The Mirror of the Sea*: see *Twenty
Letters to Joseph Conrad*, ed. G. Jean-Aubry (London: First Edition Club,
1926).

6 *The Collected Letters of Joseph Conrad*, Vol. I, ed. Frederick R. Karl and
Laurence Davies (Cambridge: Cambridge University Press, 1983), p.
408. When Henley accepted *The Nigger*, Conrad remarked: 'Now I
have conquered Henley I ain't 'fraid of the divvle himself' (ibid., p.
323).

7 *The New Review* XVII (September 1897), pp. 317, 319.

8 Henley's comment on socialism is quoted in John Connell's *W. E.
Henley* (London: Constable, 1949), p. 153.

9 W. E. Henley: *For England's Sake* (London: Nutt, 1900), p. 8. '*Pro Rege
Nostro*' first appeared in a series of poems published in Henley's *National
Observer* between 1891 and 1892; Henley noted that it 'has been set to
music by Miss Frances Allitsen (Boosey), and – chorally – by Mr Ernest
Dicks (Curwen)'.

10 When Conrad sailed in the *Duke of Sutherland* in 1878–9, the crew
included George White, from Barbados, who may have been a model
for James Wait; and the ship's chief mate was named Baker, like his
counterpart in *The Nigger*. For notable discussions of such material, see
Jocelyn Baines: *Joseph Conrad: A Critical Biography* (London: Weidenfeld
and Nicolson, 1960), pp. 76–7; Ian Watt: *Conrad in the Nineteenth
Century* (London: Chatto and Windus, 1980), pp. 88–94; and Zdzisław
Najder: *Joseph Conrad: A Chronicle* (Cambridge: Cambridge University
Press, 1983), pp. 82–3.

11 G. Jean-Aubry: *Joseph Conrad: Life and Letters* (London: Heinemann,
1927), I, p. 77.

12 *Conrad: The Critical Heritage*, pp. 83–4.

13 W. Clark Russell's popular novel, *The Wreck of the 'Grosvenor'*, had
appeared in 1877. On 5 August 1896 Conrad had said of his own
labours on *The Rescue*: 'You see I must justify – give a motive – to my
yacht people. . . . . or have a Clark Russell puppet show which would be
worse than starvation.' (*Letters from Conrad 1895 to 1924*, pp. 42–3.)

14 The statement appears in the first paragraph of Chapter V. Conrad
could have found warrants for it in the work of Flaubert, Maupassant
and Anatole France, and he may be recalling the sceptical *Maximes* of
La Rochefoucauld – e.g., *maxime* 264: 'La pitié est souvent un senti-

ment de nos propres maux dans les maux d'autrui' ('When we pity the woes of others, we are often pitying our own').

15 See Chapter IV, p. 79; Plimsoll sometimes made false allegations against ship-owners. Ian Watt suggests that Conrad's divided allegiances as a captain (loyalty to the ship-owners conflicting with loyalty to the crews) are illustrated in Conrad's evidence at the Board of Trade's enquiry in July 1894 into the manning of merchant vessels: while maintaining that the *Adowa* was under-manned, he was reluctant to say the same of the *Torrens*. See *Conrad in the Nineteenth Century*, p. 113.

16 See J. Havelock Wilson: *My Stormy Voyage through Life* (London: Co-operative Printing Society, 1925), pp. 272-5 ff.

17 Cedric Watts: *The Deceptive Text* (Brighton: Harvester, 1984), pp. 59-74.

18 'The Feast' in Beerbohm's *A Christmas Garland* (London: Heinemann, 1912), pp. 123-30.

19 See Jakob Lothe: 'Variations of Narrative in *The Nigger of the "Narcissus"*': *Conradiana* XVI (1984), pp. 215-24. I adapt the table given on pp. 221-2.

20 Marvin Mudrick: 'The Artist's Conscience and *The Nigger of the "Narcissus"*': *Nineteenth-Century Fiction* XI (1957), pp. 288-97. Ian Watt: *Conrad in the Nineteenth Century*, p. 102. The relatively sceptical critics include Vernon Young and Robert Foulke; relatively sympathetic critics include Marion C. Michael, John Lester and Daniel R. Schwarz. See Lothe, *op. cit.*, pp. 223-4.

21 The distinction between 'hard' and 'soft' primitivism is discussed by Arthur O. Lovejoy and George Boas in *Primitivism and Related Ideas in Antiquity* [1935] (New York: Octagon Books, 1973), pp. 7-11.

22 *Joseph Conrad's Letters to R. B. Cunninghame Graham*, p. 70.

23 *Metamorphoses* I, lines 125-55.

24 'To found a great empire for the sole purpose of raising up a people of customers may at first sight appear a project fit only for a nation of shopkeepers.' Adam Smith: *The Wealth of Nations*, Vol. II [1776] (London and Toronto: Dent, 1910), p. 110.

25 '"Bloody Niggers"' is reprinted in *Selected Writings of Cunninghame Graham*, ed. Cedric Watts (East Brunswick and London: Associated University Presses, 1981), pp. 58-67. The quotation is from pp. 66-7.

26 *Joseph Conrad's Letters to R. B. Cunninghame Graham*, p. 89.

27 'Racism, or Realism? Literary Apartheid, or Poetic License? Conrad's Burden in *The Nigger of the "Narcissus"*': *The Nigger of the 'Narcissus'*, ed. Robert Kimbrough (New York: Norton, 1979), pp. 358-68. The quotations are from pp. 362 and 368.

28 A common nineteenth-century stereotype depicted the negro as lazy, undisciplined and sensual. See, for example, Joseph Arthur, Comte de Gobineau: *Essai sur l'inégalité des races humaines* (1853–5), translated by Oscar Levy as *The Inequality of Human Races* (London: Heinemann, 1915), Chapters XII and XVI; Thomas Carlyle: 'The Nigger Question' (1849) and 'Shooting Niagara; and After?' (1867) in *Critical and Miscellaneous Essays*, Vol. III (London: Chapman and Hall, 1888).

29 Donkin accelerates Wait's death by abusing him as a 'black, rotten hincumbrance', and proceeds to steal his money.

30 See J. S. Mill: *On Liberty* [1859] (London: Oxford University Press, 1912), Chapter 2; Alan Sinfield: 'Against Appropriation': *Essays in Criticism* XXXI (1981), pp. 181–95; and J. W. Burrow: 'The Tragical-Historical-Racial Drama': *Times Literary Supplement*, 13 June 1986, p. 653.

SELECTED FURTHER READING

CONRAD'S LETTERS

G. Jean-Aubry: *Joseph Conrad: Life and Letters* (two volumes, London: Heinemann, 1927).

Joseph Conrad's Letters to R. B. Cunninghame Graham, ed. C. T. Watts (London: Cambridge University Press, 1969).

The Collected Letters of Joseph Conrad, ed. Frederick R. Karl and Laurence Davies (Cambridge: Cambridge University Press, 1983 onwards).

BIOGRAPHIES

Jocelyn Baines: *Joseph Conrad: A Critical Biography* (London: Weidenfeld and Nicolson, 1960).

Norman Sherry: *Conrad and His World* (London: Thames and Hudson, 1972).

Frederick R. Karl: *Joseph Conrad: The Three Lives* (New York: Farrar, Straus and Giroux; London: Faber and Faber; 1979).

Zdzisław Najder: *Joseph Conrad: A Chronicle* (London: Cambridge University Press, 1983; New Brunswick, N.J.: Rutgers University Press, 1983).

CRITICISM

Max Beerbohm: 'The Feast' in *A Christmas Garland* (London: Heinemann, 1912).

F. R. Leavis: *The Great Tradition* (London: Chatto and Windus, 1948).

Douglas Hewitt: *Conrad: A Reassessment* (Cambridge: Bowes and Bowes, 1952).

Thomas Moser: *Joseph Conrad: Achievement and Decline* (Cambridge, Mass.: Harvard University Press, 1957).

Albert Guerard: *Conrad the Novelist* (Cambridge, Mass.: Harvard University Press, 1958).

The Art of Joseph Conrad: A Critical Symposium, ed. R. W. Stallman (East Lansing: Michigan State University Press, 1960).

Eloise Knapp Hay: *The Political Novels of Joseph Conrad* (Chicago and London: Chicago University Press, 1963).

J. Hillis Miller: *Poets of Reality* (Cambridge, Mass.: Harvard University Press, 1966).

Avrom Fleishman: *Conrad's Politics* (Baltimore: Johns Hopkins Press, 1967).

Conrad: The Critical Heritage, ed. Norman Sherry (London and Boston: Routledge & Kegan Paul, 1973).

C. B. Cox: *Joseph Conrad: The Modern Imagination* (London: Dent, 1974).

Jacques Berthoud: *Joseph Conrad: The Major Phase* (London: Cambridge University Press, 1978).

Cedric Watts: *A Preface to Conrad* (London and New York: Longman, 1982).

MATERIAL CONCERNING *THE NIGGER OF THE 'NARCISSUS'*

Joseph Warren Beach: *The Twentieth Century Novel: Studies in Technique* (New York: Appleton-Century Crofts, 1932), pp. 348–52.

Ted E. Boyle: *Symbol and Meaning in the Fiction of Joseph Conrad* (The Hague: Mouton, 1965), pp. 38–59.

David R. Smith: *Conrad's Manifesto: Preface to a Career* (Philadelphia: Gehenna Press, 1966; London: Bodley Head, 1975).

Paul Kirschner: *Conrad: The Psychologist as Artist* (Edinburgh: Oliver and Boyd, 1968), pp. 102–9, 198, 200–205, 272–4, 276.

Robert Foulke: 'Postures of Belief in *The Nigger of the "Narcissus"*': *Modern Fiction Studies* XVII (Summer 1971), pp. 249–63.

William W. Bonney: 'Semantic and Structural Indeterminacy in *The Nigger of the "Narcissus"*: An Experiment in Reading': *English Literary History* XL (Winter 1973), pp. 564–83.

The Nigger of the 'Narcissus', ed. Robert Kimbrough (New York: Norton, 1979).

Ian Watt: *Conrad in the Nineteenth Century* (Berkeley: University of California Press, 1979; London: Chatto and Windus, 1980), Chapter 3.

A Concordance to Conrad's 'The Nigger of the Narcissus', ed. James W. Parrins and Todd K. Bender (New York and London: Garland, 1981).

Jacques Berthoud: 'Introduction' to *The Nigger of the 'Narcissus'* (Oxford: Oxford University Press, 1984).

The periodicals *Conradiana* (published by Texas Tech University) and *The Conradian* (published by the Joseph Conrad Society, U.K.) have included a variety of scholarly and critical articles on this novel.

NOTES ON THE TEXT

'TO MY READERS IN AMERICA'

Early in 1914 Conrad wrote this piece to introduce the forthcoming new American edition of *The Nigger of the 'Narcissus'* by Doubleday, Page & Company (Garden City, New York, 1914); initially the firm published 'To My Readers in America' together with the earlier 'Preface' as a pamphlet entitled *Joseph Conrad on the Art of Writing*.

As copy-text I have taken Conrad's manuscript, reproduced in facsimile in David R. Smith's *Conrad's Manifesto: Preface to a Career* (Philadelphia: Rosenbach Foundation, 1966). I have compared this text with that in the 1926 edition of *The Nigger of the 'Narcissus'* published by Doubleday, Page & Co., Garden City, New York. On a few occasions, listed below, I have preferred the latter to the former. Neither text gives me the authority to clarify (by means of a comma after 'preface' and another before 'was') the sentence which begins 'That preface on advice', so I have refrained from doing so. In the list, the page and line numbers refer to this Penguin edition; the manuscript reading is given in square brackets.

Page xlv, line 3: port, [port]
        xlvi, 3–4:   *New Review* [New Review]
        xlvi, 7:   "The Nigger of the 'Narcissus'" [The Nigger of the Narcissus"]
        xlvi, 13:   *New Review* [New Review]

'PREFACE'

Accounts of the textual transmission of Conrad's 'Preface' to *The Nigger of the 'Narcissus'* include the following. David R. Smith: *Conrad's Manifesto* (1966); Neill R. Joy: 'Conrad's "Preface" to *The Nigger of the "Narcissus"*: The Lost Typescript Restored': *Conradiana* IX (1977), pp. 17–33; and Thomas Lavoie's 'Textual History and Textual Notes: The "Preface"' in the Norton edition of the novel (New York, 1979).

Conrad completed *The Nigger* in February 1897; subsequently, and by 24 August of the same year, he drafted the preface, of which the manuscript survives at the Rosenbach Foundation. (A typescript, incorporating numerous small revisions, is held by Colgate University.) Heinemann declined to publish the preface with the forthcoming book of the novel; it was, however, soon published by W. E. Henley as an 'Author's Note' to the serial version of *The Nigger* in the *New Review* (December 1897). This 'Author's Note' lacks what subsequent texts give as paragraph four, and its second paragraph is merged with what subsequently became the third.

In 1902 the preface appeared as a pamphlet, entitled *The Nigger of the 'Narcissus'/Preface*, printed in a limited edition of one hundred copies by J. Lovick, High Street, Hythe, and Cheriton. This private publication was probably arranged by Conrad himself, who lived near Hythe; and even if, as some commentators have speculated, the arrangement was made by T. J. Wise (the diligent bibliographer and alleged forger), the pamphlet had Conrad's approval, for he subsequently sent copies to various people, notably Alfred A. Knopf of Doubleday, Page & Co. The preface next appeared as an essay entitled 'The Art of Fiction' in *Harper's Weekly* (New York, 1905); and in 1914 it appeared with 'To My Readers in America' in the pamphlet, *Joseph Conrad on the Art of Writing*. In the same year, again accompanied by 'To My Readers in America', it was at last incorporated in a book of *The Nigger* (Garden City, New York: Doubleday, Page & Co.).

As copy-text of the preface for this Penguin volume I have used the Hythe pamphlet; and, in particular, I have used the copy which Conrad corrected and sent to C. K. Shorter. This copy, now owned by the British Library, is inscribed 'To Clement Shorter from J. C. 1917', and in the first paragraph Conrad has corrected the word misprinted as 'prjudices'. (The transcription of the Hythe text in David R. Smith's book differs in a few small respects from the original.) I have compared the Hythe version with that in the Hofstra University set of proofs corrected by Conrad in 1920, and have consulted the manuscript reproduced in facsimile by Smith, the *New Review* text, the 1914 pamphlet, and the version in the edition of the novel published by Doubleday, Page & Co. in 1926. (I have also noted Neill R. Joy's account of variant readings in the typescript.)

On some occasions, where the Hofstra punctuation offers distinct logical clarification, I have preferred the Hofstra reading to that of the Hythe pamphlet. In one case I have preferred the manuscript to either. An important claim in the preface is rendered in the Hythe text as 'In that uneasy solitude the supreme cry of Art for Art, itself, loses the exciting ring of its apparent immortality.' Some book versions (and the Hofstra proofs) omit the comma before 'itself'; others omit, in addition, the comma which follows that word. These variations in punctuation are attempts to resolve the ambiguity of 'itself', which can be linked either to the word 'Art' (so that the postulated cry means 'Art for Art alone', i.e., Art for Art's sake) or to the word 'cry' (to mean 'even the supreme cry of Art for Art'). The manuscript offers: 'Art for Art, even, ... '. This resolves the ambiguity decisively in favour of the latter alternative; therefore I have preferred it to the customary phrase.

In the list of emendations which follows, page and line numbers refer, again, to this Penguin edition; the Hythe reading is given in square brackets.

Page xlvii, line 16: prejudices [prjudices]
    xlvii, 19:   bodies; [bodies:]
    xlvii, 20:   ambitions; [ambitions:]
    xlviii, 12:   lives; [lives:]
    xlviii, 13:   pain; [pain:]
    xlviii, 36:   appeal, [appeal]
    xlviii, 36:   effective, [effective]
    xlix, 26:   deserts: [deserts;]

I, 12:   of); [of,)]
I, 17:   Art, even, [Art, itself,]
I, 19:   at times, [at times]
I, 19:   faintly, [faintly]

I give here the defensive paragraph which, on Edward Garnett's advice, Conrad deleted from the preface. It was originally located between the paragraphs which now appear as the eighth and ninth. I retain seven words omitted by Jacques Berthoud from his version (*The Nigger of the 'Narcissus'* [Oxford: World's Classics, 1984], p.xxx); and I read as 'region' the word given there as 'reign', and as 'indulgency' the word given by Berthoud as 'inadequacy' and by Smith as 'indulgence'.

It may seem strange if not downright suspicious that so much should be said in introduction to the unimportant tale of the sea which follows. It may also appear the height of conceit or folly since every word of the preface may be brought in judgment against the work it is meant to introduce. But a preface – if anything – is spoken in perfect good faith, as one speaks to friends, and in the hope that the unprovoked confidence shall be treated with scrupulous fairness. And, after all, everyone desires to be understood: We all with mutual indulgency give way to the pressing need of explaining ourselves – the politician, the prophet, the fool, the bricklayer they all do it: and if so then why not the writer of tales who is, as far as I know, no greater criminal than any of these. It is true that the disclosure of the aim otherwise than by the effective effort towards it is a confession of doubt and so far a confession of weakness. Yet in the region of art such an awoval [*sic*] is not so fatal as it would be elsewhere. For in art alone of all the enterprises of men there is meaning in endeavour disassociated from success and merit – if any merit there be – is not wholly centred in achievement but may be faintly discerned in the aim.

THE NIGGER OF THE 'NARCISSUS'

This edition of the novel has not been commissioned as a critical edition. I have, however, adopted a procedure which gives the present text clear credentials. For reasons which are provided below, I have selected as copy-text the first British trade edition, the book published by William Heinemann (London) in December 1897. This has been compared with the set of proofs corrected by

Conrad for the Heinemann edition of 1921. My editorial policy has been conservative in the sense that I have endeavoured to keep emendations to an essential minimum.

The transmission of the text of *The Nigger of the 'Narcissus'* has been ably described by Kenneth W. Davis and Donald W. Rude in *Conradiana* V (1973), pp. 20–45, complemented by Donald Rude's discussion in *Joseph Conrad Today* V (October 1979), pp. 132–4. Within Conrad's lifetime the text underwent many revisions; some of the changes were made by Conrad, some by editors working for various publishers. The novel first appeared in print in a copyright edition of just seven copies published by William Heinemann on 29 July 1897. There followed the English serial version (*New Review*, August–December 1897); the American serial (an abridgement in *The Illustrated Buffalo Express*, August–September 1897); the first American book edition, *The Children of the Sea: A Tale of the Forecastle* (New York: Dodd, Mead, 1897); and the first British book edition for the trade, *The Nigger of the 'Narcissus': A Tale of the Sea* (London: Heinemann, 1897, bearing the incorrect date '1898'). From *The Children of the Sea* descended the Doubleday 'Personal Edition' (New York, 1914). The Heinemann edition was reprinted on various occasions; and a copy of the 1910 'Popular Edition', corrected by Conrad, served as a basis for the Doubleday 'Sun-Dial Edition' of 1920–21, from which descended the J. M. Dent 'Uniform Edition' (London, 1923) and the eventual Dent 'Collected Edition' (London, 1950). Furthermore, the 'Sun-Dial' text provided a basis for the Heinemann edition of 1921, and Conrad revised proofs for that edition (though not all of his corrections were effected). In turn, the Heinemann 1921 edition, containing not only revisions already introduced in the Sun-Dial edition but also 38 additional substantive variants, influenced the Doubleday texts published between 1923 and 1925.

The basic problem for an editor of *The Nigger of the 'Narcissus'* may be summed up as follows. If he chooses as copy-text a late edition, he thereby gains some of Conrad's considered revisions and some worthwhile clarifications provided by publishing-house editorial staff; but such a text will also contain layers of un-Conradian 'house style' accretions. If, on the other hand, he chooses an early edition, there is not only the difficulty of choice (given the differences between the copyright edition, the *New Review* serial and the first British and American editions), but also the problem occasioned by the presence of blemishes which later editorial work removed and of details subsequently changed by Conrad or with Conrad's approval. Furthermore, the perils of the endeavour are indicated by the fact that the 'Authoritative Text' of *The Nigger* published by Norton in 1979 is marred in various ways, notably by a large number of proof-errors, some of which result in the omission of words.

I have chosen an early edition as copy-text, because such an edition brings us close to Conrad's creative intentions when *The Nigger* was being written, at the start of the great decade from 1897 to 1907 which produced the preponderant number of his major works. Of the various early editions, I have selected the first Heinemann trade edition (as opposed to the copyright edition) because of its literary-historical importance. This, not the copyright edition or the serial version, is the text that most of the novel's early reviewers in Britain discussed, at that crucial period when Conrad's reputation as a major writer was being established and defined. His letters emphasize the obvious fact that it was the British (rather than the American) response which primarily concerned Conrad: he studied the reviews anxiously and attentively. I have also taken account of the fact that this first British edition contains numerous readings not found in the copyright edition or the serial instalments, and that these readings (as Davis and Rude have shown) indicate 'careful attention to accuracy, connotation and the poetic qualities of language'. Of the early impressions of that edition, I have preferred the first to the second, for the former is typographically superior.

As the main text for comparison with the copy-text, I have chosen Hofstra University's set of page-proofs for the 1921 Heinemann edition. Of the handwritten corrections on these proofs, many are clearly by Conrad, and many are in a second hand which appears to be that of a publisher's editor. Since some of the editorial annotations are queries addressed to the author, it appears likely that Conrad was in a position to see and approve changes made by his collaborator in the task of proof-checking. Naturally, I have given special consideration to Conrad's work on these proofs; and it seemed appropriate, in any case, to use a relatively late text for comparison purposes. Given my sense of the historical importance of the first Heinemann edition, however, it follows that my editorial policy has been deliberately conservative. I have departed from the 1897 text only when the Hofstra proofs correct obvious errors or effect a necessary (rather than merely desirable) gain in clarity. The Conrad of 1920, four years before his death, was not necessarily a better judge than the Conrad of 1897; and even where the later text offers considered 'second thoughts', I have usually given priority to the earlier readings. I have also preserved various grammatical errors or idiosyncrasies which seem characteristically Conradian (e.g., the use of 'such as' for 'like', and 'like does' for 'as does'). In later editions of the novel, Conrad toned down Donkin's cockney accent by greatly reducing the number of misplaced aspirates; but the heavily accentuated vernacular of the first edition seemed to me to be fully in keeping with the narratorial animus directed against Donkin, so there were thematic as well as textually historical grounds for preserving it.

In all cases where the Hofstra reading has been preferred, the original version is listed in Table A, so that the reader who wishes to do so may reconstitute fully the 1897 text. In cases where the 1897 text has been preferred, some of the more interesting differences between 1897 and Hofstra are given in Table B; the first edition is superior in a sufficient number of examples to challenge the preference of some previous editors for a later copy-text.

Table A. Emendations of the 1897 text.

I have regularized some irregularities: 'bo'sen' and 'boss'en' have been regularized as 'bosun', and 'belaying-pin' has been consistently hyphenated. On page 101, line 12, I supply a missing quotation mark after 'it.'. Where Heinemann uses double quotation marks, Penguin uses single ones, and vice versa. With these exceptions, all the emendations tally with the Hofstra proofs. Page and line numbers refer, as usual, to this Penguin edition; the 1897 readings are given in square brackets.

Page 2, line 26: bedding, [bedding]

    3, 22:   sat [set]

    3, 37:   can their rough, inexperienced souls [their rough, inexperienced souls can]

5, 23:	you! That's [you!" "That's]
11, 25:	bosun [bo'sen]
36, 9:	ship, [ship]
39, 22:	abysmal [abyssmal]
40, 20:	light, [light]
41, 19:	Mr. [Mr,]
48, 3:	belaying-pin [belaying pin]
61, 10:	Bosun [Boss'en]
61, 29:	no [on]
62, 2:	mouths [mouth]
63, 33:	belaying-pin [belaying pin]
63, 36:	now? [now,]
68, 8:	world; [world:]
68, 35:	imprecations [implications]
69, 10:	seaman [seamen]
73, 8:	shook his [shook s]
74, 10:	bloomin' condemned [blooming' condemed]
74, 35:	a-drivin' [a-drivin]
79, 1:	Donkin; [Donkin]
82, 35:	dry, [dry?]
105, 31:	well!) by [well!) and]
106, 16:	thrashed [trashed]
107, 3:	for [or]
107, 15:	tobacco, and loafed for hours, very [tobacco, loafed for hours and very]
107, 18:	prophecies [prophesies]
110, 6:	enough ['enough]
112, 33:	rage. [rage,]
116, 25:	'ead [ead]
124, 31:	crown [crown,]
126, 17:	comin' [comin]
126, 22:	'ypocrites [yrpocrits]
127, 28:	caps, [caps]

Table B. Samples of differences between the 1897 text and the Hofstra proofs.

In the 1897 text, as has been noted, Donkin's cockney accent is

given greater (and sometimes excessive) prominence: for example,
he says 'I ham a Henglishman, I ham', where Hofstra gives 'I am
an Englishman, I am'. 1897 gives the sailors 'hard hats'; later
these became 'round hats'. Some of the descriptions were subsequently shortened. Below, the square brackets enclose the
Hofstra versions.

Page 37: He watched her every motion; he kept [He kept]

42: green glass [green grass]

54: He breathed slowly, and the air [The air]

58: sang [sank]

66: existence, lest they should remember and, perchance,
regret the reward of a cup of inspiring bitterness, tasted
so often, and so often withdrawn from before their stiffening but reluctant lips. They [existence. They]

67: objectless [aimless]

71: full of a deep rumour [full of deep murmurs]

72: He slept at last. He breathed heavily, high-booted [He
slept at last, high-booted]

76: globe of fire [glove of fire]

82: chummed [chimed in]

84: The ship heeled over a little, slipping quietly over a
sombre sea towards the inaccessible and festal splendour
of a black horizon pierced by points of flickering fire.
Above [Above]

85: went over [went walking over]

86: see the fire [see the everlasting fire]

86: I can see it for you. I can't bear it. [Repent, repent! I can't
bear to think of you.]

87: Heavy breathings stirred the darkness. The sea [The sea]

91: Shadowy figures could be seen tottering, falling, leaping
up. Ringbolts [Ringbolts]

103: profound impertinence of his large eyes, that stood far
out of his head like the eyes of crabs. [impertinent
mournfulness of his languid and enormous stare.]

109: Jimmy breathed with composure. He [Jimmy]

115: depths; promising, empty, inspiring—terrible. [depths.]

119: leaped off with his arm thrown out [sprang out of the
crowd with his arm extended]

119: reluctantly to, all at once, whizz [reluctantly to whizz]

119: square the yards. Look alive, men! [Man the weather braces.]

125: maculated his [hung in his]

CONRAD'S 'TO MY READERS IN AMERICA'

From that evening when James Wait joined the ship—late for the muster of the crew—to the moment when he left us in the open sea, shrouded in sailcloth, through the open port, I had much to do with him. He was in my watch.[1] A negro in a British forecastle is a lonely being. He has no chums. Yet James Wait afraid of death and making Her his accomplice was an impostor of some character —mastering our compassion, scornful of our sentimentalism, triumphing over our suspicions.

But in the book he is nothing; he is merely the centre of the ship's collective psychology and the pivot of the action. Yet he who in the family circle and amongst my friends is familiarly referred to as The Nigger, remains very precious to me. For the book written round him is not the sort of thing that can be attempted more than once in a life-time. It is the book by which, not as a novelist perhaps, but as an artist striving for the utmost sincerity of expression, I am willing to stand or fall. Its pages are the tribute of my unalterable and profound affection for the ship, the seamen, the winds and the great sea—the moulders of my youth, the companions of the best years of my life.

After writing the last words of that book, in the revulsion of feeling before the accomplished task, I understood that I had done with the sea, and that henceforth I had to be a writer. And almost without laying down the pen I wrote a preface, trying to express the spirit in which I was entering on the task of my new life. That preface on advice (which I now think was wrong) was never published with the book. But the late W. E. Henley,[2] who had the courage at that time (1897) to serialise my 'Nigger' in the New Review judged it worthy to be printed as an Afterword at the end of the last instalment of the tale.

I am glad that this book which means so much to me is coming out again, under its proper title[3] of "The Nigger of the 'Narcissus'" and under the auspices of my good friends and publishers Messrs Doubleday Page & Cº, into the light of publicity.

Half the span of a generation has passed since W. E. Henley, after reading two chapters, sent me a verbal message: 'Tell Conrad that if the rest is up to sample it shall certainly come out in the New Review.' The most gratifying recollection of my writer's life!

And here is the Suppressed Preface.

CONRAD'S 'PREFACE'

A work that aspires, however humbly, to the condition of art should carry its justification in every line. And art itself may be defined as a single-minded attempt to render the highest kind of justice to the visible universe, by bringing to light the truth, manifold and one, underlying its every aspect. It is an attempt to find in its forms, in its colours, in its light, in its shadows, in the aspects of matter and in the facts of life, what of each is fundamental, what is enduring and essential—their one illuminating and convincing quality—the very truth of their existence. The artist, then, like the thinker or the scientist, seeks the truth and makes his appeal. Impressed by the aspect of the world the thinker plunges into ideas, the scientist into facts—whence, presently, emerging they make their appeal to those qualities of our being that fit us best for the hazardous enterprise of living. They speak authoritatively to our common-sense, to our intelligence, to our desire of peace or to our desire of unrest; not seldom to our prejudices, sometimes to our fears, often to our egoism—but always to our credulity. And their words are heard with reverence, for their concern is with weighty matters: with the cultivation of our minds and the proper care of our bodies; with the attainment of our ambitions; with the perfection of the means and the glorification of our precious aims.

It is otherwise with the artist.[4]

Confronted by the same enigmatical spectacle the artist descends within himself, and in that lonely region of stress and strife, if he be deserving and fortunate, he finds the terms of his appeal. His appeal is made to our less obvious capacities: to that part of our nature which, because of the warlike conditions of existence, is necessarily kept out of sight within the more resisting and hard qualities—like the vulnerable body within the steel armour. His appeal is less loud, more profound, less distinct, more stirring— and sooner forgotten. Yet its effect endures for ever. The changing wisdom of successive generations discards ideas, questions facts, demolishes theories. But the artist appeals to that part of our being which is not dependent on wisdom: to that in us which is a gift and not an acquisition—and, therefore, more permanently enduring. He speaks to our capacity for delight and wonder, to the sense of mystery surrounding our lives; to our sense of pity, and beauty, and pain; to the latent feeling of fellowship with all creation—and to the subtle but invincible, conviction of solidarity that knits together the loneliness of innumerable hearts: to the solidarity in dreams, in joy, in sorrow, in aspirations, in illusions, in hope, in fear, which binds men to each other, which binds together all humanity—the dead to the living and the living to the unborn.

It is only some such train of thought, or rather of feeling, that can in a measure explain the aim of the attempt, made in the tale which follows, to present an unrestful episode in the obscure lives of a few individuals out of all the disregarded multitude of the bewildered, the simple and the voiceless. For, if there is any part of truth in the belief confessed above, it becomes evident that there is not a place of splendour or a dark corner of the earth that does not deserve, if only a passing glance of wonder and pity. The motive, then, may be held to justify the matter of the work; but this preface, which is simply an avowal of endeavour, cannot end here—for the avowal is not yet complete.

Fiction—if it at all aspires to be art—appeals to temperament. And in truth it must be, like painting, like music, like all art, the appeal of one temperament to all the other innumerable temperaments whose subtle and resistless power endows passing events with their true meaning, and creates the moral, the emotional atmosphere of the place and time. Such an appeal, to be effective, must be an impression conveyed through the senses; and, in fact, it cannot be made in any other way, because temperament, whether individual or collective, is not amenable to persuasion. All art, therefore, appeals primarily to the senses, and the artistic aim when expressing itself in written words must also make its appeal through the senses, if its high desire is to reach the secret spring of responsive emotions. It must strenuously aspire to the plasticity of sculpture, to the colour of painting, and to the magic suggestiveness of music—which is the art of arts.[5] And it is only through complete, unswerving devotion to the perfect blending of form and substance; it is only through an unremitting, never-discouraged care for the shape and ring of sentences that an approach can be made to plasticity, to colour; and the light of magic suggestiveness may be brought to play for an evanescent instant over the commonplace surface of words: of the old, old words, worn thin, defaced by ages of careless usage.

The sincere endeavour to accomplish that creative task, to go as far on that road as his strength will carry him, to go undeterred by faltering, weariness or reproach, is the only valid justification for the worker in prose. And if his conscience is clear, his answer to those who, in the fulness of a wisdom which looks for immediate profit, demand specifically to be edified, consoled, amused; who demand to be promptly improved, or encouraged, or frightened, or shocked, or charmed, must run thus:—My task which I am trying to achieve is, by the power of the written word, to make you hear, to make you feel—it is, before all, to make you see.[6] That—and no more, and it is everything. If I succeed, you shall find there according to your deserts: encouragement, consolation, fear, charm—all you demand; and, perhaps, also that glimpse of truth for which you have forgotten to ask.

To snatch in a moment of courage, from the remorseless rush of time, a passing phase of life is only the beginning of the task. The task approached in tenderness and faith is to hold up unquestioningly, without choice and without fear, the rescued fragment before all eyes and in the light of a sincere mood. It is to show its vibration, its colour, its form; and through its movement, its form, and its colour, reveal the substance of its truth—disclose its inspiring secret: the stress and passion within the core of each convincing moment.[7] In a single-minded attempt of that kind, if one be deserving and fortunate, one may perchance attain to such clearness of sincerity that at last the presented vision of regret or pity, of terror or mirth, shall awaken in the hearts of the beholders that feeling of unavoidable solidarity; of the solidarity in mysterious origin, in toil, in joy, in hope, in uncertain fate, which binds men to each other and all mankind to the visible world.

It is evident that he who, rightly or wrongly, holds by the convictions expressed above cannot be faithful to any one of the temporary formulas of his craft. The enduring part of them—the truth which each only imperfectly veils—should abide with him as the most precious of his possessions, but they all: Realism, Romanticism, Naturalism, even the unofficial sentimentalism (which, like the poor, is exceedingly difficult to get rid of); all these gods must, after a short period of fellowship, abandon him—even on the very threshold of the temple—to the stammerings of his conscience and to the outspoken consciousness of the difficulties of his work. In that uneasy solitude the supreme cry of Art for Art,[8] even, loses the exciting ring of its apparent immorality. It sounds far off. It has ceased to be a cry, and is heard only as a whisper, often incomprehensible, but at times, and faintly, encouraging.

Sometimes, stretched at ease in the shade of a roadside tree, we watch the motions of a labourer in a distant field,[9] and after a time, begin to wonder languidly as to what the fellow may be at. We watch the movements of his body, the waving of his arms, we see him bend down, stand up, hesitate, begin again. It may add to the charm of an idle hour to be told the purpose of his exertions. If we know he is trying to lift a stone, to dig a ditch, to uproot a stump, we look with a more real interest at his efforts; we are disposed to condone the jar of his agitation upon the restfulness of the landscape; and even, if in a brotherly frame of mind, we may bring ourselves to forgive his failure. We understood his object, and, after all, the fellow has tried, and perhaps he had not the strength, and perhaps he had not the knowledge. We forgive, go on our way—and forget.

And so it is with the workman of art. Art is long and life is short,[10] and success is very far off. And thus, doubtful of strength to travel so far, we talk a little about the aim—the aim of art, which, like life itself, is inspiring, difficult—obscured by mists. It is not in the clear logic of a triumphant conclusion; it is not in the unveiling of one of those heartless secrets which are called the Laws of Nature. It is not less great, but only more difficult.

To arrest, for the space of a breath, the hands busy about the work of the earth, and compel men entranced by the sight of distant goals to glance for a moment at the surrounding vision of form and colour, of sunshine and shadows; to make them pause for a look, for a sigh, for a smile—such is the aim, difficult and evanescent, and reserved only for a very few to achieve. But sometimes, by the deserving and the fortunate, even that task is accomplished. And when it is accomplished—behold!—all the truth of life is there: a moment of vision, a sigh, a smile—and the return to an eternal rest.

From the NEW REVIEW, *December, 1897.*

Facsimile of the title-page of the first British trade edition, December 1897, bearing the incorrect date '1898'.

The

Nigger of the "Narcissus"

A Tale of the Sea

By

Joseph Conrad

"... My Lord in his discourse discovered a great deal of
love to this ship."—*Diary of Samuel Pepys*[11]

London
William Heinemann
1898

TO

EDWARD GARNETT[1][2]

THIS TALE
ABOUT MY FRIENDS
OF THE SEA

THE
NIGGER OF THE 'NARCISSUS'

I

<u>MR. BAKER</u>, chief mate of the ship *Narcissus*, stepped in one stride
out of his lighted cabin into the darkness of the quarter-deck.
Above his head, on the break of the poop, the night-watchman
rang a double stroke. It was nine o'clock. Mr. Baker, speaking up
to the man above him, asked:—'Are all the hands aboard,
Knowles?'

The man limped down the ladder, then said reflectively:—

'I think so, sir. All our old chaps are there, and a lot of new men
has come. . . . . They must be all there.'

'Tell the boatswain to send all hands aft,' went on Mr. Baker;
'and tell one of the youngsters to bring a good lamp here. I want to
muster our crowd.'

The main deck was dark aft, but halfway from forward, through
the open doors of the forecastle, two streaks of brilliant light cut
the shadow of the quiet night that lay upon the ship. A hum of
voices was heard there, while port and starboard, in the illuminated
doorways, silhouettes of moving men appeared for a moment, very
black, without relief, like figures cut out of sheet tin. The ship was
ready for sea. The carpenter had driven in the last wedge of the
main-hatch battens, and, throwing down his maul, had wiped his
face with great deliberation, just on the stroke of five. The decks
had been swept, the windlass oiled and made ready to heave up

the anchor; the big tow-rope lay in long bights along one side of the main deck, with one end carried up and hung over the bows, in readiness for the tug that would come paddling and hissing noisily, hot and smoky, in the limpid, cool quietness of the early morning. The captain was ashore, where he had been engaging some new hands to make up his full crew; and, the work of the day over, the ship's officers had kept out of the way, glad of a little breathing-time. Soon after dark the few liberty-men and the new hands began to arrive in shore-boats rowed by white-clad Asiatics, who clamoured fiercely for payment before coming alongside the gangway-ladder. The feverish and shrill babble of Eastern language struggled against the masterful tones of tipsy seamen, who argued against brazen claims and dishonest hopes by profane shouts. The resplendent and bestarred peace of the East was torn into squalid tatters by howls of rage and shrieks of lament raised over sums ranging from five annas to half a rupee; and every soul afloat in Bombay Harbour became aware that the new hands were joining the *Narcissus*.

Gradually the distracting noise had subsided. The boats came no longer in splashing clusters of three or four together, but dropped alongside singly, in a subdued buzz of expostulation cut short by a 'Not a pice more! You go to the devil!' from some man staggering up the accommodation-ladder – a dark figure, with a long bag poised on the shoulder. In the forecastle the newcomers, upright and swaying amongst corded boxes and bundles of bedding, made friends with the old hands, who sat one above another in the two tiers of bunks, gazing at their future shipmates with glances critical but friendly. The two forecastle lamps were turned up high, and shed an intense hard glare; shore-going hard hats were pushed far on the backs of heads, or rolled about on the deck amongst the chain-cables; white collars, undone, stuck out on each side of red faces; big arms in white sleeves gesticulated; the growling voices hummed steady amongst bursts of laughter and hoarse calls. 'Here, sonny, take that bunk! . . . . Don't you do it! . . . . What's your last ship? . . . . I know her. . . . . Three years ago, in Puget Sound . . . . This here berth leaks, I tell you! . . . . Come on; give us a chance to swing that chest! . . . . Did you bring a bottle, any of you shore toffs? .... Give us a bit of 'baccy. .... I know her; her skipper drank himself to death. .... He was a dandy boy! .... Liked his lotion inside, he did! .... No! .... Hold your row, you chaps! .... I tell you, you came on board a hooker, where they get their money's worth out of poor Jack, by——! ....'

A little fellow, called Craik and nicknamed Belfast, abused the ship violently, romancing on principle, just to give the new hands something to think over. Archie, sitting aslant on his sea-chest, kept his knees out of the way, and pushed the needle steadily through a white patch in a pair of blue trousers. Men in black jackets and stand-up collars, mixed with men bare-footed, bare-armed, with coloured shirts open on hairy chests, pushed against one another in the middle of the forecastle. The group swayed, reeled, turning upon itself with the motion of a scrimmage, in a haze of tobacco smoke. All were speaking together, swearing at every second word. A Russian Finn, wearing a yellow shirt with pink stripes, stared upwards, dreamy-eyed, from under a mop of tumbled hair. Two young giants with smooth, baby faces—two Scandinavians—helped each other to spread their bedding, silent, and smiling placidly at the tempest of good-humoured and meaningless curses. Old Singleton, the oldest able seaman in the ship, sat apart on the deck right under the lamps, stripped to the waist, tattooed like a cannibal chief all over his powerful chest and enormous biceps. Between the blue and red patterns his white skin gleamed like satin; his bare back was propped against the heel of the bowsprit, and he held a book at arm's length before his big, sunburnt face. With his spectacles and a venerable white beard, he resembled a learned and savage patriarch, the incarnation of barbarian wisdom serene in the blasphemous turmoil of the world. He was intensely absorbed, and, as he turned the pages an expression of grave surprise would pass over his rugged features. He was reading 'Pelham.'[13] The popularity of Bulwer Lytton in the forecastles of Southern-going ships is a wonderful and bizarre phenomenon. What ideas do his polished and so curiously insincere sentences awaken in the simple minds of the big children who people those dark and wandering places of the earth? What meaning can their rough, inexperienced souls find in the elegant verbiage of his pages? What excitement?—what forgetfulness?—

what appeasement? Mystery! Is it the fascination of the incomprehensible?—is it the charm of the impossible? Or are those
beings who exist beyond the pale of life stirred by his tales as by an
enigmatical disclosure of a resplendent world that exists within the
frontier of infamy and filth, within that border of dirt and hunger,
of misery and dissipation, that comes down on all sides to the
water's edge of the incorruptible ocean, and is the only thing they
know of life, the only thing they see of surrounding land—those
life-long prisoners of the sea? Mystery!

Singleton, who had sailed to the southward since the age of
twelve, who in the last forty-five years had lived (as we had calcu-
lated from his papers) no more than forty months ashore—old
Singleton, who boasted, with the mild composure of long years
well spent, that generally from the day he was paid off from one
ship till the day he shipped in another he seldom was in a condition
to distinguish daylight—old Singleton sat unmoved in the clash of
voices and cries, spelling through 'Pelham' with slow labour, and
lost in an absorption profound enough to resemble a trance. He
breathed regularly. Every time he turned the book in his enormous
and blackened hands the muscles of his big white arms rolled
slightly under the smooth skin. Hidden by the white moustache,
his lips, stained with tobacco-juice that trickled down the long
beard, moved in inward whisper. His bleared eyes gazed fixedly
from behind the glitter of black-rimmed glasses. Opposite to him,
and on a level with his face, the ship's cat sat on the barrel of the
windlass in the pose of a crouching chimera,[14] blinking its green
eyes at its old friend. It seemed to meditate a leap on to the old
man's lap over the bent back of the ordinary seaman who sat at
Singleton's feet. Young Charley was lean and long-necked. The
ridge of his backbone made a chain of small hills under the old
shirt. His face of a street-boy—a face precocious, sagacious, and
ironic, with deep downward folds on each side of the thin, wide
mouth—hung low over his bony knees. He was learning to make a
lanyard knot with a bit of an old rope. Small drops of perspiration
stood out on his bulging forehead; he sniffed strongly from time to
time, glancing out of the corners of his restless eyes at the old
seaman, who took no notice of the puzzled youngster muttering at
his work.

4

The noise increased. Little Belfast seemed, in the heavy heat of the forecastle, to boil with facetious fury. His eyes danced; in the crimson of his face, comical as a mask, the mouth yawned black, with strange grimaces. Facing him, a half-undressed man held his sides, and, throwing his head back, laughed with wet eyelashes. Others stared with amazed eyes. Men sitting doubled up in the upper bunks smoked short pipes, swinging bare brown feet above the heads of those who, sprawling below on sea-chests, listened, smiling stupidly or scornfully. Over the white rims of berths stuck out heads with blinking eyes; but the bodies were lost in the gloom of those places, that resembled narrow niches for coffins in a white-washed and lighted mortuary. Voices buzzed louder. Archie, with compressed lips, drew himself in, seemed to shrink into a smaller space, and sewed steadily, industrious and dumb. Belfast shrieked like an inspired Dervish:—'. . . . So I seez to him,'s boys, seez I, "Beggin' yer pardon, sorr," seez I to that second mate of that steamer—"beggin' your-r-r pardon, sorr, the Board of Trade must 'ave been drunk when they granted you your certificate!" "What do you say, you ——!" seez he, comin' at me like a mad bull . . . . all in his white clothes; and I up with my tarpot and capsizes it all over his blamed lovely face and his lovely jacket. . . . . "Take that!" seez I. "I am a sailor, anyhow, you nosing, skipper-licking, useless, sooperfloos bridge-stanchion, you! That's the kind of man I am!" shouts I. . . . . You should have seed him skip, boys! Drowned, blind with tar, he was! So . . . .'

'Don't 'ee believe him! He never upset no tar; I was there!' shouted somebody. The two Norwegians sat on a chest side by side, alike and placid, resembling a pair of love-birds on a perch, and with round eyes stared innocently; but the Russian Finn, in the racket of explosive shouts and rolling laughter, remained motionless, limp and dull, like a deaf man without a backbone. Near him Archie smiled at his needle. A broad-chested, slow-eyed newcomer spoke deliberately to Belfast during an exhausted lull in the noise:—'I wonder any of the mates here are alive yet with such a chap as you on board! I concloode they ain't that bad now, if you had the taming of them, sonny.'

'Not bad! Not bad!' screamed Belfast. 'If it wasn't for us sticking together. . . . . Not bad! They ain't never bad when they ain't got a chawnce, blast their black 'arts. . . . .' He foamed, whirling his arms, then suddenly grinned and, taking a tablet of black tobacco out of his pocket, bit a piece off with a funny show of ferocity. Another new hand—a man with shifty eyes and a yellow hatchet face, who had been listening open-mouthed in the shadow of the midship locker—observed in a squeaky voice:—'Well, it's a 'omeward trip, anyhow. Bad or good, I can do it hall on my 'ed—s'long as I get 'ome. And I can look after my rights! I will show 'em!' All the heads turned towards him. Only the ordinary seaman and the cat took no notice. He stood with arms akimbo, a little fellow with white eyelashes. He looked as if he had known all the degradations and all the furies. He looked as if he had been cuffed, kicked, rolled in the mud; he looked as if he had been scratched, spat upon, pelted with unmentionable filth . . . . and he smiled with a sense of security at the faces around. His ears were bending down under the weight of his battered hard hat. The torn tails of his black coat flapped in fringes about the calves of his legs. He unbuttoned the only two buttons that remained and every one saw he had no shirt under it. It was his deserved misfortune that those rags which nobody could possibly be supposed to own looked on him as if they had been stolen. His neck was long and thin; his eyelids were red; rare hairs hung about his jaws; his shoulders were peaked and drooped like the broken wings of a bird; all his left side was caked with mud which showed that he had lately slept in a wet ditch. He had saved his inefficient carcass from violent destruction by running away from an American ship[16] where, in a moment of forgetful folly, he had dared to engage himself; and he had knocked about for a fortnight ashore in the native quarter, cadging for drinks, starving, sleeping on rubbish-heaps, wandering in sun-shine: a startling visitor from a world of nightmares. He stood repulsive and smiling in the sudden silence. This clean white forecastle was his refuge; the place where he could be lazy; where he could wallow, and lie and eat—and curse the food he ate; where he could display his talents for shirking work, for cheating, for cadging; where he could find surely some one to wheedle and some one to bully—and where he would be paid for doing all this. They all knew him. Is there a spot on earth where such a man is unknown, an ominous survival testifying to the eternal fitness of

6

lies and impudence? A taciturn long-armed shellback, with hooked
fingers, who had been lying on his back smoking, turned in his bed
to examine him dispassionately, then, over his head, sent a long jet
of clear saliva towards the door. They all knew him! He was the
man that cannot steer, that cannot splice, that dodges the work on
dark nights; that, aloft, holds on frantically with both arms and
legs, and swears at the wind, the sleet, the darkness; the man who
curses the sea while others work. The man who is the last out and
the first in when all hands are called. The man who can't do most
things and won't do the rest. The pet of philanthropists and self-
seeking landlubbers.[17] The sympathetic and deserving creature
that knows all about his rights, but knows nothing of courage, of
endurance, and of the unexpressed faith, of the unspoken loyalty
that knits together a ship's company. The independent offspring of
the ignoble freedom of the slums full of disdain and hate for the
austere servitude of the sea.

Some one cried at him: 'What's your name?'—'Donkin,' he said,
looking round with cheerful effrontery.—'What are you?' asked
another voice.—'Why, a sailor like you, old man,' he replied, in a
tone that meant to be hearty but was impudent.—'Blamme if you
don't look a blamed sight worse[18] than a broken-down fireman,'
was the comment in a convinced mutter. Charley lifted his head
and piped in a cheeky voice: 'He is a man and a sailor'—then
wiping his nose with the back of his hand bent down industriously
over his bit of rope. A few laughed. Others stared doubtfully. The
ragged newcomer was indignant.—'That's a fine way to welcome
a chap into a fo'c'sle,' he snarled. 'Are you men or a lot of 'artless
cannybals?'—'Don't take your shirt off for a word, shipmate,' called
out Belfast, jumping up in front, fiery, menacing, and friendly at
the same time.—'Is that 'ere bloke blind?' asked the indomitable
scarecrow, looking right and left with affected surprise. 'Can't 'ee
see I 'aven't got no shirt?'

He held both his arms out crosswise and shook the rags that
hung over his bones with dramatic effect.

''Cos why?' he continued very loud. 'The bloody Yankees been
tryin' to jump my guts hout 'cos I stood up for my rights like a
good 'un. I ham a Henglishman, I ham. They set upon me an' I 'ad
to run. That's why. A'n't yer never seed a man 'ard up? Yah!

What kind of blamed ship is this? I'm dead broke. I 'aven't got nothink. No bag, no bed, no blanket, no shirt—not a bloomin' rag but what I stand in. But I 'ad the 'art to stand hup agin' them Yankees. 'As any of you 'art enough to spare a pair of old pants for a chum?'

He knew how to conquer the naïve instincts of that crowd. In a moment they gave him their compassion, jocularly, contemptuously, or surlily; and at first it took the shape of a blanket thrown at him as he stood there with the white skin of his limbs showing his human kinship through the black fantasy of his rags. Then a pair of old shoes fell at his muddy feet. With a cry:—'From under,' a rolled-up pair of trousers, heavy with tar stains, struck him on the shoulder. The gust of their benevolence sent a wave of sentimental pity through their doubting hearts. They were touched by their own readiness to alleviate a shipmate's misery. Voices cried:— 'We will fit you out, old man.' Murmurs: 'Never seed seech a hard case. . . . . Poor beggar. . . . . I've got an old singlet. . . . . Will that be of any use to you?. . . . Take it, matey. . . . .' Those friendly murmurs filled the forecastle. He pawed around with his naked foot, gathering the things in a heap and looked about for more. Unemotional Archie perfunctorily contributed to the pile an old cloth cap with the peak torn off. Old Singleton, lost in the serene regions of fiction, read on unheeding. Charley, pitiless with the wisdom of youth, squeaked:—'If you want brass buttons for your new unyforms I've got two for you.' The filthy object of universal charity shook his fist at the youngster.—'I'll make you keep this 'ere fo'c'sle clean, young feller,' he snarled viciously. 'Never you fear. I will learn you to be civil to an able seaman, you hignorant hass.' He glared harmfully, but saw Singleton shut his book, and his little beady eyes began to roam from berth to berth.—'Take that bunk by the door there—it's pretty fair,' suggested Belfast. So advised, he gathered the gifts at his feet, pressed them in a bundle against his breast, then looked cautiously at the Russian Finn, who stood on one side with an unconscious gaze, contemplating, perhaps, one of those weird visions that haunt the men of his race.[19] 'Get out of my road, Dutchy,' said the victim of Yankee brutality. The Finn did not move—did not hear. 'Get out, blast ye,' shouted the other, shoving him aside with his elbow. 'Get out, you blanked deaf and dumb fool. Get out.' The man staggered, recovered him-self, and gazed at the speaker in silence.—'Those damned furriners should be kept hunder,' opined the amiable Donkin to the fore-castle. 'If you don't teach 'em their place they put on you like hanythink.' He flung all his worldly possessions into the empty bed-place, gauged with another shrewd look the risks of the pro-ceeding, then leaped up to the Finn, who stood pensive and dull.— 'I'll teach you to swell around,' he yelled. 'I'll plug your eyes for you, you blooming square-head.' Most of the men were now in their bunks and the two had the forecastle clear to themselves. The development of the destitute Donkin aroused interest. He danced all in tatters before the amazed Finn, squaring from a distance at the heavy, unmoved face. One or two men cried encouragingly: 'Go it, Whitechapel!' settling themselves luxuriously in their beds to survey the fight. Others shouted: 'Shut yer row! . . . . Go an' put yer 'ed in a bag! . . . .' The hubbub was recommencing. Suddenly many heavy blows struck with a handspike on the deck above boomed like discharges of small cannon through the forecastle. Then the boatswain's voice rose outside the door with an authori-tative note in its drawl:—'D'ye hear, below there? Lay aft! Lay aft to muster all hands!'

There was a moment of surprised stillness. Then the forecastle floor disappeared under men whose bare feet flopped on the planks as they sprang clear out of their berths. Caps were rooted for amongst tumbled blankets. Some, yawning, buttoned waistbands. Half-smoked pipes were knocked hurriedly against woodwork and stuffed under pillows. Voices growled:—'What's up? . . . . Is there no rest for us?' Donkin yelped:—'If that's the way of this ship, we'll 'ave to change hall that. . . . . You leave me alone. . . . . I will soon. . . . .' None of the crowd noticed him. They were lurching in twos and threes through the doors, after the manner of merchant Jacks who cannot go out of a door fairly, like mere landsmen. The votary of change followed them. Singleton, struggling into his jacket, came last, tall and fatherly, bearing high his head of a weatherbeaten sage on the body of an old athlete. Only Charley remained alone in the white glare of the empty place, sitting be-tween the two rows of iron links that stretched into the narrow gloom forward. He pulled hard at the strands in a hurried

9

endeavour to finish his knot. Suddenly he started up, flung the rope at the cat, and skipped after the black tom that went off leaping sedately over chain compressors, with the tail carried stiff and upright, like a small flag pole.

Outside the glare of the steaming forecastle the serene purity of the night enveloped the seamen with its soothing breath, with its tepid breath flowing under the stars that hung countless above the mastheads in a thin cloud of luminous dust. On the town side the blackness of the water was streaked with trails of light which undulated gently on slight ripples, similar to filaments that float rooted to the shore. Rows of other lights stood away in straight lines as if drawn up on parade between towering buildings; but on the other side of the harbour sombre hills arched high their black spines, on which, here and there, the point of a star resembled a spark fallen from the sky. Far off, Byculla way, the electric lamps at the dock gates shone on the end of lofty standards with a glow blinding and frigid like captive ghosts of some evil moons. Scattered all over the dark polish of the roadstead, the ships at anchor floated in perfect stillness under the feeble gleam of their riding-lights, looming up, opaque and bulky, like strange and monumental structures abandoned by men to an everlasting repose.

Before the cabin door Mr. Baker was mustering the crew. As they stumbled and lurched along past the mainmast, they could see aft his round, broad face with a white paper before it, and beside his shoulder the sleepy head, with dropped eyelids, of the boy, who held, suspended at the end of his raised arm, the luminous globe of a lamp. Even before the shuffle of naked soles had ceased along the decks, the mate began to call over the names. He called distinctly in a serious tone befitting this roll-call to unquiet loneliness, to inglorious and obscure struggle, or to the more trying endurance of small privations and wearisome duties. As the chief mate read out a name, one of the men would answer: 'Yes, sir!' or 'Here!' and, detaching himself from the shadowy mob of heads visible above the blackness of starboard bulwarks, would step barefooted into the circle of light, and in two noiseless strides pass into the shadows on the port side of the quarter-deck. They answered in divers tones: in thick mutters, in clear, ringing voices; and some, as if the whole thing had been an outrage on their feelings, used an injured intonation: for discipline is not ceremonious in merchant ships, where the sense of hierarchy is weak, and where all feel themselves equal before the unconcerned immensity of the sea and the exacting appeal of the work.

Mr. Baker read on steadily:—'Hanssen—Campbell—Smith—Wamibo. Now, then, Wamibo. Why don't you answer? Always got to call your name twice.'[20] The Finn emitted at last an uncouth grunt, and, stepping out, passed through the patch of light, weird and gaudy, with the face of a man marching through a dream. The mate went on faster:—'Craik—Singleton—Donkin. . . . . O Lord!' he involuntarily ejaculated as the incredibly dilapidated figure appeared in the light. It stopped; it uncovered pale gums and long, upper teeth in a malevolent grin.—'Is there anythink wrong with me, Mister Mate?' it asked, with a flavour of insolence in the forced simplicity of its tone. On both sides of the deck subdued titters were heard.—'That'll do. Go over,' growled Mr. Baker, fixing the new hand with steady blue eyes. And Donkin vanished suddenly out of the light into the dark group of mustered men, to be slapped on the back and to hear flattering whispers. Round him men muttered to one another:—'He ain't afeard, he'll give sport to 'em, see if he don't. . . . . Reg'lar Punch and Judy show. . . . . Did ye see the mate start at him?. . . . Well! Damme, if I ever! . . . .'

The last man had gone over, and there was a moment of silence while the mate peered at his list.—'Sixteen, seventeen,' he muttered. 'I am one hand short, bosun,' he said aloud. The big west-countryman at his elbow, swarthy and bearded like a gigantic Spaniard, said in a rumbling bass:—'There's no one left forward, sir. I had a look round. He ain't aboard, but he may turn up before daylight.'—'Ay. He may or he may not,' commented the mate; 'can't make out that last name. It's all a smudge. . . . . That will do, men. Go below.'

The indistinct and motionless group stirred, broke up, began to move forward.

'Wait!'[21] cried a deep, ringing voice.

All stood still. Mr. Baker, who had turned away yawning, spun round open-mouthed. At last, furious, he blurted out:—'What's this? Who said "Wait"? What . . . .'

But he saw a tall figure standing on the rail. It came down and pushed through the crowd, marching with a heavy tread towards the light on the quarter-deck. Then again the sonorous voice said with insistence:—'Wait!' The lamplight lit up the man's body. He was tall. His head was away up in the shadows of lifeboats that stood on skids above the deck. The whites of his eyes and his teeth gleamed distinctly, but the face was indistinguishable. His hands were big and seemed gloved.

Mr. Baker advanced intrepidly. 'Who are you? How dare you . . . .' he began.

The boy, amazed like the rest, raised the light to the man's face. It was black. A surprised hum—a faint hum that sounded like the suppressed mutter of the word 'Nigger'—ran along the deck and escaped out into the night. The nigger seemed not to hear. He balanced himself where he stood in a swagger that marked time. After a moment he said calmly:—'My name is Wait—James Wait.'

'Oh!' said Mr. Baker. Then, after a few seconds of smouldering silence, his temper blazed out. 'Ah! Your name is Wait. What of that? What do you want? What do you mean, coming shouting here?'

The nigger was calm, cool, towering, superb. The men had approached and stood behind him in a body. He overtopped the tallest by half a head. He said: 'I belong to the ship.' He enunciated distinctly, with soft precision. The deep, rolling tones of his voice filled the deck without effort. He was naturally scornful, unaffectedly condescending, as if from his height of six foot three he had surveyed all the vastness of human folly and had made up his mind not to be too hard on it. He went on:—'The captain shipped me this morning. I couldn't get aboard sooner. I saw you all aft as I came up the ladder, and could see directly you were mustering the crew. Naturally I called out my name. I thought you had it on your list, and would understand. You misapprehended.' He stopped short. The folly around him was confounded. He was right as ever, and as ever ready to forgive. The disdainful tones had ceased, and, breathing heavily, he stood still, surrounded by all these white men. He held his head up in the glare of the lamp—a head vigorously modelled into deep shadows and shining lights—a head powerful and misshapen with a tormented and flattened face—a face pathetic and brutal: the tragic, the mysterious, the repulsive mask of a nigger's soul.[22]

Mr. Baker, recovering his composure, looked at the paper close. 'Oh, yes; that's so. All right, Wait. Take your gear forward,' he said.

Suddenly the nigger's eyes rolled wildly, became all whites. He put his hand to his side and coughed twice, a cough metallic, hollow, and tremendously loud; it resounded like two explosions in a vault; the dome of the sky rang to it, and the iron plates of the ship's bulwarks seemed to vibrate in unison; then he marched off forward with the others. The officers lingering by the cabin door could hear him say: 'Won't some of you chaps lend a hand with my dunnage? I've got a chest and a bag.' The words, spoken sonorously, with an even intonation, were heard all over the ship, and the question was put in a manner that made refusal impossible. The short, quick shuffle of men carrying something heavy went away forward, but the tall figure of the nigger lingered by the main hatch in a knot of smaller shapes. Again he was heard asking: 'Is your cook a coloured gentleman?'²³ Then a disappointed and disapproving 'Ah! h'm!' was his comment upon the information that the cook happened to be a mere white man. Yet, as they went all together towards the forecastle, he condescended to put his head through the galley door and boom out inside a magnificent 'Good evening, doctor!' that made all the saucepans ring. In the dim light the cook dozed on the coal locker in front of the captain's supper. He jumped up as if he had been cut with a whip, and dashed wildly on deck to see the backs of several men going away laughing. Afterwards, when talking about that voyage, he used to say:—'The poor fellow had scared me. I thought I had seen the devil.' The cook had been seven years in the ship with the same captain. He was a serious-minded man with a wife and three children, whose society he enjoyed on an average one month out of twelve. When on shore he took his family to church twice every Sunday.²⁴ At sea he went to sleep every evening with his lamp turned up full, a pipe in his mouth, and an open Bible in his hand. Some one had always to go during the night to put out the light, take the book from his hand, and the pipe from between his teeth. 'For'—Belfast used to say, irritated and complaining—'some night, you stupid cookie, you'll swallow your ould clay, and we will have no cook.'—'Ah! sonny, I am ready for my Maker's call . . . . wish you all were,' the other would answer with a benign serenity that was altogether imbecile and touching. Belfast outside the galley door danced with vexation. 'You holy fool! I don't want you to die,' he howled, looking up with furious, quivering face and tender eyes. 'What's the hurry? you blessed wooden-headed ould heretic, the divvle will have you soon enough. Think of Us . . . . of Us . . . . of Us!' And he would go away, stamping, spitting aside, disgusted and worried; while the other, stepping out, saucepan in hand, hot, begrimed, and placid, watched with a superior, cock-sure smile the back of his 'queer little man' reeling in a rage. They were great friends.

Mr. Baker, lounging over the after-hatch, sniffed the humid night in the company of the second mate.—'Those West India niggers run fine and large—some of them . . . . Ough! . . . . Don't they? A fine, big man that, Mr. Creighton. Feel him on a rope. Hey? Ough! I will take him into my watch, I think.' The second mate, a fair, gentlemanly young fellow, with a resolute face and a splendid physique, observed quietly that it was just about what he expected. There could be felt in his tone some slight bitterness which Mr. Baker very kindly set himself to argue away. 'Come, come, young man,' he said, grunting between the words. 'Come! Don't be too greedy. You had that big Finn in your watch all the voyage. I will do what's fair. You may have those two young Scandinavians and I . . . . Ough! . . . . I get the nigger, and will take that . . . . Ough! that cheeky costermonger chap in a black frock-coat. I'll make him . . . . Ough! . . . . make him toe the mark, or my . . . . Ough! . . . . name isn't Baker. Ough! Ough! Ough!'

He grunted thrice—ferociously. He had that trick of grunting so between his words and at the end of sentences. It was a fine, effective grunt that went well with his menacing utterance, with his heavy, bull-necked frame, his jerky, rolling gait; with his big, seamed face, his steady eyes, and sardonic mouth. But its effect had been long ago discounted by the men. They liked him; Belfast—who was a favourite, and knew it—mimicked him, not quite behind his back. Charley—but with greater caution—imitated his walk. Some of his sayings became established, daily quotations in the forecastle. Popularity can go no farther! Besides, all hands were ready to admit that on a fitting occasion the mate could 'jump down a fellow's throat in a reg'lar Western Ocean style.'

Now he was giving his last orders. 'Ough! .... You, Knowles! Call all hands at four. I want .... Ough! .... to heave short before the tug comes. Look out for the captain. I am going to lay down in my clothes..... Ough! .... Call me when you see the boat coming. Ough! Ough! .... The old man is sure to have something to say when he comes aboard,' he remarked to Creighton. 'Well, good-night..... Ough! A long day before us to-morrow..... Ough! .... Better turn in now. Ough! Ough!'

Upon the dark deck a band of light flashed, then a door slammed, and Mr. Baker was gone into his neat cabin. Young Creighton stood leaning over the rail, and looked dreamily into the night of the East. And he saw in it a long country lane, a lane of waving leaves and dancing sunshine. He saw stirring boughs of old trees outspread, and framing in their arch the tender, the caressing blueness of an English sky. And through the arch a girl in a clear dress, smiling under a sunshade, seemed to be stepping out of the tender sky.

At the other end of the ship the forecastle, with only one lamp burning now, was going to sleep in a dim emptiness traversed by loud breathings, by sudden short sighs. The double row of berths yawned black, like graves tenanted by uneasy corpses. Here and there a curtain of gaudy chintz, half drawn, marked the resting-place of a sybarite. A leg hung over the edge very white and lifeless. An arm stuck straight out with a dark palm turned up, and thick fingers half closed. Two light snores, that did not synchronise, quarrelled in funny dialogue. Singleton stripped again—the old man suffered much from prickly heat—stood cooling his back in the doorway, with his arms crossed on his bare and adorned chest. His head touched the beam of the deck above. The nigger, half undressed, was busy casting adrift the lashing of his box, and spreading his bedding in an upper berth. He moved about in his socks, tall and noiseless, with a pair of braces beating about his heels. Amongst the shadows of stanchions and bowsprit, Donkin munched a piece of hard ship's bread, sitting on the deck with upturned feet and restless eyes; he held the biscuit up before his mouth in the whole fist, and snapped his jaws at it with a raging face. Crumbs fell between his outspread legs. Then he got up.

'Where's our water-cask?' he asked in a contained voice.

THE NIGGER OF THE 'NARCISSUS'

Singleton, without a word, pointed with a big hand that held a short smouldering pipe. Donkin bent over the cask, drank out of the tin, splashing the water, turned round and noticed the nigger looking at him over the shoulder with calm loftiness. He moved up sideways.

'There's a blooming supper for a man,' he whispered bitterly. 'My dorg at 'ome wouldn't 'ave it. It's fit enouf for you an' me. 'Ere's a big ship's fo'c'sle! .... Not a blooming scrap of meat in the kids. I've looked in all the lockers. . . . .'

The nigger stared like a man addressed unexpectedly in a foreign language. Donkin changed his tone:—'Giv' us a bit of 'baccy, mate,' he breathed out confidentially, 'I 'aven't 'ad smoke or chew for the last month. I am rampin' mad for it. Come on, old man!'

'Don't be familiar,' said the nigger. Donkin started and sat down on a chest near by, out of sheer surprise. 'We haven't kept pigs together,'[25] continued James Wait in a deep undertone. 'Here's your tobacco.' Then, after a pause, he asked:—'What ship?'— '*Golden State*,' muttered Donkin indistinctly, biting the tobacco. The nigger whistled low.—'Ran?' he said curtly. Donkin nodded: one of his cheeks bulged out.—'In course I ran,' he mumbled. 'They booted the life hout of one Dago chap on the passage 'ere, then started on me. I cleared hout 'ere.'—'Left your dunnage behind?'—'Yes, dunnage and money,' answered Donkin, raising his voice a little; 'I got nothink. No clothes, no bed. A bandy-legged little Hirish chap 'ere 'as give me a blanket. . . . . Think I'll go an' sleep in the fore topmast staysail to-night.'

He went on deck trailing behind his back a corner of the blanket. Singleton, without a glance, moved slightly aside to let him pass. The nigger put away his shore togs and sat in clean working clothes on his box, one arm stretched over his knees. After staring at Singleton for some time he asked without emphasis:—'What kind of ship is this? Pretty fair? Eh?'

Singleton didn't stir. A long while after he said, with unmoved face:—'Ship! .... Ships are all right. It is the men in them!'

He went on smoking in the profound silence. The wisdom of half a century spent in listening to the thunder of the waves had spoken unconsciously through his old lips. The cat purred on the windlass. Then James Wait had a fit of roaring, rattling cough, that shook him, tossed him like a hurricane, and flung him panting with staring eyes headlong on his sea-chest. Several men woke up. One said sleepily out of his bunk: "Struth! what a blamed row!'—'I have a cold on my chest,' gasped Wait.—'Cold! you call it,' grumbled the man; 'should think 'twas something more. . . . .'— 'Oh! you think so,' said the nigger upright and loftily scornful again. He climbed into his berth and began coughing persistently while he put his head out to glare all round the forecastle. There was no further protest. He fell back on the pillow, and could be heard there wheezing regularly like a man oppressed in his sleep.

Singleton stood at the door with his face to the light and his back to the darkness. And alone in the dim emptiness of the sleeping forecastle he appeared bigger, colossal, very old; old as Father Time himself, who should have come there into this place as quiet as a sepulchre to contemplate with patient eyes the short victory of sleep, the consoler. Yet he was only a child of time, a lonely relic of a devoured and forgotten generation. He stood, still strong, as ever unthinking; a ready man with a vast empty past and with no future, with his childlike impulses and his man's passions already dead within his tattooed breast. The men who could understand his silence were gone—those men who knew how to exist beyond the pale of life and within sight of eternity. They had been strong, as those are strong who know neither doubts nor hopes. They had been impatient and enduring, turbulent and devoted, unruly and faithful. Well-meaning people had tried to represent those men as whining over every mouthful of their food; as going about their work in fear of their lives.[26] But in truth they had been men who knew toil,[27] privation, violence, debauchery—but knew not fear, and had no desire of spite in their hearts. Men hard to manage, but easy to inspire; voiceless men— but men enough to scorn in their hearts the sentimental voices that bewailed the hardness of their fate. It was a fate unique and their own; the capacity to bear it appeared to them the privilege of the chosen! Their generation lived inarticulate and indispensable, without knowing the sweetness of affections or the refuge of a home—and died free from the dark menace of a narrow grave. They were the everlasting children of the mysterious sea. Their successors are the grown-up children of a discontented earth. They

17

are less naughty, but less innocent; less profane, but perhaps also less believing; and if they had learned how to speak they have also learned how to whine.[28] But the others were strong and mute; they were effaced, bowed and enduring, like stone caryatides that hold up in the night the lighted halls of a resplendent and glorious edifice. They are gone now—and it does not matter. The sea and the earth are unfaithful to their children: a truth, a faith, a generation of men goes—and is forgotten, and it does not matter! Except, perhaps, to the few of those who believed the truth, confessed the faith—or loved the men.

A breeze was coming. The ship that had been lying tide-rode swung to a heavier puff; and suddenly the slack of the chain cable between the windlass and the hawse-pipe clinked, slipped forward an inch, and rose gently off the deck with a startling suggestion as of unsuspected life that had been lurking stealthily in the iron. In the hawse-pipe the grinding links sent through the ship a sound like a low groan of a man sighing under a burden. The strain came on the windlass, the chain tautened like a string, vibrated—and the handle of the screw-brake moved in slight jerks. Singleton stepped forward.

Till then he had been standing meditative and unthinking, reposeful and hopeless, with a face grim and blank—a sixty-year-old child of the mysterious sea. The thoughts of all his lifetime could have been expressed in six words, but the stir of those things that were as much part of his existence as his beating heart called up a gleam of alert understanding upon the sternness of his aged face. The flame of the lamp swayed, and the old man, with knitted and bushy eyebrows, stood over the brake, watchful and motionless in the wild saraband of dancing shadows. Then the ship, obedient to the call of her anchor, forged ahead slightly and eased the strain. The cable relieved, hung down, and after swaying imperceptibly to and fro dropped with a loud tap on the hard wood planks. Singleton seized the high lever, and, by a violent throw forward of his body, wrung out another half-turn from the brake. He recovered himself, breathed largely, and remained for awhile glaring down at the powerful and compact engine that squatted on the deck at his feet, like some quiet monster—a creature amazing and tame.

'You . . . . hold!' he growled at it masterfully, in the incult tangle of his white beard.

NEXT morning, at daylight, the *Narcissus* went to sea. A slight haze blurred the horizon. Outside the harbour the measureless expanse of smooth water lay sparkling like a floor of jewels, and as empty as the sky. The short black tug gave a pluck to windward, in the usual way, then let go the rope, and hovered for a moment on the quarter with her engines stopped; while the slim, long hull of the ship moved ahead slowly under lower top-sails. The loose upper canvas blew out in the breeze with soft round contours, resembling small white clouds snared in the maze of ropes. Then the sheets were hauled home, the yards hoisted, and the ship became a high and lonely pyramid, gliding, all shining and white, through the sunlit mist. The tug turned short round and went away towards the land. Twenty-six pairs of eyes watched her low broad stern crawling languidly over the smooth swell between the two paddle-wheels that turned fast, beating the water with fierce hurry. She resembled an enormous and aquatic blackbeetle, surprised by the light, overwhelmed by the sunshine, trying to escape with ineffectual effort into the distant gloom of the land. She left a lingering smudge of smoke on the sky, and two vanishing trails of foam on the water. On the place where she had stopped a round black patch of soot remained, undulating on the swell—an unclean mark of the creature's rest.

The *Narcissus* left alone, heading south, seemed to stand resplendent and still upon the restless sea, under the moving sun. Flakes of foam swept past her sides; the water struck her with flashing blows; the land glided away, slowly fading; a few birds screamed on motionless wings over the swaying mastheads. But soon the land disappeared, the birds went away; and to the west the pointed sail of an Arab dhow running for Bombay, rose triangular and upright above the sharp edge of the horizon, lingered, and vanished like an illusion. Then the ship's wake, long and straight, stretched itself out through a day of immense solitude. The setting sun, burning on the level of the water, flamed crimson below the blackness of heavy rain clouds. The sunset squall, coming up from behind, dissolved itself into the short deluge of a hissing shower. It left the ship glistening from trucks to waterline, and with darkened sails. She ran easily before a fair monsoon, with her decks cleared for the night; and, moving along with her, was heard the sustained and monotonous swishing of the waves, mingled with the low whispers of men mustered aft for the setting of watches; the short plaint of some block aloft; or, now and then, a loud sigh of wind.

Mr. Baker, coming out of his cabin, called out the first name sharply before closing the door behind him. He was going to take charge of the deck. On the homeward trip, according to an old custom of the sea, the chief officer takes the first night-watch—from eight till midnight. So Mr. Baker, after he had heard the last 'Yes, sir!' said moodily, 'Relieve the wheel and look-out'; and climbed with heavy feet the poop ladder to windward. Soon after Mr. Creighton came down, whistling softly, and went into the cabin. On the doorstep the steward lounged, in slippers, meditative, and with his shirt-sleeves rolled up to the armpits. On the main deck the cook, locking up the galley doors, had an altercation with young Charley about a pair of socks. He could be heard saying impressively, in the darkness amidships: 'You don't deserve a kindness. I've been drying them for you, and now you complain about the holes—and you swear, too! Right in front of me! If I hadn't been a Christian—which you ain't, you young ruffian—I would give you a clout on the head. . . . . Go away!' Men in couples or threes stood pensive or moved silently along the bulwarks in the waist. The first busy day of a homeward passage was sinking into the dull peace of resumed routine. Aft, on the high poop, Mr. Baker walked shuffling; grunted to himself in the pauses of his thoughts. Forward, the look-out man, erect between the flukes of the two anchors, hummed an endless tune, keeping his eyes fixed dutifully ahead in a vacant stare. A multitude of stars coming out into the clear night peopled the emptiness of the sky. They glittered, as if alive above the sea; they surrounded the running ship on all sides; more intense than the eyes of a staring crowd, and as inscrutable as the souls of men.

The passage had begun; and the ship, a fragment detached from the earth, went on lonely and swift like a small planet. Round her the abysses of sky and sea met in an unattainable frontier. A great circular solitude moved with her, ever changing and ever the same, always monotonous and always imposing. Now and then another wandering white speck, burdened with life, appeared far off—disappeared; intent on its own destiny. The sun looked upon her all day, and every morning rose with a burning, round stare of undying curiosity. She had her own future; she was alive with the lives of those beings who trod her decks; like that earth which had given her up to the sea, she had an intolerable load of regrets and hopes. On her lived timid truth and audacious lies; and, like the earth, she was unconscious, fair to see—and condemned by men to an ignoble fate. The august loneliness of her path lent dignity to the sordid inspiration of her pilgrimage. She drove foaming to the southward, as if guided by the courage of a high endeavour. The smiling greatness of the sea dwarfed the extent of time. The days raced after one another, brilliant and quick like the flashes of a lighthouse, and the nights, eventful and short, resembled fleeting dreams.

The men had shaken into their places, and the half-hourly voice of the bells ruled their life of unceasing care. Night and day the head and shoulders of a seaman could be seen aft by the wheel, outlined high against sunshine or starlight, very steady above the stir of revolving spokes. The faces changed, passing in rotation. Youthful faces, bearded faces, dark faces: faces serene, or faces moody, but all akin with the brotherhood of the sea; all with the same attentive expression of eyes, carefully watching the compass or the sails. Captain Allistoun, serious, and with an old red muffler round his throat, all day long pervaded the poop. At night, many times he rose out of the darkness of the companion, such as a phantom above a grave, and stood watchful and mute under the stars, his night-shirt fluttering like a flag—then, without a sound, sank down again. He was born on the shores of the Pentland Firth. In his youth he attained the rank of harpooner in Peterhead whalers. When he spoke of that time his restless grey eyes became still and cold, like the loom of ice. Afterwards he went into the East Indian trade for the sake of change. He had commanded the *Narcissus* since she was built. He loved his ship, and drove her unmercifully; for his secret ambition was to make her accomplish some day a brilliantly quick passage which would be mentioned in nautical papers. He pronounced his owner's name with a sardonic smile, spoke but seldom to his officers, and reproved errors in a gentle voice, with words that cut to the quick. His hair was iron-grey, his face hard and of the colour of pump-leather. He shaved every morning of his life—at six—but once (being caught in a fierce hurricane eighty miles south-west of Mauritius) he had missed three consecutive days. He feared naught but an unforgiving God, and wished to end his days in a little house, with a plot of ground attached—far in the country—out of sight of the sea.

He, the ruler of that minute world, seldom descended from the Olympian heights of his poop. Below him—at his feet, so to speak— common mortals led their busy and insignificant lives. Along the main deck Mr. Baker grunted in a manner bloodthirsty and innocuous; and kept all our noses to the grindstone, being—as he once remarked—paid for doing that very thing. The men working about the deck were healthy and contented—as most seamen are, when once well out to sea. The true peace of God begins at any spot a thousand miles from the nearest land; and when He sends there the messengers of His might it is not in terrible wrath against crime, presumption, and folly, but paternally, to chasten simple hearts—ignorant hearts that know nothing of life, and beat undisturbed by envy or greed.

In the evening the cleared decks had a reposeful aspect, resembling the autumn of the earth. The sun was sinking to rest, wrapped in a mantle of warm clouds. Forward, on the end of the spare spars, the boatswain and the carpenter sat together with crossed arms; two men friendly, powerful, and deep-chested. Beside them the short, dumpy sailmaker—who had been in the Navy—related, between the whiffs of his pipe, impossible stories about Admirals. Couples tramped backwards and forwards, keeping step and balance without effort, in a confined space. Pigs grunted in the big pigstye. Belfast, leaning thoughtfully on his elbow, above the bars, communed with them through the silence of his meditation. Fellows with shirts open wide on sunburnt breasts sat upon the mooring bits, and all up the steps of the forecastle ladders. By the foremast a few discussed in a circle the characteristics of a gentleman.[29] One said:—'It's money as does it.' Another maintained:— 'No, it's the way they speak.' Lame Knowles stumped up with an unwashed face (he had the distinction of being the dirty man of the forecastle), and, showing a few yellow fangs in a shrewd smile, explained craftily that he 'had seen some of their pants.' The backsides of them—he had observed—were thinner than paper from constant sitting down in offices, yet otherwise they looked first-rate and would last for years. It was all appearance. 'It was,' he said, 'bloomin' easy to be a gentleman when you had a clean job for life.' They disputed endlessly, obstinate and childish; they repeated in shouts and with inflamed faces their amazing arguments; while the soft breeze, eddying down the enormous cavity of the foresail, that stood out distended above their bare heads, stirred the tumbled hair with a touch passing and light like an indulgent caress.

They were forgetting their toil, they were forgetting themselves. The cook approached to hear, and stood by, beaming with the inward consciousness of his faith, like a conceited saint unable to forget his glorious reward; Donkin, solitary and brooding over his wrongs on the forecastle-head, moved closer to catch the drift of the discussion below him; he turned his sallow face to the sea, and his thin nostrils moved, sniffing the breeze, as he lounged negligently by the rail. In the glow of sunset faces shone with interest, teeth flashed, eyes sparkled. The walking couples stood still suddenly, with broad grins; a man, bending over a washtub, sat up, entranced, with the soapsuds flecking his wet arms. Even the three petty officers listened leaning back, comfortably propped, and with superior smiles. Belfast left off scratching the ear of his favourite pig, and, open mouthed, tried with eager eyes to have his say. He lifted his arms, grimacing and baffled. From a distance Charley screamed at the ring:—'I know about gentlemen morn'n any of you. I've been hintymate with 'em . . . . I've blacked their boots.' The cook, craning his neck to hear better, was scandalised. 'Keep your mouth shut when your elders speak, you impudent young heathen—you.' 'All right, old Hallelujah, I'm done,' answered Charley, soothingly. At some opinion of dirty Knowles, delivered with an air of supernatural cunning, a ripple of laughter ran along, rose like a wave, burst with a startling roar. They stamped with both feet; they turned their shouting faces to the sky; many, spluttering, slapped their thighs; while one or two, bent double, gasped, hugging themselves with both arms like men in pain. The carpenter and the boatswain, without changing their attitude, shook with laughter where they sat; the sailmaker, charged with an anecdote about a Commodore, looked sulky; the cook was wiping his eyes with a greasy rag; and lame Knowles, astonished at his own success, stood in their midst showing a slow smile.

Suddenly the face of Donkin leaning high-shouldered over the after-rail became grave. Something like a weak rattle was heard through the forecastle door. It became a murmur; it ended in a sighing groan. The washerman plunged both his arms into the tub abruptly; the cook became more crestfallen than an exposed backslider; the boatswain moved his shoulders uneasily; the carpenter got up with a spring and walked away—while the sailmaker seemed mentally to give his story up, and began to puff at his pipe with sombre determination. In the blackness of the doorway a pair of eyes glimmered white, and big, and staring. Then James Wait's head protruding, became visible, as if suspended between the two hands that grasped a doorpost on each side of the face. The tassel of his blue woollen nightcap, cocked forward, danced gaily over his left eyelid. He stepped out in a tottering stride. He looked powerful as ever, but showed a strange and affected unsteadiness in his gait; his face was perhaps a trifle thinner, and his eyes appeared rather startlingly prominent. He seemed to hasten the

24

retreat of departing light by his very presence; the setting sun dipped sharply, as though fleeing before our nigger; a black mist emanated from him; a subtle and dismal influence; a something cold and gloomy that floated out and settled on all the faces like a mourning veil. The circle broke up. The joy of laughter died on stiffened lips. There was not a smile left among all the ship's company. Not a word was spoken. Many turned their backs, trying to look unconcerned; others, with averted heads, sent half-reluctant glances out of the corners of their eyes. They resembled criminals conscious of misdeeds more than honest men distracted by doubt; only two or three stared frankly, but stupidly, with lips slightly open. All expected James Wait to say something, and, at the same time, had the air of knowing beforehand what he would say. He leaned his back against the doorpost, and with heavy eyes swept over us a glance domineering and pained, like a sick tyrant overawing a crowd of abject but untrustworthy slaves.

No one went away. They waited in fascinated dread. He said ironically, with gasps between the words:—

'Thank you . . . . chaps. You . . . . are nice . . . . and . . . . quiet . . . . you are! Yelling so . . . . before . . . . the door . . . .'

He made a longer pause, during which he worked his ribs in an exaggerated labour of breathing. It was intolerable. Feet were shuffled. Belfast let out a groan; but Donkin above blinked his red eyelids with invisible eyelashes, and smiled bitterly over the nigger's head.

The nigger went on again with surprising ease. He gasped no more, and his voice rang, hollow and loud, as though he had been talking in an empty cavern. He was contemptuously angry.

'I tried to get a wink of sleep. You know I can't sleep o' nights. And you come jabbering near the door here like a blooming lot of old women. . . . . You think yourselves good shipmates. Do you? . . . . Much you care for a dying man!'

Belfast spun away from the pigstye. 'Jimmy,' he cried tremulously, 'if you hadn't been sick I would——'

He stopped. The nigger waited awhile, then said, in a gloomy tone:—'You would. . . . . What? Go an' fight another such one as yourself. Leave me alone. It won't be for long. I'll soon die. . . . . It's coming right enough!'

Men stood around very still, breathing lightly, and with exasperated eyes. It was just what they had expected, and hated to hear, that idea of a stalking death, thrust at them many times a day like a boast and like a menace by this obnoxious nigger. He seemed to take a pride in that death which, so far, had attended only upon the ease of his life; he was overbearing about it, as if no one else in the world had ever been intimate with such a companion; he paraded it unceasingly before us with an affectionate persistence that made its presence indubitable, and at the same time incredible. No man could be suspected of such monstrous friendship! Was he a reality—or was he a sham—this ever-expected visitor of Jimmy's? We hesitated between pity and mistrust, while, on the slightest provocation, he shook before our eyes the bones of his bothersome and infamous skeleton. He was for ever trotting him out. He would talk of that coming death as though it had been already there, as if it had been walking the deck outside, as if it would presently come in to sleep in the only empty bunk; as if it had sat by his side at every meal. It interfered daily with our occupations, with our leisure, with our amusements. We had no songs and no music in the evening, because Jimmy (we all lovingly called him Jimmy, to conceal our hate of his accomplice) had managed, with that prospective decease of his, to disturb even Archie's mental balance. Archie was the owner of the concertina; but after a couple of stinging lectures from Jimmy he refused to play any more. He said:—'Yon's an uncanny joker. I dinna ken what's wrang wi' him,[30] but there's something verra wrang, verra wrang. It's nae manner of use asking me. I won't play.' Our singers became mute because Jimmy was a dying man. For the same reason no chap—as Knowles remarked—could 'drive in a nail to hang his few poor rags upon,' without being made aware of the enormity he committed in disturbing Jimmy's interminable last moments. At night, instead of the cheerful yell, 'One bell! Turn out! Do you hear there? Hey! hey! hey! Show leg!' the watches were called man by man, in whispers, so as not to interfere with Jimmy's, possibly, last slumber on earth. True, he was always awake, and managed, as we sneaked out on deck, to plant in our backs some cutting remark that, for the moment, made us feel as if we had been brutes, and afterwards made us suspect ourselves of being fools. We spoke in low tones within that fo'c'sle as though it had been a church. We ate our meals in silence and dread, for Jimmy was capricious with his food, and railed bitterly at the salt meat, at the biscuits, at the tea, as at articles unfit for human consumption—'let alone for a dying man!' He would say:—'Can't you find a better slice of meat for a sick man who's trying to get home to be cured—or buried? But there! If I had a chance, you fellows would do away with it. You would poison me. Look at what you have given me!' We served him in his bed with rage and humility, as though we had been the base courtiers of a hated prince; and he rewarded us by his unconciliating criticism. He had found the secret of keeping for ever on the run the fundamental imbecility of mankind; he had the secret of life, that confounded dying man, and he made himself master of every moment of our existence. We grew desperate, and remained submissive. Emotional little Belfast was for ever on the verge of assault or on the verge of tears. One evening he confided to Archie:—'For a ha'penny I would knock his ugly black head off—the skulking dodger!' And the straightforward Archie pretended to be shocked! Such was the infernal spell which that casual St. Kitt's nigger had cast upon our guileless manhood! But the same night Belfast stole from the galley the officers' Sunday fruit pie, to tempt the fastidious appetite of Jimmy. He endangered not only his long friendship with the cook but also—as it appeared—his eternal welfare. The cook was overwhelmed with grief; he did not know the culprit but he knew that wickedness flourished; he knew that Satan was abroad amongst those men, whom he looked upon as in some way under his spiritual care. Whenever he saw three or four of us standing together he would leave his stove, to run out and preach. We fled from him; and only Charley (who knew the thief) affronted the cook with a candid gaze which irritated the good man. 'It's you, I believe,' he groaned, sorrowful, and with a patch of soot on his chin. 'It's you. You are a brand for the burning! No more of YOUR socks in my galley.' Soon, unofficially, the information was spread about that, should there be another case of stealing, our marmalade (an extra allowance: half a pound per man) would be stopped. Mr. Baker ceased to heap jocular abuse upon his favourites, and grunted suspiciously at all. The captain's cold eyes, high up on the poop, glittered mistrustful, as he surveyed us trooping in a small mob from halyards to braces for the usual evening pull at all the ropes. Such stealing in a merchant ship is difficult to check, and may be taken as a declaration by men of their dislike for their officers. It is a bad symptom. It may end in God knows what trouble. The *Narcissus* was still a peaceful ship, but mutual confidence was shaken. Donkin did not conceal his delight. We were dismayed.

Then illogical Belfast reproached our nigger with great fury. James Wait, with his elbow on the pillow, choked, gasped out:— 'Did I ask you to bone the dratted thing? Blow your blamed pie. It has made me worse—you little Irish lunatic, you!' Belfast, with scarlet face and trembling lips, made a dash at him. Every man in the forecastle rose with a shout. There was a moment of wild tumult. Some one shrieked piercingly:—'Easy, Belfast! Easy! . . . .' We expected Belfast to strangle Wait without more ado. Dust flew. We heard through it the nigger's cough, metallic and explosive like a gong. Next moment we saw Belfast hanging over him. He was saying plaintively:—'Don't! Don't, Jimmy! Don't be like that. An angel couldn't put up with ye—sick as ye are.' He looked round at us from Jimmy's bedside, his comical mouth twitching, and through tearful eyes; then he tried to put straight the disarranged blankets. The unceasing whisper of the sea filled the forecastle. Was James Wait frightened, or touched, or repentant? He lay on his back with a hand to his side, and as motionless as if his expected visitor had come at last. Belfast fumbled about his feet, repeating with emotion:—'Yes. We know. Ye are bad, but . . . . Just say what ye want done, and . . . . We all know ye are bad—very bad. . . . .' No! Decidedly James Wait was not touched or repentant. Truth to say, he seemed rather startled. He sat up with incredible suddenness and ease. 'Ah! You think I am bad, do you?' he said gloomily, in his clearest baritone voice (to hear him speak sometimes you would never think there was anything wrong with that man). 'Do you? . . . . Well, act according! Some of you haven't sense enough to put a blanket shipshape over a sick man. There! Leave it alone! I can die anyhow!' Belfast turned away limply with a gesture of discouragement. In the silence of the forecastle, full of interested men, Donkin pronounced distinctly:—'Well, I'm blowed!' and sniggered. Wait looked at him. He looked at him in a quite friendly manner. Nobody could tell what would please our incomprehensible invalid: but for us the scorn of that snigger was hard to bear.

Donkin's position in the forecastle was distinguished but unsafe. He stood on the bad eminence of a general dislike. He was left alone; and in his isolation he could do nothing but think of the gales of the Cape of Good Hope and envy us the possession of warm clothing and waterproofs. Our sea-boots, our oilskin coats, our well-filled sea-chests, were to him so many causes for bitter meditation: he had none of those things, and he felt instinctively that no man, when the need arose, would offer to share them with him. He was impudently cringing to us and systematically insolent to the officers. He anticipated the best results, for himself, from such a line of conduct—and was mistaken. Such natures forget that under extreme provocation men will be just—whether they want to be so or not. Donkin's insolence to long-suffering Mr. Baker became at last intolerable to us, and we rejoiced when the mate, one dark night, tamed him for good. It was done neatly, with great decency and decorum, and with little noise. We had been called—just before midnight—to trim the yards, and Donkin—as usual—made insulting remarks. We stood sleepily in a row with the forebrace in our hands waiting for the next order, and heard in the darkness a scuffly trampling of feet, an exclamation of surprise, sounds of cuffs and slaps, suppressed, hissing whispers:—'Ah! Will you!' .... 'Don't!' .... Don't!' .... 'Then behave.'.... 'Oh! Oh! ....' Afterwards there were soft thuds mixed with the rattle of iron things as if a man's body had been tumbling helplessly amongst the main-pump rods. Before we could realise the situation, Mr. Baker's voice was heard very near and a little impatient:—'Haul away, men! Lay back on that rope!' And we did lay back on the rope with great alacrity. As if nothing had happened, the chief mate went on trimming the yards with his usual and exasperating fastidiousness. We didn't at the time see anything of Donkin, and did not care. Had the chief officer thrown him overboard, no man would have said as much as 'Hallo! he's gone!' But, in truth, no great harm was done—even if Donkin did lose one of his front teeth. We perceived this in the morning, and preserved a ceremonious silence: the etiquette of the forecastle commanded us to be blind and dumb in such a case, and we cherished the decencies of our life more than ordinary landsmen respect theirs. Charley, with unpardonable want of *savoir vivre*, yelled out:—''Ave you been to your dentyst?. . . . Hurt ye, didn't it?' He got a box on the ear from one of his best friends. The boy was surprised, and remained plunged in grief for at least three hours. We were sorry for him, but youth requires even more discipline than age. Donkin grinned venomously. From that day he became pitiless; told Jimmy that he was a 'black fraud'; hinted to us that we were an imbecile lot, daily taken in by a vulgar nigger. And Jimmy seemed to like the fellow!

Singleton lived untouched by human emotions. Taciturn and unsmiling, he breathed amongst us—in that alone resembling the rest of the crowd. We were trying to be decent chaps, and found it jolly difficult; we oscillated between the desire of virtue and the fear of ridicule; we wished to save ourselves from the pain of remorse, but did not want to be made the contemptible dupes of our sentiment. Jimmy's hateful accomplice seemed to have blown with his impure breath undreamt-of subtleties into our hearts. We were disturbed and cowardly. That we knew. Singleton seemed to know nothing, understand nothing. We had thought him till then as wise as he looked, but now we dared, at times, suspect him of being stupid—from old age. One day, however, at dinner, as we sat on our boxes round a tin dish that stood on the deck within the circle of our feet, Jimmy expressed his general disgust with men and things in words that were particularly disgusting. Singleton lifted his head. We became mute. The old man, addressing Jimmy, asked:—'Are you dying?' Thus interrogated, Jame Wait appeared horribly startled and confused. We all were startled. Mouths remained open; hearts thumped; eyes blinked; a dropped tin fork rattled in the dish; a man rose as if to go out, and stood still. In less than a minute Jimmy pulled himself together.—'Why? Can't you see I am?' he answered shakily. Singleton lifted a piece of soaked biscuit ('his teeth'—he declared—'had no edge on them now') to his lips.—'Well, get on with your dying,' he said with venerable mildness; 'don't raise a blamed fuss with us over that job. We can't help you.' Jimmy fell back in his bunk, and for a long time lay very still wiping the perspiration off his chin. The dinner-tins were put away quickly. On deck we discussed the incident in whispers. Some showed a chuckling exultation. Many looked grave. Wamibo, after long periods of staring dreaminess, attempted abortive smiles; and one of the young Scandinavians, much tormented by doubt, ventured in the second dog-watch to approach Singleton (the old man did not encourage us much to speak to him) and ask sheepishly:—'You think he will die?' Singleton looked up.—'Why, of course he will die,' he said deliberately. This seemed decisive. It was promptly imparted to every one by him who had consulted the oracle. Shy and eager, he would step up and with averted gaze recite his formula:—'Old Singleton says he will die.' It was a relief! At last we knew that our compassion would not be misplaced, and we could again smile without misgivings—but we reckoned without Donkin. Donkin 'didn't want to 'ave no truck with 'em dirty furriners.' When Neillssen came to him with the news: 'Singleton says he will die,' he answered him by a spiteful 'And so will you— you fat-headed Dutchman. Wish you Dutchmen were hall dead— 'stead comin' takin' our money hinto your starvin' country.' We were appalled. We perceived that after all Singleton's answer meant nothing. We began to hate him for making fun of us. All our certitudes were going; we were on doubtful terms with our officers; the cook had given us up for lost; we had overheard the boatswain's opinion that 'we were a crowd of softies.' We suspected Jimmy, one another, and even our very selves. We did not know what to do. At every insignificant turn of our humble life we met Jimmy overbearing and blocking the way, arm-in-arm with his awful and veiled familiar. It was a weird servitude.

It began a week after leaving Bombay and came on us stealthily like any other great misfortune. Every one had remarked that Jimmy from the first was very slack at his work; but we thought it simply the outcome of his philosophy of life. Donkin said:—'You put no more weight on a rope than a bloody sparrer.' He disdained him. Belfast, ready for a fight, exclaimed provokingly:—'You don't kill yourself, old man!'—'Would you?' he retorted with extreme scorn—and Belfast retired. One morning, as we were washing decks, Mr. Baker called to him:—'Bring your broom over here, Wait.' He strolled languidly. 'Move yourself! Ough!' grunted Mr. Baker; 'what's the matter with your hind legs?' He stopped dead

THE NIGGER OF THE 'NARCISSUS'

short. He gazed slowly with eyes that bulged out, with an expression audacious and sad.—'It isn't my legs,' he said, 'it's my lungs.' Everybody listened.—'What's .... Ough! .... What's wrong with them?' inquired Mr. Baker. All the watch stood around on the wet deck, grinning, and with brooms or buckets in their hands. He said mournfully:—'Going—or gone. Can't you see I'm a dying man? I know it!' Mr. Baker was disgusted.—'Then why the devil did you ship aboard here?'—'I must live till I die—mustn't I?' he replied. The grins became audible.—'Go off the deck—get out of my sight,' said Mr. Baker. He was nonplussed. It was an unique experience. James Wait, obedient, dropped his broom, and walked slowly forward. A burst of laughter followed him. It was too funny. All hands laughed. . . . . They laughed! . . . . Alas!

He became the tormentor of all our moments; he was worse than a nightmare. You couldn't see that there was anything wrong with him: a nigger does not show. He was not very fat—certainly— but then he was no leaner than other niggers we had known. He coughed often, but the most prejudiced person could perceive that, mostly, he coughed when it suited his purpose. He wouldn't, or couldn't, do his work—and he wouldn't lie-up. One day he would skip aloft with the best of them, and next time we would be obliged to risk our lives to get his limp body down. He was reported, he was examined; he was remonstrated with, threatened, cajoled, lectured. He was called into the cabin to interview the captain. There were wild rumours. It was said he had cheeked the old man; it was said he had frightened him. Charley maintained that the 'skipper, weepin', 'as giv' 'im 'is blessin' an' a pot of jam.' Knowles had it from the steward that the unspeakable Jimmy had been reeling against the cabin furniture; that he had groaned; that he had complained of general brutality and disbelief; and had ended by coughing all over the old man's meteorological journals which were then spread on the table. At any rate, Wait returned forward supported by the steward, who, in a pained and shocked voice, entreated us:—'Here! Catch hold of him, one of you. He is to lie-up.' Jimmy drank a tin mugful of coffee, and, after bullying first one and then another, went to bed. He remained there most of the time, but when it suited him would come on deck and appear amongst us. He was scornful and brooding; he looked ahead upon

32

the sea; and no one could tell what was the meaning of that black man sitting apart in a meditative attitude and as motionless as a carving.

He refused steadily all medicine; he threw sago and cornflour overboard till the steward got tired of bringing it to him. He asked for paregoric. They sent him a big bottle; enough to poison a wilderness of babies. He kept it between his mattress and the deal lining of the ship's side; and nobody ever saw him take a dose. Donkin abused him to his face, jeered at him while he gasped; and the same day Wait would lend him a warm jersey. Once Donkin reviled him for half an hour; reproached him with the extra work his malingering gave to the watch; and ended by calling him 'a black-faced swine.' Under the spell of our accursed perversity we were horror-struck. But Jimmy positively seemed to revel in that abuse. It made him look cheerful—and Donkin had a pair of old sea boots thrown at him. 'Here, you East-end trash,' boomed Wait, 'you may have that.'

At last Mr. Baker had to tell the captain that James Wait was disturbing the peace of the ship. 'Knock discipline on the head—he will, Ough,' grunted Mr. Baker. As a matter of fact, the starboard watch came as near as possible to refusing duty, when ordered one morning by the boatswain to wash out their forecastle. It appears Jimmy objected to a wet floor—and that morning we were in a compassionate mood. We thought the boatswain a brute, and, practically, told him so. Only Mr. Baker's delicate tact prevented an all-fired row: he refused to take us seriously. He came bustling forward, and called us many unpolite names, but in such a hearty and seamanlike manner that we began to feel ashamed of ourselves. In truth, we thought him much too good a sailor to annoy him willingly: and after all Jimmy might have been a fraud—probably was! The forecastle got a clean up that morning; but in the afternoon a sick-bay was fitted up in the deck-house. It was a nice little cabin opening on deck, and with two berths. Jimmy's belongings were transported there, and then—notwithstanding his protests—Jimmy himself. He said he couldn't walk. Four men carried him on a blanket. He complained that he would have to die there alone, like a dog. We grieved for him, and were delighted to have him removed from the forecastle. We attended him as before.

33

The galley was next door, and the cook looked in many times a day. Wait became a little more cheerful. Knowles affirmed having heard him laugh to himself in peals one day. Others had seen him walking about on deck at night. His little place, with the door ajar on a long hook, was always full of tobacco smoke. We spoke through the crack cheerfully, sometimes abusively, as we passed by, intent on our work. He fascinated us. He would never let doubt die. He overshadowed the ship. Invulnerable in his promise of speedy corruption he trampled on our self-respect, he demonstrated to us daily our want of moral courage; he tainted our lives. Had we been a miserable gang of wretched immortals, unhallowed alike by hope and fear, he could not have lorded it over us with a more pitiless assertion of his sublime privilege.

III

MEANTIME the *Narcissus*, with square yards, ran out of the fair monsoon. She drifted slowly, swinging round and round the compass, through a few days of baffling light airs. Under the patter of short warm showers, grumbling men whirled the heavy yards from side to side; they caught hold of the soaked ropes with groans and sighs, while their officers, sulky and dripping with rain water, unceasingly ordered them about in wearied voices. During the short respites they looked with disgust into the smarting palms of their stiff hands, and asked one another bitterly:—'Who would be a sailor if he could be a farmer?' All the tempers were spoilt, and no man cared what he said. One black night, when the watch, panting in the heat and half-drowned with the rain, had been through four mortal hours hunted from brace to brace, Belfast declared that he would 'chuck going to sea for ever and go in a steamer.' This was excessive, no doubt. Captain Allistoun, with great self-control, would mutter sadly to Mr. Baker:—'It is not so bad—not so bad,' when he had managed to shove, and dodge, and manœuvre his smart ship through sixty miles in twenty-four hours. From the doorstep of the little cabin, Jimmy, chin in hand, watched our distasteful labours with insolent and melancholy eyes. We spoke to him gently—and out of his sight exchanged sour smiles.

Then, again, with a fair wind and under a clear sky, the ship went on piling up the South Latitude. She passed outside Mada-gascar and Mauritius without a glimpse of the land. Extra lashings were put on the spare spars. Hatches were looked to. The steward in his leisure moments and with a worried air tried to fit wash-boards to the cabin doors. Stout canvas was bent with care. Anxi-ous eyes looked to the westward, towards the cape of storms. The ship began to dip into a south-west swell, and the softly luminous sky of low latitudes took on a harder sheen from day to day above our heads: it arched high above the ship, vibrating and pale, like an immense dome of steel, resonant with the deep voice of fresh-ening gales. The sunshine gleamed cold on the white curls of black waves. Before the strong breath of westerly squalls the ship, with reduced sail, lay slowly over, obstinate and yielding. She drove to and fro in the unceasing endeavour to fight her way through the invisible violence of the winds: she pitched headlong into dark smooth hollows; she struggled upwards over the snowy ridges of great running seas; she rolled, restless, from side to side, like a thing in pain. Enduring and valiant, she answered to the call of men; and her slim spars waving for ever in abrupt semicircles, seemed to beckon in vain for help towards the stormy sky.

It was a bad winter off the Cape that year. The relieved helmsmen came off flapping their arms, or ran stamping hard and blowing into swollen, red fingers. The watch on deck dodged the sting of cold sprays or, crouching in sheltered corners, watched dismally the high and merciless seas boarding the ship time after time in unappeasable fury. Water tumbled in cataracts over the forecastle doors. You had to dash through a waterfall to get into your damp bed. The men turned in wet and turned out stiff to face the re-deeming and ruthless exactions of their glorious and obscure fate. Far aft, and peering watchfully to windward, the officers could be seen through the mist of squalls. They stood by the weather-rail, holding on grimly, straight and glistening in their long coats; then, at times, in the disordered plunges of the hard-driven ship, they appeared high up, attentive, tossing violently above the grey line of a clouded horizon, and in motionless attitudes.

They watched the weather and the ship as men on shore watch the momentous chances of fortune. Captain Allistoun never left the deck, as though he had been part of the ship's fittings. Now and then the steward, shivering, but always in shirt sleeves, would struggle towards him with some hot coffee, half of which the gale blew out of the cup before it reached the master's lips. He drank what was left gravely in one long gulp, while heavy sprays pattered loudly on his oilskin coat, the seas swishing broke about his high boots; and he never took his eyes off the ship. He watched her every motion; he kept his gaze riveted upon her as a loving man who watches the unselfish toil of a delicate woman upon the slender thread of whose existence is hung the whole meaning and joy of the world. We all watched her. She was beautiful and had a weakness.[11] We loved her no less for that. We admired her qualities aloud, we boasted of them to one another, as though they had been our own, and the consciousness of her only fault we kept buried in the silence of our profound affection. She was born in the thundering peal of hammers beating upon iron, in black eddies of smoke, under a grey sky, on the banks of the Clyde. The clamorous and sombre stream gives birth to things of beauty that float away into the sunshine of the world to be loved by men. The *Narcissus* was one of that perfect brood. Less perfect than many perhaps, but she was ours, and, consequently, incomparable. We were proud of her. In Bombay, ignorant landlubbers alluded to her as that 'pretty grey ship.' Pretty! A scurvy meed of commendation! We knew she was the most magnificent sea-boat ever launched. We tried to forget that, like many good sea-boats, she was at times rather crank. She was exacting. She wanted care in loading and handling, and no one knew exactly how much care would be enough. Such are the imperfections of mere men! The ship knew, and sometimes would correct the presumptuous human ignorance by the wholesome discipline of fear. We had heard ominous stories about past voyages. The cook (technically a seaman, but in reality no sailor)—the cook, when unstrung by some misfortune, such as the rolling over of a saucepan, would mutter gloomily while he wiped the floor:—'There! Look at what she has done! Some voy'ge she will drown all hands! You'll see if she won't.' To which the steward, snatching in the galley a moment to draw breath in the hurry of his worried life, would remark philosophically:—'Those that see won't tell, anyhow. I don't want to see it.' We derided those fears. Our hearts went out to the old man when he pressed her hard so as to make her hold her own, hold to every inch gained to windward; when he made her, under reefed sails, leap obliquely at enormous waves. The men, knitted together aft into a ready group by the first sharp order of an officer coming to take charge of the deck in bad weather:—'Keep handy the watch,' stood admiring her valiance. Their eyes blinked in the wind; their dark faces were wet with drops of water more salt and bitter than human tears; beards and moustaches, soaked, hung straight and dripping like fine seaweed. They were fantastically misshapen; in high boots, in hats like helmets, and swaying clumsily, stiff and bulky in glistening oilskins, they resembled men strangely equipped for some fabulous adventure. Whenever she rose easily to a towering green sea, elbows dug ribs, faces brightened, lips murmured:—'Didn't she do it cleverly,' and all the heads turning like one watched with sardonic grins the foiled wave go roaring to leeward, white with the foam of a monstrous rage. But when she had not been quick enough and, struck heavily, lay over trembling under the blow, we clutched at ropes, and looking up at the narrow bands of drenched and strained sails waving desperately aloft, we thought in our hearts:—'No wonder. Poor thing!'

The thirty-second day out of Bombay began inauspiciously. In the morning a sea smashed one of the galley doors. We dashed in through lots of steam and found the cook very wet and indignant with the ship:—'She's getting worse every day. She's trying to drown me in front of my own stove!' He was very angry. We pacified him, and the carpenter, though washed away twice from there, managed to repair the door. Through that accident our dinner was not ready till late, but it didn't matter in the end because Knowles, who went to fetch it, got knocked down by a sea and the dinner went over the side. Captain Allistoun, looking more hard and thin-lipped than ever, hung on to full topsails and foresail, and would not notice that the ship, asked to do too much, appeared to lose heart altogether for the first time since we knew her. She refused to rise, and bored her way sullenly through the seas. Twice running, as though she had been blind or weary of life, she put her nose deliberately into a big wave and swept the decks from end to end. As the boatswain observed with marked annoyance, while we were splashing about in a body to try and save a worthless wash-tub:—'Every blooming thing in the ship is going overboard this afternoon.' Venerable Singleton broke his habitual silence and said with a glance aloft:—'The old man's in a temper with the weather, but it's no good bein' angry with the winds of heaven.' Jimmy had shut his door, of course. We knew he was dry and comfortable within his little cabin, and in our absurd way were pleased one moment, exasperated the next, by that certitude. Donkin skulked shamelessly, uneasy and miserable. He grumbled:—'I'm perishin' with cold houtside in bloomin' wet rags, an' that 'ere black sojer sits dry on a blamed chest full of bloomin' clothes; blank his black soul!' We took no notice of him; we hardly gave a thought to Jimmy and his bosom friend. There was no leisure for idle probing of hearts. Sails blew adrift. Things broke loose. Cold and wet, we were washed about the deck while trying to repair damages. The ship tossed about, shaken furiously, like a toy in the hand of a lunatic. Just at sunset there was a rush to shorten sail before the menace of a sombre hail cloud. The hard gust of wind came brutal like the blow of a fist. The ship relieved of her canvas in time received it pluckily: she yielded reluctantly to the violent onset; then, coming up with a stately and irresistible motion, brought her spars to windward in the teeth of the screeching squall. Out of the abysmal darkness of the black cloud overhead white hail streamed on her, rattled on the rigging, leaped in handfuls off the yards, rebounded on the deck—round and gleaming in the murky turmoil like a shower of pearls. It passed away. For a moment a livid sun shot horizontally the last rays of sinister light between the hills of steep, rolling waves. Then a wild night rushed in—stamped out in a great howl that dismal remnant of a stormy day.

There was no sleep on board that night. Most seamen remember in their life one or two such nights of a culminating gale. Nothing seems left of the whole universe but darkness, clamour, fury—and the ship. And like the last vestige of a shattered creation she drifts, bearing an anguished remnant of sinful mankind, through the distress, tumult, and pain of an avenging terror. No one slept in the forecastle. The tin oil-lamp suspended on a long string, smoking, described wide circles; wet clothing made dark heaps on the glistening floor; a thin layer of water rushed to and fro. In the bed-places men lay booted, resting on elbows and with open eyes. Hung-up suits of oilskin swung out and in, lively and disquieting like reckless ghosts of decapitated seamen dancing in a tempest. No one spoke and all listened. Outside the night moaned and sobbed to the accompaniment of a continuous loud tremor as of innumerable drums beating far off. Shrieks passed through the air. Tremendous dull blows made the ship tremble while she rolled under the weight of the seas toppling on her deck. At times she soared up swiftly as if to leave this earth for ever, then during interminable moments fell through a void with all the hearts on board of her standing still, till a frightful shock, expected and sudden, started them off again with a big thump. After every dislocating jerk of the ship, Wamibo, stretched full length, his face on the pillow, groaned slightly with the pain of his tormented universe. Now and then, for the fraction of an intolerable second, the ship, in the fiercer burst of a terrible uproar, remained on her side, vibrating and still, with a stillness more appalling than the wildest motion. Then upon all those prone bodies a stir would pass, a shiver of suspense. A man would protrude his anxious head and a pair of eyes glistened in the sway of light, glaring wildly. Some moved their legs a little as if making ready to jump out. But several, motionless on their backs and with one hand gripping hard the edge of the bunk, smoked nervously with quick puffs, staring upwards; immobilised in a great craving for peace.

At midnight, orders were given to furl the fore and mizen topsails. With immense efforts men crawled aloft through a merciless buffeting, saved the canvas, and crawled down almost exhausted, to bear in panting silence the cruel battering of the seas. Perhaps for the first time in the history of the merchant service the watch, told to go below, did not leave the deck, as if compelled to remain there by the fascination of a venomous violence. At every heavy gust men, huddled together, whispered to one another:—'It can blow no harder'—and presently the gale would give them the lie with a piercing shriek, and drive their breath back into their throats. A fierce squall seemed to burst asunder the thick mass of sooty vapours; and above the wrack of torn clouds glimpses could be caught of the high moon rushing backwards with frightful speed over the sky, right into the wind's eye. Many hung their heads, muttering that it 'turned their inwards out' to look at it. Soon the clouds closed up, and the world again became a raging, blind darkness that howled, flinging at the lonely ship salt sprays and sleet.

About half-past seven the pitchy obscurity round us turned a ghastly grey, and we knew that the sun had risen. This unnatural and threatening daylight, in which we could see one another's wild eyes and drawn faces, was only an added tax on our endurance. The horizon seemed to have come on all sides within arm's length of the ship. Into that narrowed circle furious seas leaped in, struck, and leaped out. A rain of salt, heavy drops flew aslant like mist. The main-topsail had to be goose-winged,[32] and with stolid resignation every one prepared to go aloft once more; but the officers yelled, pushed back, and at last we understood that no more men would be allowed to go on the yard than were absolutely necessary for the work. As at any moment the masts were likely to be jumped out or blown overboard, we concluded that the captain didn't want to see all his crowd go over the side at once. That was reasonable. The watch then on duty, led by Mr. Creighton, began to struggle up the rigging. The wind flattened them against the ratlines; then, easing a little, would let them ascend a couple of steps; and again, with a sudden gust, pin all up the shrouds the whole crawling line in attitudes of crucifixion. The other watch plunged down on the main deck to haul up the sail. Men's heads bobbed up as the water flung them irresistibly from side to side. Mr. Baker grunted encouragingly in our midst, spluttering and blowing amongst the tangled ropes like an energetic porpoise. Favoured by an ominous and untrustworthy lull, the work was done without any one being lost either off the deck or from the yard. For the moment the gale seemed to take off, and the ship, as if grateful for our efforts, plucked up heart and made better weather of it.

At eight the men off duty, watching their chance, ran forward over the flooded deck to get some rest. The other half of the crew remained aft for their turn of 'seeing her through her trouble,' as they expressed it. The two mates urged the master to go below. Mr. Baker grunted in his ear:—'Ough! surely now .... Ough! .... confidence in us .... nothing more to do .... she must lay it out or go. Ough! Ough!' Tall young Mr. Creighton smiled down at him cheerfully:—'. . . . She's right as a trivet! Take a spell, sir.' He looked at them stonily with bloodshot, sleepless eyes. The rims of his eyelids were scarlet, and he moved his jaw unceasingly with a slow effort, as though he had been masticating a lump of india-rubber. He shook his head. He repeated:—'Never mind me. I must see it out—I must see it out,' but he consented to sit down for a moment on the skylight, with his hard face turned unflinchingly to windward. The sea spat at it—and, stoical, it streamed with water as though he had been weeping. On the weather side of the poop the watch, hanging on to the mizen rigging and to one another, tried to exchange encouraging words. Singleton, at the wheel, yelled out:—'Look out for yourselves!' His voice reached them in a warning whisper. They were startled.

A big, foaming sea came out of the mist; it made for the ship, roaring wildly, and in its rush it looked as mischievous and dis-composing as a madman with an axe. One or two, shouting, scrambled up the rigging; most, with a convulsive catch of the breath, held on where they stood. Singleton dug his knees under the wheel-box, and carefully eased the helm to the headlong pitch of the ship, but without taking his eyes off the coming wave. It towered close-to and high, like a wall of green glass topped with snow. The ship rose to it as though she had soared on wings, and for a moment rested poised upon the foaming crest, as if she had been a great sea-bird. Before we could draw breath a heavy gust struck her, another roller took her unfairly under the weather bow, she gave a toppling lurch, and filled her decks. Captain Allistoun leaped up, and fell; Archie rolled over him, screaming:—'She will rise!' She gave another lurch to leeward; the lower deadeyes dipped heavily; the men's feet flew from under them, and they hung kicking above the slanting poop. They could see the ship putting her side in the water, and shouted all together:—'She's going!' Forward the forecastle doors flew open, and the watch below were seen leaping out one after another, throwing their arms up; and, falling on hands and knees, scrambled aft on all fours along the high side of the deck, sloping more than the roof of a house. From leeward the seas rose, pursuing them; they looked wretched in a hopeless struggle, like vermin fleeing before a flood;

42

they fought up the weather ladder of the poop one after another, half naked and staring wildly; and as soon as they got up they shot to leeward in clusters, with closed eyes, till they brought up heavily with their ribs against the iron stanchions of the rail; then, groaning, they rolled in a confused mass. The immense volume of water thrown forward by the last scend of the ship had burst the lee door of the forecastle. They could see their chests, pillows, blankets, clothing, come out floating upon the sea. While they struggled back to windward they looked in dismay. The straw beds swam high, the blankets, spread out, undulated; while the chests, waterlogged and with a heavy list, pitched heavily, like dismasted hulks, before they sank; Archie's big coat passed with outspread arms, resembling a drowned seaman floating with his head under water. Men were slipping down while trying to dig their fingers into the planks; others, jammed in corners, rolled enormous eyes. They all yelled unceasingly:—'The masts! Cut! Cut! . . . .'³³ A black squall howled low over the ship, that lay on her side with the weather yard-arms pointing to the clouds; while the tall masts, inclined nearly to the horizon, seemed to be of an unmeasurable length. The carpenter let go his hold, rolled against the skylight, and began to crawl to the cabin entrance, where a big axe was kept ready for just such an emergency. At that moment the topsail sheet parted, the end of the heavy chain racketed aloft, and sparks of red fire streamed down through the flying sprays. The sail flapped once with a jerk that seemed to tear our hearts out through our teeth, and instantly changed into a bunch of fluttering narrow ribbons that tied themselves into knots and became quiet along the yard. Captain Allistoun struggled, managed to stand up with his face near the deck, upon which men swung on the ends of ropes, like nest robbers upon a cliff. One of his feet was on somebody's chest; his face was purple; his lips moved. He yelled also; he yelled, bending down:—'No! No!' Mr. Baker, one leg over the binnacle-stand, roared out:—'Did you say no? Not cut?' He shook his head madly. 'No! No!' Between his legs the crawling carpenter heard, collapsed at once, and lay full length in the angle of the skylight. Voices took up the shout—'No! No!' Then all became still. They waited for the ship to turn over altogether, and shake them out into the sea; and upon the terrific noise of wind and sea not a

43

murmur of remonstrance came out from those men, who each would have given ever so many years of life to see 'them damned sticks go overboard!' They all believed it their only chance; but a little hard-faced man shook his grey head and shouted 'No!' without giving them as much as a glance. They were silent, and gasped. They gripped rails, they had wound ropes'-ends under their arms; they clutched ringbolts, they crawled in heaps where there was foothold; they held on with both arms, hooked themselves to anything to windward with elbows, with chins, almost with their teeth: and some, unable to crawl away from where they had been flung, felt the sea leap up, striking against their backs as they struggled upwards. Singleton had stuck to the wheel. His hair flew out in the wind; the gale seemed to take its life-long adversary by the beard and shake his old head. He wouldn't let go, and, with his knees forced between the spokes, flew up and down like a man on a bough. As Death appeared unready, they began to look about. Donkin, caught by one foot in a loop of some rope, hung, head down, below us, and yelled, with his face to the deck:—'Cut! Cut!' Two men lowered themselves cautiously to him; others hauled on the rope. They caught him up, shoved him into a safer place, held him. He shouted curses at the master, shook his fist at him with horrible blasphemies, called upon us in filthy words to 'Cut! Don't mind that murdering fool! Cut, some of you!' One of his rescuers struck him a back-handed blow over the mouth; his head banged on the deck, and he became suddenly very quiet, with a white face, breathing hard, and with a few drops of blood trickling from his cut lip. On the lee side another man could be seen stretched out as if stunned; only the washboard prevented him from going over the side. It was the steward. We had to sling him up like a bale, for he was paralysed with fright. He had rushed up out of the pantry when he felt the ship go over, and had rolled down helplessly, clutching a china mug. It was not broken. With difficulty we tore it from him, and when he saw it in our hands he was amazed. 'Where did you get that thing?' he kept on asking, in a trembling voice. His shirt was blown to shreds; the ripped sleeves flapped like wings. Two men made him fast, and, doubled over the rope that held him, he resembled a bundle of wet rags. Mr. Baker crawled along the line of men, asking:—'Are you all there?' and looking them over. Some blinked vacantly, others shook convulsively; Wamibo's head hung over his breast; and in painful attitudes, cut by lashings, exhausted with clutching, screwed up in corners, they breathed heavily. Their lips twitched, and at every sickening heave of the overturned ship they opened them wide as if to shout. The cook, embracing a wooden stanchion, unconsciously repeated a prayer. In every short interval of the fiendish noises around he could be heard there, without cap or slippers, imploring in that storm the Master of our lives not to lead him into temptation. Soon he also became silent. In all that crowd of cold and hungry men, waiting wearily for a violent death, not a voice was heard; they were mute, and in sombre thoughtfulness listened to the horrible imprecations of the gale.

Hours passed. They were sheltered by the heavy inclination of the ship from the wind that rushed in one long unbroken moan above their heads, but cold rain showers fell at times into the uneasy calm of their refuge. Under the torment of that new infliction a pair of shoulders would writhe a little. Teeth chattered. The sky was clearing, and bright sunshine gleamed over the ship. After every burst of battering seas, vivid and fleeting rainbows arched over the drifting hull in the flick of sprays. The gale was ending in a clear blow, which gleamed and cut like a knife. Between two bearded shellbacks Charley, fastened with somebody's long muffler to a deck ring-bolt, wept quietly, with rare tears wrung out by bewilderment, cold, hunger, and general misery. One of his neighbours punched him in the ribs, asking roughly:—'What's the matter with your cheek? In fine weather there's no holding you, youngster.' Turning about with prudence he worked himself out of his coat and threw it over the boy. The other man closed up, muttering:—"Twill make a bloomin' man of you, sonny.' They flung their arms over and pressed against him. Charley drew his feet up and his eyelids dropped. Sighs were heard, as men, perceiving that they were not to be 'drowned in a hurry,' tried easier positions. Mr. Creighton, who had hurt his leg, lay amongst us with compressed lips. Some fellows belonging to his watch set about securing him better. Without a word or a glance he lifted his arms òne after another to facilitate the operation, and not a muscle moved in his stern, young face. They asked him with solicitude:—

45

'Easier now, sir?' He answered with a curt:—'That'll do.' He was a hard young officer, but many of his watch used to say they liked him well enough because he had 'such a gentlemanly way of damning us up and down the deck.' Others, unable to discern such fine shades of refinement, respected him for his smartness. For the first time since the ship had gone on her beam ends Captain Allistoun gave a short glance down at his men. He was almost upright—one foot against the side of the skylight, one knee on the deck; and with the end of the vang round his waist swung back and forth with his gaze fixed ahead, watchful, like a man looking out for a sign. Before his eyes the ship, with half her deck below water, rose and fell on heavy seas that rushed from under her flashing in the cold sunshine. We began to think she was wonderfully buoyant—considering. Confident voices were heard shouting:—'She'll do, boys!' Belfast exclaimed with fervour:—'I would giv' a month's pay for a draw at a pipe!' One or two, passing dry tongues on their salt lips, muttered something about a 'drink of water.' The cook, as if inspired, scrambled up with his breast against the poop water-cask and looked in. There was a little at the bottom. He yelled, waving his arms, and two men began to crawl backwards and forwards with the mug. We had a good mouthful all round. The master shook his head impatiently, refusing. When it came to Charley one of his neighbours shouted:—'That bloomin' boy's asleep.' He slept as though he had been dosed with narcotics. They let him be. Singleton held to the wheel with one hand while he drank, bending down to shelter his lips from the wind. Wamibo had to be poked and yelled at before he saw the mug held before his eyes. Knowles said sagaciously:—'It's better'n a tot o' rum.' Mr. Baker grunted:—'Thank ye.' Mr Creighton drank and nodded. Donkin gulped greedily, glaring over the rim. Belfast made us laugh when with grimacing mouth he shouted:—'Pass it this way. We're all taytottlers here.' The master, presented with the mug again by a crouching man, who screamed up at him:—'We all had a drink, captain,' groped for it without ceasing to look ahead, and handed it back stiffly as though he could not spare half a glance away from the ship. Faces brightened. We shouted to the cook:— 'Well done, doctor!' He sat to leeward, propped by the water-cask and yelled back abundantly, but the seas were breaking in thunder

46

just then, and we only caught snatches that sounded like: 'Providence' and 'born again.' He was at his old game of preaching. We made friendly but derisive gestures at him, and from below he lifted one arm, holding on with the other, moved his lips; he beamed up to us, straining his voice—earnest, and ducking his head before the sprays.

Suddenly some one cried:—'Where's Jimmy?' and we were appalled once more. On the end of the row the boatswain shouted hoarsely:—'Has any one seed him come out?' Voices exclaimed dismally:—'Drowned—is he?.... No! In his cabin!.... Good Lord!.... Caught like a bloomin' rat in a trap..... Couldn't open his door.... Aye! She went over too quick and the water jammed it.... Poor beggar!.... No help for 'im..... Let's go and see....' 'Damn him, who could go?' screamed Donkin.—'Nobody expects you to,' growled the man next to him; 'you're only a thing.'—'Is there half a chance to get at 'im?' inquired two or three men together. Belfast untied himself with blind impetuosity, and all at once shot down to leeward quicker than a flash of lightning. We shouted all together with dismay; but with his legs overboard he held and yelled for a rope. In our extremity nothing could be terrible; so we judged him funny kicking there, and with his scared face. Some one began to laugh, and, as if hysterically infected with screaming merriment, all those haggard men went off laughing, wild-eyed, like a lot of maniacs tied up on a wall. Mr. Baker swung off the binnacle-stand and tendered him one leg. He scrambled up rather scared, and consigning us with abominable words to the 'divvle.' 'You are.... Ough! You're a foul-mouthed beggar, Craik,' grunted Mr. Baker. He answered, stuttering with indignation:— 'Look at 'em, sorr. The bloomin' dirty images! laughing at a chum going overboard. Call themselves men, too.' But from the break of the poop the boatswain called out:—'Come along,' and Belfast crawled away in a hurry to join him. The five men, poised and gazing over the edge of the poop, looked for the best way to get forward. They seemed to hesitate. The others, twisting in their lashings, turning painfully, stared with open lips. Captain Allistoun saw nothing; he seemed with his eyes to hold the ship up in a superhuman concentration of effort. The wind screamed loud in sunshine; columns of spray rose straight up; and in the glitter of

47

rainbows bursting over the trembling hull the men went over cautiously, disappearing from sight with deliberate movements.

They went swinging from belaying-pin to cleat above the seas that beat the half-submerged deck. Their toes scraped the planks. Lumps of green cold water toppled over the bulwark and on their heads. They hung for a moment on strained arms, with the breath knocked out of them, and with closed eyes—then, letting go with one hand, balanced with lolling heads, trying to grab some rope or stanchion further forward. The long-armed and athletic boatswain swung quickly, gripping things with a fist hard as iron, and re-membering suddenly snatches of the last letter from his 'old woman.' Little Belfast scrambled rageously, muttering 'cursed nigger.' Wamibo's tongue hung out with excitement; and Archie, intrepid and calm, watched his chance to move with intelligent coolness.

When above the side of the house, they let go one after another, and falling heavily, sprawled, pressing their palms to the smooth teak wood. Round them the backwash of waves seethed white and hissing. All the doors had become trap-doors, of course. The first was the galley door. The galley extended from side to side, and they could hear the sea splashing with hollow noises in there. The next door was that of the carpenter's shop. They lifted it, and looked down. The room seemed to have been devastated by an earthquake. Everything in it had tumbled on the bulkhead facing the door, and on the other side of that bulkhead there was Jimmy, dead or alive. The bench, a half-finished meat-safe, saws, chisels, wire rods, axes, crowbars, lay in a heap besprinkled with loose nails. A sharp adze stuck up with a shining edge that gleamed dangerously down there like a wicked smile. The men clung to one another peering. A sickening, sly lurch of the ship nearly sent them overboard in a body. Belfast howled 'Here goes!' and leaped down. Archie followed cannily, catching at shelves that gave way with him, and eased himself in a great crash of ripped wood. There was hardly room for three men to move. And in the sunshiny blue square of the door, the boatswain's face, bearded and dark, Wamibo's face, wild and pale, hung over—watching.

Together they shouted: 'Jimmy! Jim!' From above the boatswain contributed a deep growl: 'You . . . . Wait!' In a pause, Belfast entreated: 'Jimmy, darlin', are ye aloive?' The boatswain said: 'Again! All together, boys!' All yelled excitedly. Wamibo made noises resembling loud barks. Belfast drummed on the side of the bulkhead with a piece of iron. All ceased suddenly. The sound of screaming and hammering went on thin and distinct—like a solo after a chorus. He was alive. He was screaming and knocking below us with the hurry of a man prematurely shut up in a coffin. We went to work. We attacked with desperation the abominable heap of things heavy, of things sharp, of things clumsy to handle. The boatswain crawled away to find somewhere a flying end of a rope; and Wamibo, held back by shouts:—'Don't jump! . . . . Don't come in here, muddle-head!'—remained glaring above us—all shining eyes, gleaming fangs, tumbled hair; resembling an amazed and half-witted fiend gloating over the extraordinary agitation of the damned. The boatswain adjured us to 'bear a hand,' and a rope descended. We made things fast to it and they went up spinning, never to be seen by man again. A rage to fling things overboard possessed us. We worked fiercely, cutting our hands, and speaking brutally to one another. Jimmy kept up a distracting row; he screamed piercingly, without drawing breath, like a tortured woman; he banged with hands and feet. The agony of his fear wrung our hearts so terribly that we longed to abandon him, to get out of that place deep as a well and swaying like a tree, to get out of his hearing, back on the poop where we could wait passively for death in incomparable repose. We shouted to him to 'shut up, for God's sake.' He redoubled his cries. He must have fancied we could not hear him. Probably he heard his own clamour but faintly. We could picture him crouching on the edge of the upper berth, letting out with both fists at the wood, in the dark, and with his mouth wide open for that unceasing cry. Those were loathsome moments. A cloud driving across the sun would darken the doorway menacingly. Every movement of the ship was pain. We scrambled about with no room to breathe, and felt frightfully sick. The boatswain yelled down at us:—'Bear a hand! Bear a hand! We two will be washed away from here directly if you ain't quick!' Three times a sea leaped over the high side and flung bucketfuls of water on our heads. Then Jimmy, startled by the shock, would stop his noise for a moment—waiting for the ship to sink, perhaps—and began again, distressingly loud, as if invigorated by the gust of fear. At the bottom the nails lay in a layer several inches thick. It was ghastly. Every nail in the world, not driven in firmly somewhere, seemed to have found its way into that carpenter's shop. There they were, of all kinds, the remnants of stores from seven voyages. Tin-tacks, copper tacks (sharp as needles), pump nails, with big heads, like tiny iron mushrooms; nails without any heads (horrible); French nails polished and slim. They lay in a solid mass more inabordable than a hedgehog. We hesitated, yearning for a shovel, while Jimmy below us yelled as though he had been flayed. Groaning, we dug our fingers in, and very much hurt, shook our hands, scattering nails and drops of blood. We passed up our hats full of assorted nails to the boatswain, who, as if performing a mysterious and appeasing rite, cast them wide upon a raging sea.

We got to the bulkhead at last. Those were stout planks. She was a ship, well finished in every detail—the Narcissus was. They were the stoutest planks ever put into a ship's bulkhead—we thought—and then we perceived that, in our hurry, we had sent all the tools overboard. Absurd little Belfast wanted to break it down with his own weight, and with both feet leaped straight up like a springbok, cursing the Clyde shipwrights for not scamping their work. Incidentally he reviled all North Britain, the rest of the earth, the sea—and all his companions. He swore, as he alighted heavily on his heels, that he would never, never any more associate with any fool that 'hadn't savee enough to know his knee from his elbow.' He managed by his thumping to scare the last remnant of wits out of Jimmy. We could hear the object of our exasperated solicitude darting to and fro under the planks. He had cracked his voice at last, and could only squeak miserably. His back or else his head rubbed the planks, now here, now there, in a puzzling manner. He squeaked as he dodged the invisible blows. It was more heartrending even than his yells. Suddenly Archie produced a crowbar. He had kept it back; also a small hatchet. We howled with satisfaction. He struck a mighty blow and small chips flew at our eyes. The boatswain above shouted:—'Look out! Look out there. Don't kill the man. Easy does it!' Wamibo, maddened with excitement, hung head down and insanely urged us:—'Hoo! Strook 'im! Hoo! Hoo!' We were afraid he would fall in and kill one of us and, hurriedly, we entreated the boatswain to 'shove the blamed Finn overboard.' Then, all together, we yelled down at the planks:—'Stand from under! Get forward,' and listened. We only heard the deep hum and moan of the wind above us, the mingled roar and hiss of the seas. The ship, as if overcome with despair, wallowed lifelessly, and our heads swam with that unnatural motion. Belfast clamoured:—'For the love of God, Jimmy, where are ye? . . . . Knock! Jimmy darlint! . . . . Knock! You bloody black beast! Knock!' He was as quiet as a dead man inside a grave; and, like men standing above a grave, we were on the verge of tears—but with vexation, the strain, the fatigue; with the great longing to be done with it, to get away, and lay down to rest somewhere where we could see our danger and breathe. Archie shouted:—'Gi'e me room!' We crouched behind him, guarding our heads, and he struck time after time in the joint of planks. They cracked. Suddenly the crowbar went halfway in through a splintered oblong hole. It must have missed Jimmy's head by less than an inch. Archie withdrew it quickly, and that infamous nigger rushed at the hole, put his lips to it, and whispered 'Help' in an almost extinct voice; he pressed his head to it, trying madly to get out through that opening one inch wide and three inches long. In our disturbed state we were absolutely paralysed by his incredible action. It seemed impossible to drive him away. Even Archie at last lost his composure. 'If ye don't clear oot I'll drive the crowbar thro' your head,' he shouted in a determined voice. He meant what he said, and his earnestness seemed to make an impression on Jimmy. He disappeared suddenly, and we set to prising and tearing at the planks with the eagerness of men trying to get at a mortal enemy, and spurred by the desire to tear him limb from limb. The wood split, cracked, gave way. Belfast plunged in head and shoulders and groped viciously. 'I've got 'im! Got 'im,' he shouted. 'Oh! There! . . . . He's gone; I've got 'im! . . . . Pull at my legs! . . . . Pull!' Wamibo hooted unceasingly. The boatswain shouted directions:—'Catch hold of his hair, Belfast; pull straight up, you two! . . . . Pull fair!' We pulled fair. We pulled Belfast out with a jerk, and dropped him with disgust. In a sitting posture, purple-faced, he sobbed despairingly:—'How can I hold on to 'is blooming short wool?'

Suddenly Jimmy's head and shoulders appeared. He stuck halfway, and with rolling eyes foamed at our feet. We flew at him
with brutal impatience, we tore the shirt off his back, we tugged
at his ears, we panted over him; and all at once he came away
in our hands as though somebody had let go his legs. With the
same movement, without a pause, we swung him up. His breath
whistled, he kicked our upturned faces, he grasped two pairs
of arms above his head, and he squirmed up with such precipi-
tation that he seemed positively to escape from our hands like a
bladder full of gas. Streaming with perspiration, we swarmed up
the rope, and, coming into the blast of cold wind, gasped like
men plunged into icy water. With burning faces we shivered to
the very marrow of our bones. Never before had the gale seemed
to us more furious, the sea more mad, the sunshine more merciless and mocking, and the position of the ship more hopeless
and appalling. Every movement of her was ominous of the end
of her agony and of the beginning of ours. We staggered away
from the door, and, alarmed by a sudden roll, fell down in a
bunch. It appeared to us that the side of the house was more
smooth than glass and more slippery than ice. There was nothing to hang on to but a long brass hook used sometimes to keep
back an open door. Wamibo held on to it and we held on to
Wamibo, clutching our Jimmy. He had completely collapsed now.
He did not seem to have the strength to close his hand. We stuck
to him blindly in our fear. We were not afraid of Wamibo letting go
(we remembered that the brute was stronger than any three men
in the ship), but we were afraid of the hook giving way, and we
also believed that the ship had made up her mind to turn over at
last. But she didn't. A sea swept over us. The boatswain spluttered:—'Up and away. There's a lull. Away aft with you, or we
will all go to the devil here.' We stood up surrounding Jimmy.
We begged him to hold up, to hold on, at least. He glared with
his bulging eyes, mute as a fish, and with all the stiffening
knocked out of him. He wouldn't stand; he wouldn't even as
much as clutch at our necks; he was only a cold black skin
loosely stuffed with soft cotton wool; his arms and legs swung
jointless and pliable; his head rolled about; the lower lip hung
down, enormous and heavy. We pressed round him, bothered

and dismayed; sheltering him we swung here and there in a body; and on the very brink of eternity we tottered all together with concealing and absurd gestures, like a lot of drunken men embarrassed with a stolen corpse.

Something had to be done. We had to get him aft. A rope was tied slack under his armpits, and, reaching up at the risk of our lives, we hung him on the foresheet cleet. He emitted no sound; he looked as ridiculously lamentable as a doll that had lost half its sawdust, and we started on our perilous journey over the main deck, dragging along with care that pitiful, that limp, that hateful burden. He was not very heavy, but had he weighed a ton he could not have been more awkward to handle. We literally passed him from hand to hand. Now and then we had to hang him up on a handy belaying-pin, to draw a breath and reform the line. Had the pin broken he would have irretrievably gone into the Southern Ocean, but he had to take his chance of that; and after a little while, becoming apparently aware of it, he groaned slightly, and with a great effort whispered a few words. We listened eagerly. He was reproaching us with our carelessness in letting him run such risks: 'Now, after I got myself out from there,' he breathed out weakly. 'There' was his cabin. And he got himself out. We had nothing to do with it apparently! . . . . No matter. . . . . We went on and let him take his chances, simply because we could not help it; for though at that time we hated him more than ever—more than anything under heaven—we did not want to lose him. We had so far saved him; and it had become a personal matter between us and the sea. We meant to stick to him. Had we (by an incredible hypothesis) undergone similar toil and trouble for an empty cask, that cask would have become as precious to us as Jimmy was. More precious, in fact, because we would have had no reason to hate the cask. And we hated James Wait. We could not get rid of the monstrous suspicion that this astounding black-man was shamming sick, had been malingering heartlessly in the face of our toil, of our scorn, of our patience—and now was malingering in the face of our devotion—in the face of death. Our vague and imperfect morality rose with disgust at his unmanly lie. But he stuck to it manfully—amazingly. No! It couldn't be. He was at all extremity. His cantankerous temper was only the result of the provoking invincibleness of that death he felt by his side. Any man may be angry with such a masterful chum. But, then, what kind of men were we—with our thoughts! Indignation and doubt grappled within us in a scuffle that trampled upon the finest of our feelings. And we hated him because of the suspicion; we detested him because of the doubt. We could not scorn him safely—neither could we pity him without risk to our dignity. So we hated him, and passed him carefully from hand to hand. We cried, 'Got him?'—'Yes. All right. Let go.' And he swung from one enemy to another, showing about as much life as an old bolster would do. His eyes made two narrow white slits in the black face. He breathed slowly, and the air escaped through his lips with a noise like the sound of bellows. We reached the poop ladder at last, and it being a comparatively safe place, we lay for a moment in an exhausted heap to rest a little. He began to mutter. We were always incurably anxious to hear what he had to say. This time he mumbled peevishly, 'It took you some time to come. I began to think the whole smart lot of you had been washed overboard. What kept you back? Hey? Funk?' We said nothing. With sighs we started again to drag him up. The secret and ardent desire of our hearts was the desire to beat him viciously with our fists about the head: and we handled him as tenderly as though he had been made of glass. . . . .

The return on the poop was like the return of wanderers after many years amongst people marked by the desolation of time. Eyes were turned slowly in their sockets glancing at us. Faint murmurs were heard, 'Have you got 'im after all?' The well-known faces looked strange and familiar; they seemed faded and grimy; they had a mingled expression of fatigue and eagerness. They seemed to have become much thinner during our absence, as if all these men had been starving for a long time in their abandoned attitudes. The captain, with a round turn of a rope on his wrist, and kneeling on one knee, swung with a face cold and stiff; but with living eyes he was still holding the ship up, heeding no one, as if lost in the unearthly effort of that endeavour. We fastened up James Wait in a safe place. Mr. Baker scrambled along to lend a hand. Mr. Creighton, on his back, and very pale, muttered, 'Well done,' and gave us, Jimmy and the sky, a scornful glance, then closed his eyes slowly. Here and there a man stirred a little, but most remained

54

apathetic, in cramped positions, muttering between shivers. The sun was setting. A sun enormous, unclouded and red, declining low as if bending down to look into their faces. The wind whistled across long sunbeams that, resplendent and cold, struck full on the dilated pupils of staring eyes without making them wink. The wisps of hair and the tangled beards were grey with the salt of the sea. The faces were earthy, and the dark patches under the eyes extended to the ears, smudged into the hollows of sunken cheeks. The lips were livid and thin, and when they moved it was with difficulty, as though they had been glued to the teeth. Some grinned sadly in the sunlight, shaking with cold. Others were sad and still. Charley, subdued by the sudden disclosure of the insignificance of his youth, darted fearful glances. The two smooth-faced Norwegians resembled decrepid children, staring stupidly. To leeward, on the edge of the horizon, black seas leaped up towards the glowing sun. It sank slowly, round and blazing, and the crests of waves splashed on the edge of the luminous circle. One of the Norwegians appeared to catch sight of it, and, after giving a violent start, began to speak. His voice, startling the others, made them stir. They moved their heads stiffly, or turning with difficulty, looked at him with surprise, with fear, or in grave silence. He chattered at the setting sun, nodding his head, while the big seas began to roll across the crimson disc; and over miles of turbulent waters the shadows of high waves swept with a running darkness the faces of men. A crested roller broke with a loud hissing roar, and the sun, as if put out, disappeared. The chattering voice faltered, went out together with the light. There were sighs. In the sudden lull that follows the crash of a broken sea a man said wearily, 'Here's that blooming Dutchman gone off his chump.' A seaman, lashed by the middle, tapped the deck with his open hand with unceasing quick flaps. In the gathering greyness of twilight a bulky form was seen rising aft, and began marching on all fours with the movements of some big cautious beast. It was Mr. Baker passing along the line of men. He grunted encouragingly over every one, felt their fastenings. Some, with half-open eyes, puffed like men oppressed by heat; others mechanically and in dreamy voices answered him, 'Aye! aye! sir!' He went from one to another grunting, 'Ough! . . . . See her through it yet;' and unexpectedly, with loud angry outbursts, blew up Knowles for cutting off a long piece from the fall of the relieving tackle. 'Ough!——Ashamed of yourself——Relieving tackle——Don't you know better!——Ough! ——Able seaman! Ough!' The lame man was crushed. He muttered, 'Get som'think for a lashing for myself, sir.'—'Ough! Lashing——yourself. Are you a tinker or a sailor——What? Ough!—— May want that tackle directly——Ough!——More use to the ship than your lame carcass. Ough!——Keep it!——Keep it, now you've done it.' He crawled away slowly, muttering to himself about some men being 'worse than children.' It had been a comforting row. Low exclamations were heard: 'Hallo . . . . Hallo.' . . . . Those who had been painfully dozing asked with convulsive starts, 'What's up?. . . . What is it?' The answers came with unexpected cheerfulness: 'The mate is going bald-headed for lame Jack about something or other.' 'No!'. . . .'What 'as he done?' Some one even chuckled. It was like a whiff of hope, like a reminder of safe days. Donkin, who had been stupefied with fear, revived suddenly and began to shout: —"Ear 'im; that's the way they tawlk to hus. Vy donch 'ee 'it 'im[34]—one ov yer? 'It 'im. 'It 'im! Comin' the mate hover hus. We are as good men as 'ee! We're hall goin' to 'ell now. We 'ave been starved in this rotten ship, an' now we're goin' to be drowned for them black-'earted bullies! 'It 'im!' He shrieked in the deepening gloom, he blubbered and sobbed, screaming:—"It 'im! 'It 'im!' The rage and fear of his disregarded right to live tried the steadfastness of hearts more than the menacing shadows of the night that advanced through the unceasing clamour of the gale. From aft Mr. Baker was heard:—'Is one of you men going to stop him—must I come along?' 'Shut up!' . . . . 'Keep quiet!' cried various voices, exasperated, trembling with cold.—'You'll get one across the mug from me directly,' said an invisible seaman, in a weary tone, 'I won't let the mate have the trouble.' He ceased and lay still with the silence of despair. On the black sky the stars, coming out, gleamed over an inky sea that, speckled with foam, flashed back at them the evanescent and pale light of a dazzling whiteness born from the black turmoil of the waves. Remote in the eternal calm they glittered hard and cold above the uproar of the earth; they surrounded the vanquished and tormented ship on all sides: more pitiless than the eyes of a triumphant mob, and as unapproachable as the hearts of men.

The icy south wind howled exultingly under the sombre splendour of the sky. The cold shook the men with a resistless violence as though it had tried to shake them to pieces. Short moans were swept unheard off the stiff lips. Some complained in mutters of 'not feeling themselves below the waist'; while those who had closed their eyes, imagined they had a block of ice on their chests. Others, alarmed at not feeling any pain in their fingers, beat the deck feebly with their hands—obstinate and exhausted. Wamibo stared vacant and dreamy. The Scandinavians kept on a meaningless mutter through chattering teeth. The spare Scotchmen, with determined efforts, kept their lower jaws still. The West-country men lay big and stolid in an invulnerable surliness. A man yawned and swore in turns. Another breathed with a rattle in his throat. Two elderly hard-weather shellbacks, fast side by side, whispered dismally to one another about the landlady of a boarding-house in Sunderland, whom they both knew. They extolled her motherliness and her liberality; they tried to talk about the joint of beef and the big fire in the downstairs kitchen. The words dying faintly on their lips, ended in light sighs. A sudden voice cried into the cold night, 'Oh Lord!' No one changed his position or took any notice of the cry. One or two passed, with a repeated and vague gesture, their hand over their faces, but most of them kept very still. In the benumbed immobility of their bodies they were excessively wearied by their thoughts, that rushed with the rapidity and vividness of dreams. Now and then, by an abrupt and startling exclamation, they answered the weird hail of some illusion; then, again, in silence contemplated the vision of known faces and familiar things. They recalled the aspect of forgotten shipmates and heard the voice of dead and gone skippers. They remembered the noise of gaslit streets, the steamy heat of tap-rooms, or the scorching sunshine of calm days at sea.

Mr. Baker left his insecure place, and crawled, with stoppages, along the poop. In the dark and on all fours he resembled some carnivorous animal prowling amongst corpses. At the break, propped to windward of a stanchion, he looked down on the main deck. It seemed to him that the ship had a tendency to stand up a little more. The wind had eased a little, he thought, but the sea ran as high as ever. The waves foamed viciously, and the lee side of the

deck disappeared under a hissing whiteness as of boiling milk,
while the rigging sang steadily with a deep vibrating note, and, at
every upward swing of the ship, the wind rushed with a long-
drawn clamour amongst the spars. Mr. Baker watched very still. A
man near him began to make a blabbing noise with his lips, all at
once and very loud, as though the cold had broken brutally
through him. He went on:—'Ba—ba—ba—brrr—brr—ba—ba.'—
'Stop that!' cried Mr. Baker, groping in the dark. 'Stop it!' He went
on shaking the leg he found under his hand.—'What is it, sir?'
called out Belfast, in the tone of a man awakened suddenly; 'we
are looking after that 'ere Jimmy.'—'Are you? Ough! Don't make
that row then. Who's that near you?'—'It's me—the boatswain,
sir,' growled the West-country man; 'we are trying to keep life in
that poor devil.'—'Aye, aye!' said Mr. Baker, 'Do it quietly, can't
you.'—'He wants us to hold him up above the rail,' went on the
boatswain, with irritation, 'says he can't breathe here under our
jackets.'—'If we lift 'im, we drop 'im overboard,' said another voice,
'we can't feel our hands with cold.'—'I don't care. I am choking!'
exclaimed James Wait in a clear tone.—'Oh, no, my son,' said the
boatswain, desperately, 'you don't go till we all go on this fine
night.'—'You will see yet many a worse,' said Mr. Baker, cheerfully.—'It's no child's play, sir!' answered the boatswain. 'Some of
us further aft, here, are in a pretty bad way.'—'If the blamed sticks
had been cut out of her she would be running along on her bottom
now like any decent ship, an' giv' us all a chance,' said some one,
with a sigh.—'The old man wouldn't have it . . . . much he cares
for us,' whispered another.—'Care for you!' exclaimed Mr. Baker,
angrily. 'Why should he care for you? Are you a lot of women
passengers to be taken care of? We are here to take care of the
ship—and some of you ain't up to that. Ough! . . . . What have
you done so very smart to be taken care of? Ough! . . . . Some of
you can't stand a bit of a breeze without crying over it.'—'Come,
sorr. We ain't so bad,' protested Belfast, in a voice shaken by
shivers; 'we ain't . . . . brrr . . . .'—'Again,' shouted the mate,
grabbing at the shadowy form; 'again! . . . . Why, you're in your
shirt! What have you done?'—'I've put my oilskin and jacket over
that half-dead nayggur—and he says he chokes,' said Belfast, com-
plainingly.—'You wouldn't call me nigger if I wasn't half dead,

you Irish beggar!' boomed James Wait, vigorously.—'You . . . .
brrr . . . . You wouldn't be white if you were ever so well I
will fight you . . . . brrrr . . . . in fine weather . . . . brrr . . . .
with one hand tied behind my back . . . . brrrrrr . . . .'—'I don't
want your rags—I want air,' gasped out the other faintly, as if
suddenly exhausted.

The sprays swept over whistling and pattering. Men disturbed
in their peaceful torpor by the pain of quarrelsome shouts, moaned,
muttering curses. Mr. Baker crawled off a little way to leeward
where a water-cask loomed up big, with something white against
it. 'Is it you, Podmore?' asked Mr. Baker. He had to repeat the
question twice before the cook turned, coughing feebly.—'Yes, sir.
I've been praying in my mind for a quick deliverance; for I am
prepared for any call. . . . . I——'—'Look here, cook,' interrupted
Mr. Baker, 'the men are perishing with cold.'—'Cold!' said the
cook, mournfully; 'they will be warm enough before long.'—
'What?' asked Mr. Baker, looking along the deck into the faint
sheen of frothing water.—'They are a wicked lot,' continued the
cook solemnly, but in an unsteady voice, 'about as wicked as any
ship's company in this sinful world! Now, I'—he trembled so that
he could hardly speak; his was an exposed place, and in a cotton
shirt, a thin pair of trousers, and with his knees under his nose, he
received, quaking, the flicks of stinging, salt drops; his voice
sounded exhausted—'now, I—any time . . . . My eldest youngster,
Mr. Baker . . . . a clever boy . . . . last Sunday on shore before this
voyage he wouldn't go to church, sir. Says I, "You go and clean
yourself, or I'll know the reason why!" What does he do? . . . .
Pond, Mr. Baker—fell into the pond in his best rig, sir! . . . . Accident?
. . . . "Nothing will save you, fine scholar though you are!" says
I . . . . . Accident! . . . . I whopped him, sir, till I couldn't lift my
arm. . . . . .' His voice faltered. 'I whopped 'im!' he repeated, rattling
his teeth; then, after a while, let out a mournful sound that was
half a groan, half a snore. Mr. Baker shook him by the shoulders.
'Hey! Cook! Hold up, Podmore! Tell me—is there any fresh water
in the galley tank? The ship is lying along less, I think; I would try
to get forward. A little water would do them good. Hallo! Look out!
Look out!' The cook struggled.—'Not you, sir—not you!' He began
to scramble to windward. 'Galley! . . . . my business!' he shouted.—

59

'Cook's going crazy now,' said several voices. He yelled:—'Crazy, am I? I am more ready to die than any of you, officers incloosive—there! As long as she swims I will cook! I will get you coffee.'—'Cook, ye are a gentleman!' cried Belfast. But the cook was already going over the weather ladder. He stopped for a moment to shout back on the poop:—'As long as she swims I will cook!' and disappeared as though he had gone overboard. The men who had heard sent after him a cheer that sounded like a wail of sick children. An hour or more afterwards some one said distinctly: 'He's gone for good.'—'Very likely,' assented the boatswain; 'even in fine weather he was as smart about the deck as a milch-cow on her first voyage. We ought to go and see.' Nobody moved. As the hours dragged slowly through the darkness Mr. Baker crawled back and forth along the poop several times. Some men fancied they had heard him exchange murmurs with the master, but at that time the memories were incomparably more vivid than anything actual, and they were not certain whether the murmurs were heard now or many years ago. They did not try to find out. A mutter more or less did not matter. It was too cold for curiosity, and almost for hope. They could not spare a moment or a thought from the great mental occupation of wishing to live. And the desire of life kept them alive, apathetic and enduring, under the cruel persistence of wind and cold; while the bestarred black dome of the sky revolved slowly above the ship, that drifted, bearing their patience and their suffering, through the stormy solitude of the sea.

Huddled close to one another, they fancied themselves utterly alone. They heard sustained loud noises, and again bore the pain of existence through long hours of profound silence. In the night they saw sunshine, felt warmth, and suddenly, with a start, thought that the sun would never rise upon a freezing world. Some heard laughter, listened to songs; others, near the end of the poop, could hear loud human shrieks, and, opening their eyes, were surprised to hear them still, though very faint, and far away. The boatswain said:—'Why, it's the cook, hailing from forward, I think.' He hardly believed his own words or recognised his own voice. It was a long time before the man next to him gave a sign of life. He punched hard his other neighbour and said:—'The cook's shouting!' Many did not understand, others did not care; the majority further aft did not believe. But the boatswain and another man had the pluck to crawl away forward to see. They seemed to have been gone for hours, and were very soon forgotten. Then suddenly men that had been plunged in a hopeless resignation became as if possessed with a desire to hurt. They belaboured one another with fists. In the darkness they struck persistently anything soft they could feel near, and, with a greater effort than for a shout, whispered excitedly:—'They've got some hot coffee . . . . . Bosun got it. . . . .' 'No! . . . . Where?' . . . . 'It's coming! Cook made it.' James Wait moaned. Donkin scrambled viciously, caring not where he kicked, and anxious that the officers should have none of it. It came in a pot, and they drank in turns. It was hot, and while it blistered the greedy palates, it seemed incredible. The men sighed out parting with the mug:—'How 'as he done it?' Some cried weakly:—'Bully for you, doctor!'

He had done it somehow. Afterwards Archie declared that the thing was 'meeraculous.' For many days we wondered,[55] and it was the one ever-interesting subject of conversation to the end of the voyage. We asked the cook, in fine weather, how he felt when he saw his stove 'reared up on end.' We inquired, in the north-east trade and on serene evenings, whether he had to stand on his head to put things right somewhat. We suggested he had used his bread-board for a raft, and from there comfortably had stoked his grate; and we did our best to conceal our admiration under the wit of fine irony. He affirmed not to know anything about it, rebuked our levity, declared himself, with solemn animation, to have been the object of a special mercy for the saving of our unholy lives. Fundamentally he was right, no doubt; but he need not have been so offensively positive about it—he need not have hinted so often that it would have gone hard with us had he not been there, meritorious and pure, to receive the inspiration and the strength for the work of grace. Had we been saved by his recklessness or his agility, we could have at length become reconciled to the fact; but to admit our obligation to anybody's virtue and holiness alone was as difficult for us as for any other handful of mankind. Like many benefactors of humanity, the cook took himself too seriously, and reaped the reward of irreverence. We were not ungrateful, however. He remained heroic. His saying—*the* saying of his life—became proverbial in the mouths of men as are the sayings of conquerors or sages. Later on, whenever one of us was puzzled by a task and advised to relinquish it, he would express his determination to persevere and to succeed by the words:—'As long as she swims I will cook!'

The hot drink helped us through the bleak hours that precede the dawn. The sky low by the horizon took on the delicate tints of pink and yellow like the inside of a rare shell. And higher, where it glowed with a pearly sheen, a small black cloud appeared, like a forgotten fragment of the night set in a border of dazzling gold. The beams of light skipped on the crests of waves. The eyes of men turned to the eastward. The sunlight flooded their weary faces. They were giving themselves up to fatigue as though they had done for ever with their work. On Singleton's black oilskin coat the dried salt glistened like hoar frost. He hung on by the wheel, with open and lifeless eyes. Captain Allistoun, unblinking, faced the rising sun. His lips stirred, opened for the first time in twenty-four hours, and with a fresh firm voice he cried, 'Wear ship!'[36]

The commanding sharp tones made all these torpid men start like a sudden flick of a whip. Then again, motionless where they lay, the force of habit made some of them repeat the order in hardly audible murmurs. Captain Allistoun glanced down at his crew, and several, with fumbling fingers and hopeless movements, tried to cast themselves adrift. He repeated impatiently, 'Wear ship. Now then, Mr. Baker, get the men along. What's the matter with them?'—'Wear ship. Do you hear there?—Wear ship!' thundered out the boatswain suddenly. His voice seemed to break through a deadly spell. Men began to stir and crawl.—'I want the fore-top-mast stay-sail run up smartly,' said the master, very loudly; 'if you can't manage it standing up you must do it lying down—that's all. Bear a hand!'—'Come along! Let's give the old girl a chance,' urged the boatswain.—'Aye! aye! Wear ship!' exclaimed quavering voices. The forecastle men, with reluctant faces, prepared to go forward. Mr. Baker pushed ahead grunting on all fours to show the way, and they followed him over the break. The others lay still with a vile hope in their hearts of not being required to move till they got saved or drowned in peace.

After some time they could be seen forward appearing on the forecastle head, one by one in unsafe attitudes; hanging on to the rails; clambering over the anchors; embracing the cross-head of the windlass or hugging the fore-capstan. They were restless with strange exertions, waved their arms, knelt, lay flat down, staggered up, seemed to strive their hardest to go overboard. Suddenly a small white piece of canvas fluttered amongst them, grew larger, beating. Its narrow head rose in jerks—and at last it stood distended and triangular in the sunshine.—'They have done it!' cried the voices aft. Captain Allistoun let go the rope he had round his wrist and rolled to leeward headlong. He could be seen casting the lee main braces off the pins while the backwash of waves splashed over him.—'Square the main yard!' he shouted up to us—who stared at him in wonder. We hesitated to stir. 'The main brace, men. Haul! haul anyhow! Lay on your backs and haul!' he screeched, half drowned down there. We did not believe we could move the main yard, but the strongest and the less discouraged tried to execute the order. Others assisted half-heartedly. Singleton's eyes blazed suddenly as he took a fresh grip of the spokes. Captain Allistoun fought his way up to windward.—'Haul men! Try to move it! Haul, and help the ship.' His hard face worked suffused and furious. 'Is she going off, Singleton?' he cried.—'Not a move yet, sir,' croaked the old seaman in a horribly hoarse voice.— 'Watch the helm, Singleton,' spluttered the master. 'Haul men! Have you no more strength than rats? Haul, and earn your salt.' Mr. Creighton, on his back, with a swollen leg and a face as white as a piece of paper, blinked his eyes; his bluish lips twitched. In the wild scramble men grabbed at him, crawled over his hurt leg, knelt on his chest. He kept perfectly still, setting his teeth without a moan, without a sigh. The master's ardour, the cries of that silent man inspired us. We hauled and hung in bunches on the rope. We heard him say with violence to Donkin, who sprawled abjectly on his stomach,—'I will brain you with this belaying-pin if you don't catch hold of the brace,' and that victim of men's injustice, cowardly and cheeky, whimpered:—'Are you goin' ter murder hus now?' while with sudden desperation he gripped the rope. Men sighed, shouted, hissed meaningless words, groaned. The yards moved, came slowly square against the wind, that hummed loudly on the yard-arms.—'Going off, sir,' shouted Singleton, 'she's just started.'—'Catch a turn with that brace. Catch a turn!' clamoured the master. Mr. Creighton, nearly suffocated and unable to move, made a mighty effort, and with his left hand managed to nip the rope.—'All fast!' cried some one. He closed his eyes as if going off into a swoon, while huddled together about the brace we watched with scared looks what the ship would do now.

She went off slowly as though she had been weary and disheartened like the men she carried. She paid off very gradually, making us hold our breath till we choked, and as soon as she had brought the wind abaft the beam she started to move, and fluttered our hearts. It was awful to see her, nearly overturned, begin to gather way and drag her submerged side through the water. The dead-eyes of the rigging churned the breaking seas. The lower half of the deck was full of mad whirlpools and eddies; and the long line of the lee rail could be seen showing black now and then in the swirls of a field of foam as dazzling and white as a field of snow. The wind sang shrilly amongst the spars; and at every slight lurch we expected her to slip to the bottom sideways from under our backs. When dead before it she made the first distinct attempt to stand up, and we encouraged her with a feeble and discordant howl. A great sea came running up aft and hung for a moment over us with a curling top; then crashed down under the counter and spread out on both sides into a great sheet of bursting froth. Above its fierce hiss we heard Singleton's croak:—'She is steering!' He had both his feet now planted firmly on the grating, and the wheel spun fast as he eased the helm.—'Bring the wind on the port quarter and steady her!' called out the master, staggering to his feet, the first man up from amongst our prostrate heap. One or two screamed with excitement:—She rises! Far away forward, Mr. Baker and three others were seen erect and black on the clear sky, lifting their arms, and with open mouths as though they had been shouting all together. The ship trembled, trying to lift her side, lurched back, seemed to give up with a nerveless dip, and suddenly with an unexpected jerk swung violently to windward, as though she had torn herself out from a deadly grasp. The whole immense volume of water, lifted by her deck, was thrown bodily across to starboard. Loud cracks were heard. Iron ports breaking open thundered with ringing blows. The water topped over the starboard rail with the rush of a river falling over a dam. The sea on deck, and the seas on every side of her, mingled together in a deafening roar. She rolled violently. We got up and were helplessly run or flung about from side to side. Men, rolling over and over, yelled,—'The house will go!'—'She clears herself!' Lifted by a towering sea she ran along with it for a moment, spouting thick streams of water through every opening of her wounded sides. The lee braces having been carried away or washed off the pins, all the ponderous yards on the fore swung from side to side and with appalling rapidity at every roll. The men forward were seen crouching here and there with fearful glances upwards at the enormous spars that whirled about over their heads. The torn canvas and the ends of broken gear streamed in the wind like wisps of hair. Through the clear sunshine, over the flashing turmoil and uproar of the seas, the ship ran blindly, dishevelled and headlong, as if fleeing for her life; and on the poop we spun, we tottered about, distracted and noisy. We all spoke at once in a thin babble; we had the aspect of invalids and the gestures of maniacs. Eyes shone, large and haggard, in smiling, meagre faces that seemed to have been dusted over with powdered chalk. We stamped, clapped our hands, feeling ready to jump and do any-thing; but in reality hardly able to keep on our feet. Captain Allistoun, hard and slim, gesticulated madly from the poop at Mr. Baker: 'Steady these fore-yards! Steady them the best you can!' On the main deck, men excited by his cries, splashed, dashing aimlessly here and there with the foam swirling up to their waists. Apart, far aft, and alone by the helm, old Singleton had deliberately tucked his white beard under the top button of his glistening coat. Swaying upon the din and tumult of the seas, with the whole battered length of the ship launched forward in a rolling rush before his steady old eyes, he stood rigidly still, forgotten by all, and with an attentive face. In front of his erect figure only the two arms moved crosswise with a swift and sudden readiness to check or urge again the rapid stir of circling spokes. He steered with care.

IV

ON men reprieved by its disdainful mercy, the immortal sea confers in its justice the full privilege of desired unrest. Through the perfect wisdom of its grace they are not permitted to meditate at ease upon the complicated and acrid savour of existence, lest they should remember and, perchance, regret the reward of a cup of inspiring bitterness, tasted so often, and so often withdrawn from before their stiffening but reluctant lips. They must without pause justify their life to the eternal pity that commands toil to be hard and unceasing, from sunrise to sunset, from sunset to sunrise: till the weary succession of nights and days tainted by the obstinate clamour of sages, demanding bliss and an empty heaven,[37] is redeemed at last by the vast silence of pain and labour, by the dumb fear and the dumb courage of men obscure, forgetful, and enduring.

The master and Mr. Baker coming face to face stared for a moment, with the intense and amazed looks of men meeting unexpectedly after years of trouble. Their voices were gone, and they whispered desperately at one another.—'Any one missing?' asked Captain Allistoun.—'No. All there.'—'Anybody hurt?'—'Only the second mate.'—'I will look after him directly. We're lucky.'—'Very,' articulated Mr. Baker, faintly. He gripped the rail and rolled bloodshot eyes. The little grey man made an effort to raise his voice above a dull mutter, and fixed his chief mate with a cold gaze,

piercing like a dart.—'Get sail on the ship,' he said, speaking authoritatively, and with an inflexible snap of his thin lips. 'Get sail on her
as soon as you can. This is a fair wind. At once, sir—Don't give the
men time to feel themselves. They will get done up and stiff, and
we will never . . . . We must get her along now' . . . . He reeled to
a long heavy roll; the rail dipped into the glancing hissing water.
He caught a shroud, swung helplessly against the mate . . . . 'now
we have a fair wind at last.——Make——sail.' His head rolled
from shoulder to shoulder. His eyelids began to beat rapidly. 'And
the pumps——pumps, Mr. Baker.' He peered as though the face
within a foot of his eyes had been half a mile off. 'Keep the men
on the move to——to get her along,' he mumbled in a drowsy
tone, like a man going off into a doze. He pulled himself together suddenly. 'Mustn't stand. Won't do,' he said with a painful attempt at a smile. He let go his hold, and, propelled by the
dip of the ship, ran aft unwillingly, with small steps, till he
brought up against the binnacle stand. Hanging on there he
looked up in an objectless manner at Singleton, who, unheeding
him, watched anxiously the end of the jib-boom—'Steering gear
works all right?' he asked. There was a noise in the old seaman's
throat, as though the words had been rattling there together
before they could come out.—'Steers . . . . like a little boat,' he
said, at last, with hoarse tenderness, without giving the master
as much as half a glance—then, watchfully, spun the wheel
down, steadied, flung it back again. Captain Allistoun tore himself away from the delight of leaning against the binnacle, and
began to walk the poop, swaying and reeling to preserve his
balance. . . . . *kind of like corll*

The pump-rods, clanking, stamped in short jumps, while the fly-
wheels turned smoothly, with great speed, at the foot of the
mainmast, flinging back and forth with a regular impetuosity two
limp clusters of men clinging to the handles. They abandoned
themselves, swaying from the hip with twitching faces and stony
eyes. The carpenter, sounding from time to time, exclaimed
mechanically: 'Shake her up! Keep her going!' Mr. Baker could not
speak, but found his voice to shout; and under the goad of his
objurgations, men looked to the lashings, dragged out new sails;
and thinking themselves unable to move, carried heavy blocks

aloft—overhauled the gear. They went up the rigging with faltering and desperate efforts. Their heads swam as they shifted their hold, stepped blindly on the yards like men in the dark; or trusted themselves to the first rope to hand with the negligence of exhausted strength. The narrow escapes from falls did not disturb the languid beat of their hearts; the roar of the seas seething far below them sounded continuous and faint like an indistinct noise from another world; the wind filled their eyes with tears, and with heavy gusts tried to push them off from where they swayed in insecure positions. With streaming faces and blowing hair they flew up and down between sky and water, bestriding the ends of yard-arms, crouching on foot-ropes, embracing lifts to have their hands free, or standing up against chain ties. Their thoughts floated vaguely between the desire of rest and the desire of life, while their stiffened fingers cast off head-earrings, fumbled for knives, or held with tenacious grip against the violent shocks of beating canvas. They glared savagely at one another, made frantic signs with one hand while they held their life in the other, looked down on the narrow strip of flooded deck, shouted along to leeward: 'Light-to!' . . . . 'Haul out!' . . . . 'Make fast!' Their lips moved, their eyes started, furious and eager with the desire to be understood, but the wind tossed their words unheard upon the disturbed sea. In an unendurable and unending strain they worked like men driven by a merciless dream to toil in an atmosphere of ice or flame. They burnt and shivered in turns. Their eyeballs smarted as if in the smoke of a conflagration; their heads were ready to burst with every shout. Hard fingers seemed to grip their throats. At every roll they thought: Now I must let go. It will shake us all off—and thrown about aloft they cried wildly: 'Look out there—catch the end.' . . . . 'Reeve clear' . . . . 'Turn this block. . . . .' They nodded desperately; shook infuriated faces, 'No! No! From down up.' They seemed to hate one another with a deadly hate. The longing to be done with it all gnawed their breasts, and the wish to do things well was a burning pain. They cursed their fate, contemned their life, and wasted their breath in deadly imprecations upon one another. The sailmaker, with his bald head bared, worked feverishly, forgetting his intimacy with so many admirals. The boatswain, climbing up with marlinspikes and bunches of spunyarn rovings, or kneeling on the yard and ready to take a turn with the midship-stop, had acute and fleeting visions of his old woman and the youngsters in a moorland village. Mr. Baker, feeling very weak, tottered here and there, grunting and inflexible, like a man of iron. He waylaid those who, coming from aloft, stood gasping for breath. He ordered, encouraged, scolded. 'Now then—to the main topsail now! Tally on to that gantline. Don't stand about there!'—'Is there no rest for us?' muttered voices. He spun round fiercely, with a sinking heart.—'No! No rest till the work is done. Work till you drop. That's what you're here for.' A bowed seaman at his elbow gave a short laugh.—'Do or die,' he croaked bitterly, then spat into his broad palms, swung up his long arms, and grasping the rope high above his head sent out a mournful, wailing cry for a pull all together. A sea boarded the quarter-deck and sent the whole lot sprawling to leeward. Caps, handspikes floated. Clenched hands, kicking legs, with here and there a spluttering face, stuck out of the white hiss of foaming water. Mr. Baker, knocked down with the rest, screamed—'Don't let go that rope! Hold on to it! Hold!' And sorely bruised by the brutal fling, they held on to it, as though it had been the fortune of their life. The ship ran, rolling heavily, and the topping crests glanced past port and starboard flashing their white heads. Pumps were freed. Braces were rove. The three topsails and foresail were set. She spurted faster over the water, outpacing the swift rush of waves. The menacing thunder of distanced seas rose behind her—filled the air with the tremendous vibrations of its voice. And devastated, battered, and wounded she drove foaming to the northward, as though inspired by the courage of a high endeavour. . . . . .

The forecastle was a place of damp desolation. They looked at their dwelling with dismay. It was slimy, dripping; it hummed hollow with the wind, and was strewn with shapeless wreckage like a half-tide cavern in a rocky and exposed coast. Many had lost all they had in the world, but most of the starboard watch had preserved their chests; thin streams of water trickled out of them, however. The beds were soaked; the blankets spread out and saved by some nail squashed under foot. They dragged wet rags from evil-smelling corners, and, wringing the water out, recognised their property. Some smiled stiffly. Others looked round blank and mute.

There were cries of joy over old waistcoats, and groans of sorrow over shapeless things found amongst the black splinters of smashed bed boards. One lamp was discovered jammed under the bowsprit. Charley whimpered a little. Knowles stumped here and there, sniffing, examining dark places for salvage. He poured dirty water out of a boot, and was concerned to find the owner. Those who, overwhelmed by their losses, sat on the forepeak hatch, remained elbows on knees, and, with a fist against each cheek, disdained to look up. He pushed it under their noses. 'Here's a good boot. Yours?' They snarled, 'No—get out.' One snapped at him, 'Take it to hell out of this.' He seemed surprised. 'Why? It's a good boot,' but remembering suddenly that he had lost every stitch of his clothing, he dropped his find and began to swear. In the dim light cursing voices clashed. A man came in and, dropping his arms, stood still, repeating from the doorstep, 'Here's a bloomin' old go! Here's a bloomin' old go!' A few rooted anxiously in flooded chests for tobacco. They breathed hard, clamoured with heads down. 'Look at that, Jack!' .... 'Here! Sam! Here's my shore-going rig spoilt for ever.' One blasphemed tearfully holding up a pair of dripping trousers. No one looked at him. The cat came out from somewhere. He had an ovation. They snatched him from hand to hand, caressed him in a murmur of pet names. They wondered where he had 'weathered it out;' disputed about it. A squabbling argument began. Two men came in with a bucket of fresh water, and all crowded round it; but Tom, lean and mewing, came up with every hair astir and had the first drink. A couple of men went aft for oil and biscuits.

Then in the yellow light and in the intervals of mopping the deck they crunched hard bread, arranging to 'worry through somehow.' Men chummed as to beds. Turns were settled for wearing boots and having the use of oilskin coats. They called one another 'old man' and 'sonny' in cheery voices. Friendly slaps resounded. Jokes were shouted. One or two stretched on the wet deck, slept with heads pillowed on their bent arms, and several, sitting on the hatch, smoked. Their weary faces appeared through a thin blue haze, pacified and with sparkling eyes. The boatswain put his head through the door. 'Relieve the wheel, one of you'—he shouted inside—'it's six. Blamme if that old Singleton hasn't been there more'n thirty hours. You are a fine lot.' He slammed the door again. 'Mate's watch on deck,' said some one. 'Hey, Donkin, it's your relief!' shouted three or four together. He had crawled into an empty bunk and on wet planks lay still. 'Donkin, your wheel.' He made no sound. 'Donkin's dead,' guffawed some one. 'Sell 'is bloomin' clothes,' shouted another. 'Donkin, if ye don't go to the bloomin' wheel they will sell your clothes—d'ye hear?' jeered a third. He groaned from his dark hole. He complained about pains in all his bones, he whimpered pitifully. 'He won't go,' exclaimed a contemptuous voice, 'your turn, Davies.' The young seaman rose painfully squaring his shoulders. Donkin stuck his head out, and it appeared in the yellow light, fragile and ghastly. 'I will giv' yer a pound of tobaccer,' he whined in a conciliating voice, 'so soon as I draw it from haft. I will—s'elp me. . . . .' Davies swung his arm backhanded and the head vanished. 'I'll go,' he said, 'but you will pay for it.' He walked unsteady but resolute to the door. 'So I will,' yelped Donkin, popping out behind him. 'So I will—s'elp me . . . . a pound . . . . three bob they chawrge.' Davies flung the door open. 'You will pay my price . . . . in fine weather,' he shouted over his shoulder. One of the men unbuttoned his wet coat rapidly, threw it at his head. 'Here, Taffy—take that, you thief!'[38] 'Thank you!' he cried from the darkness above the swish of rolling water. He could be heard splashing; a sea came on board with a thump. 'He's got his bath already,' remarked a grim shellback. 'Aye, aye!' grunted others. Then, after a long silence, Wamibo made strange noises. 'Hallo, what's up with you?' said some one grumpily. 'He says he would have gone for Davy,' explained Archie, who was the Finn's interpreter generally. 'I believe him!' cried voices . . . . 'Never mind, Dutchy . . . . You'll do, muddle-head . . . . Your turn will come soon enough . . . . You don't know when ye're well off.' They ceased, and all together turned their faces to the door. Singleton stepped in, made two paces, and stood swaying slightly. The sea hissed, flowed roaring past the bows, and the forecastle trembled, full of a deep rumour; the lamp flared, swinging like a pendulum. He looked with a dreamy and puzzled stare, as though he could not distinguish the still men from their restless shadows. There were awe-struck murmurs:—'Hallo, hallo' . . . . 'How does it look outside now, Singleton?' Those who sat

on the hatch lifted their eyes in silence, and the next oldest seaman
in the ship (those two understood one another, though they hardly
exchanged three words in a day) gazed up at his friend attentively
for a moment, then taking a short clay pipe out of his mouth,
offered it without a word. Singleton put out his arm towards it,
missed, staggered, and suddenly fell forward, crashing down, stiff
and headlong like an uprooted tree. There was a swift rush. Men
pushed, crying:—'He's done!' .... 'Turn him over!' .... 'Stand
clear there!' Under a crowd of startled faces bending over him he
lay on his back, staring upwards in a continuous and intolerable
manner. In the breathless silence of a general consternation, he
said in a grating murmur:—'I am all right,' and clutched with his
hands. They helped him up. He mumbled despondently:—'I am getting old .... old.'—'Not you,' cried Belfast, with ready tact. Supported on all sides, he hung his head.—'Are you better?' they asked.
He glared at them from under his eyebrows with large black eyes,
spreading over his chest the bushy whiteness of a beard long and
thick.—'Old! old!' he repeated sternly. Helped along, he reached
his bunk. There was in it a slimy soft heap of something that smelt,
like does at dead low water a muddy foreshore. It was his soaked
straw bed. With a convulsive effort he pitched himself on it, and in
the darkness of the narrow place could be heard growling angrily,
like an irritated and savage animal uneasy in its den:—'Bit of
breeze .... small thing .... can't stand up .... old!' He slept at
last. He breathed heavily, high-booted, sou'wester on head, and
his oilskin clothes rustled, when with a deep sighing groan he
turned over. Men conversed about him in quiet concerned whispers. 'This will break 'im up' .... 'Strong as a horse' .... 'Aye. But
he ain't what he used to be.' .... In sad murmurs they gave him
up. Yet at midnight he turned out to duty as if nothing had been
the matter, and answered to his name with a mournful 'Here!' He
brooded alone more than ever, in an impenetrable silence and
with a saddened face. For many years he had heard himself called
'Old Singleton,' and had serenely accepted the qualification, taking
it as a tribute of respect due to a man who through half a century
had measured his strength against the favours and the rages of the
sea. He had never given a thought to his mortal self. He lived
unscathed, as though he had been indestructible, surrendering to

all the temptations, weathering many gales. He had panted in sunshine, shivered in the cold; suffered hunger, thirst, debauch; passed through many trials—known all the furies. Old! It seemed to him he was broken at last. And like a man bound treacherously while he sleeps, he woke up fettered by the long chain of disregarded years. He had to take up at once the burden of all his existence, and found it almost too heavy for his strength. Old! He moved his arms, shook his head, felt his limbs. Getting old .... and then? He looked upon the immortal sea with the awakened and groping perception of its heartless might; he saw it unchanged, black and foaming under the eternal scrutiny of the stars; he heard its impatient voice calling for him out of a pitiless vastness full of unrest, of turmoil, and of terror. He looked afar upon it, and he saw an immensity tormented and blind, moaning and furious, that claimed all the days of his tenacious life, and, when life was over, would claim the worn-out body of its slave.

This was the last of the breeze. It veered quickly, changed to a black south-easter, and blew itself out, giving the ship a famous shove to the northward into the joyous sunshine of the trade. Rapid and white she ran homewards in a straight path, under a blue sky and upon the plain of a blue sea. She carried Singleton's completed wisdom, Donkin's delicate susceptibilities, and the conceited folly of us all. The hours of ineffective turmoil were forgotten; the fear and anguish of these dark moments were never mentioned in the glowing peace of fine days. Yet from that time our life seemed to start afresh as though we had died and had been resuscitated. All the first part of the voyage, the Indian Ocean on the other side of the Cape, all that was lost in a haze, like an ineradicable suspicion of some previous existence. It had ended—then there were blank hours: a livid blurr—and again we lived! Singleton was possessed of sinister truth; Mr. Creighton of a damaged leg; the cook of fame—and shamefully abused the opportunities of his distinction. Donkin had an added grievance. He went about repeating with insistence:—"'E said 'e would brain me—did yer 'ear? They hare goin' to murder hus now for the least little thing.' We began at last to think it was rather awful. And we were conceited! We boasted of our pluck, of our capacity for work, of our energy. We remembered honourable episodes: our devotion,

our indomitable perseverance—and were proud of them as though
they had been the outcome of our unaided impulses. We remembered our danger, our toil—and conveniently forgot our horrible scare. We decried our officers—who had done nothing—and
listened to the fascinating Donkin. His care for our rights, his
disinterested concern for our dignity, were not discouraged by the
invariable contumely of our words, by the disdain of our looks.
Our contempt for him was unbounded—and we could not but
listen with interest to that consummate artist. He told us we were
good men—a 'bloomin' condemned lot of good men.' Who thanked
us? Who took any notice of our wrongs? Didn't we lead a 'dorg's
loife for two poun' ten a month?' Did we think that miserable pay
enough to compensate us for the risk to our lives and for the loss of
our clothes? 'We've lost hevery rag!' he cried. He made us forget
that he, at any rate, had lost nothing of his own. The younger men
listened, thinking—this 'ere Donkin's a long-headed chap, though
no kind of man, anyhow. The Scandinavians were frightened at
his audacities; Wamibo did not understand; and the older seamen
thoughtfully nodded their heads making the thin gold earrings
glitter in the fleshy lobes of hairy ears. Severe, sun-burnt faces were
propped meditatively on tattooed forearms. Veined, brown fists
held in their knotted grip the dirty white clay of smouldering pipes.
They listened, impenetrable, broad-backed, with bent shoulders,
and in grim silence. He talked with ardour, despised and irrefutable.
His picturesque and filthy loquacity flowed like a troubled stream
from a poisoned source.[39] His beady little eyes danced, glancing
right and left, ever on the watch for the approach of an officer.
Sometimes Mr. Baker going forward to take a look at the head
sheets would roll with his uncouth gait through the sudden
stillness of the men; or Mr. Creighton limped along, smooth-faced,
youthful, and more stern than ever, piercing our short silence with
a keen glance of his clear eyes. Behind his back Donkin would
begin again darting stealthy, sidelong looks.—"Ere's one of 'em.
Some of yer 'as made 'im fast that day. Much thanks yer got for
hit. Ain't 'ee a-drivin' yer wusse'n hever? .... Let 'im slip hoverboard .... Vy not? It would 'ave been less trouble. Vy not?' He
advanced confidentially, backed away with great effect; he whispered, he screamed, waved his miserable arms no thicker than

pipe-stems—stretched his lean neck—spluttered—squinted. In the pauses of his impassioned orations the wind sighed quietly aloft, the calm sea unheeded murmured in a warning whisper[40] along the ship's side. We abominated the creature and could not deny the luminous truth of his contentions. It was all so obvious. We were indubitably good men; our deserts were great and our pay small. Through our exertions we had saved the ship and the skipper would get the credit of it. What had he done? we wanted to know. Donkin asked:—'What 'ee could do without hus?' and we could not answer. We were oppressed by the injustice of the world, surprised to perceive how long we had lived under its burden without realising our unfortunate state, annoyed by the uneasy suspicion of our undiscerning stupidity. Donkin assured us it was all our 'good 'eartedness,' but we would not be consoled by such shallow sophistry. We were men enough to courageously admit to ourselves our intellectual shortcomings; though from that time we refrained from kicking him, tweaking his nose, or from accidentally knocking him about, which last, after we had weathered the Cape, had been rather a popular amusement. Davies ceased to talk at him provokingly about black eyes and flattened noses. Charley, much subdued since the gale, did not jeer at him. Knowles deferentially and with a crafty air propounded questions such as:—'Could we all have the same grub as the mates? Could we all stop ashore till we got it? What would be the next thing to try for if we got that?' He answered readily with contemptuous certitude; he strutted with assurance in clothes that were much too big for him as though he had tried to disguise himself. These were Jimmy's clothes mostly—though he would accept anything from anybody; but nobody, except Jimmy, had anything to spare. His devotion to Jimmy was unbounded. He was for ever dodging in the little cabin, ministering to Jimmy's wants, humoring his whims, submitting to his exacting peevishness, often laughing with him. Nothing could keep him away from the pious work of visiting the sick, especially when there was some heavy hauling to be done on deck. Mr. Baker had on two occasions jerked him out from there by the scruff of the neck to our inexpressible scandal. Was a sick chap to be left without attendance? Were we to be ill-used for attending a shipmate?—'What?' growled Mr.

Baker, turning menacingly at the mutter, and the whole half-circle like one man stepped back a pace. 'Set the topmast stunsail. Away aloft, Donkin, overhaul the gear,' ordered the mate inflexibly. 'Fetch the sail along; bend the down-haul clear. Bear a hand.' Then, the sail set, he would go slowly aft and stand looking at the compass for a long time, careworn, pensive, and breathing hard as if stifled by the taint of unaccountable ill-will that pervaded the ship. 'What's up amongst them?' he thought. 'Can't make out this hanging back and growling. A good crowd, too, as they go now-adays.' On deck the men exchanged bitter words, suggested by a silly exasperation against something unjust and irremediable that would not be denied, and would whisper into their ears long after Donkin had ceased speaking. Our little world went on its curved and unswerving path carrying a discontented and aspiring popu-lation. They found comfort of a gloomy kind in an interminable and conscientious analysis of their unappreciated worth; and inspired by Donkin's hopeful doctrines they dreamed enthusiastic-ally of the time when every lonely ship would travel over a serene sea, manned by a wealthy and well-fed crew of satisfied skippers.[41]

It looked as if it would be a long passage. The south-east trades, light and unsteady, were left behind; and then, on the equator and under a low grey sky, the ship, in close heat, floated upon a smooth sea that resembled a sheet of ground glass. Thunder squalls hung on the horizon, circled round the ship, far off and growling angrily, like a troop of wild beasts afraid to charge home. The invisible sun, sweeping above the upright masts, made on the clouds a blurred stain of rayless light, and a similar patch of faded radiance kept pace with it from east to west over the unglittering level of the waters. At night, through the impenetrable darkness of earth and heaven, broad sheets of flame waved noiselessly; and for half a second the becalmed craft stood out with its masts and rigging, with every sail and every rope distinct and black in the centre of a fiery outburst, like a charred ship enclosed in a globe of fire. And, again, for long hours she remained lost in a vast universe of night and silence where gentle sighs wandering here and there like forlorn souls, made the still sails flutter as in sudden fear, and the ripple of a beshrouded ocean whisper its compassion afar—in a voice mournful, immense, and faint. . . . .

When the lamp was put out, and through the door thrown wide open, Jimmy, turning on his pillow, could see vanishing beyond the straight line of top-gallant rail, the quick, repeated visions of a fabulous world made up of leaping fire and sleeping water. The lightning gleamed in his big sad eyes that seemed in a red flicker to burn themselves out in his black face, and then he would lay blinded and invisible in the midst of an intense darkness. He could hear on the quiet deck soft footfalls, the breathing of some man lounging on the doorstep; the low creak of swaying masts; or the calm voice of the watch-officer reverberating aloft, hard and loud, amongst the unstirring sails. He listened with avidity, taking a rest in the attentive perception of the slightest sound from the fatiguing wanderings of his sleeplessness. He was cheered by the rattling of blocks, reassured by the stir and murmur of the watch, soothed by the slow yawn of some sleepy and weary seaman settling himself deliberately for a snooze on the planks. Life seemed an indestructible thing. It went on in darkness, in sunshine, in sleep; tireless, it hovered affectionately round the imposture of his ready death. It was bright, like the twisted flare of lightning, and more full of surprises than the dark night. It made him safe, and the calm of its overpowering darkness was as precious as its restless and dangerous light.

But in the evening, in the dog-watches, and even far into the first night-watch, a knot of men could always be seen congregated before Jimmy's cabin. They leaned on each side of the door, peacefully interested and with crossed legs; they stood astride the doorstep discoursing, or sat in silent couples on his sea-chest; while against the bulwark along the spare topmast, three or four in a row stared meditatively, with their simple faces lit up by the projected glare of Jimmy's lamp. The little place, repainted white, had, in the night, the brilliance of a silver shrine where a black idol, reclining stiffly under a blanket, blinked its weary eyes and received our homage. Donkin officiated. He had the air of a demonstrator showing a phenomenon, a manifestation bizarre, simple, and meritorious, that, to the beholders, should be a profound and an everlasting lesson. 'Just look at 'im, 'ee knows what's what—never fear!' he exclaimed now and then, flourishing a hand hard and fleshless like the claw of a snipe. Jimmy, on his back, smiled with

77

reserve and without moving a limb. He affected the languor of extreme weakness, so as to make it manifest to us that our delay in hauling him out from his horrible confinement, and then that night spent on the poop among our selfish neglect of his needs, had 'done for him.' He rather liked to talk about it, and of course we were always interested. He spoke spasmodically, in fast rushes with long pauses between, as a tipsy man walks. . . . . 'Cook had just given me a pannikin of hot coffee. . . . . Slapped it down there, on my chest—banged the door to. . . . . I felt a heavy roll coming; tried to save my coffee, burnt my fingers . . . . and fell out of my bunk. . . . . She went over so quick. . . . . Water came in through the ventilator. . . . . I couldn't move the door . . . . dark as a grave . . . . tried to scramble up into the upper berth. . . . . Rats . . . . a rat bit my finger as I got up. . . . . I could hear him swimming below me. . . . . I thought you would never come . . . . . I thought you were all gone overboard . . . . of course . . . . Could hear nothing but the wind. . . . . Then you came . . . . to look for the corpse, I suppose. A little more and . . . .'

'Man! But ye made a rare lot of noise in here,' observed Archie, thoughtfully.

'You chaps kicked up such a confounded row above. . . . . Enough to scare any one. . . . . I didn't know what you were up to. . . . . Bash in the blamed planks . . . . my head. . . . . Just what a silly, scary gang of fools would do. . . . . Not much good to me anyhow. . . . . Just as well . . . . drown. . . . . Pah.'

He groaned, snapped his big white teeth, and gazed with scorn. Belfast lifted a pair of dolorous eyes, with a broken-hearted smile, clenched his fists stealthily; blue-eyed Archie caressed his red whiskers with a hesitating hand; the boatswain at the door stared a moment, and brusquely went away with a loud guffaw. Wamibo dreamed. . . . . Donkin felt all over his sterile chin for the few rare hairs, and said, triumphantly, with a sidelong glance at Jimmy:— 'Look at 'im! Wish I was 'arf has 'ealthy has 'e his—I do.' He jerked a short thumb over his shoulder towards the after end of the ship. 'That's the blooming way to do 'em!' he yelped, with forced heartiness. Jimmy said:—'Don't be a dam' fool,' in a pleasant voice. Knowles, rubbing his shoulder against the doorpost, remarked shrewdly:—'We can't all go an' be took sick—it would be mutiny.'—'Mutiny—gawn!' jeered Donkin; 'there's no bloomin' law against bein' sick.'—'There's six weeks' hard for refoosing dooty,' argued Knowles, 'I mind I once seed in Cardiff the crew of an overloaded ship—leastways she weren't overloaded, only a fatherly old gentleman with a white beard and an umbreller came along the quay and talked to the hands. Said as how it was crool hard to be drownded in winter just for the sake of a few pounds more for the owner—he said. Nearly cried over them—he did; and he had a square mainsail coat, and a gaff-topsail hat too—all proper. So they chaps they said they wouldn't go to be drownded in winter—depending upon that 'ere Plimsoll man[42] to see 'em through the court. They thought to have a bloomin' lark and two or three days' spree. And the beak giv' 'em six weeks—coss the ship warn't overloaded. Anyways they made it out in court that she wasn't. There wasn't one overloaded ship in Penarth Dock at all. 'Pears that old coon he was only on pay and allowance from some kind people, under orders to look for overloaded ships, and he couldn't see no further than the length of his umbreller. Some of us in the boarding-house, where I live when I'm looking for a ship in Cardiff, stood by to duck that old weeping spunger in the dock. We kept a good look out, too—but he topped his boom directly he was outside the court. . . . . Yes. They got six weeks' hard. . . . .'

They listened, full of curiosity, nodding in the pauses their rough pensive faces. Donkin opened his mouth once or twice, but restrained himself. Jimmy lay still with open eyes and not at all interested. A seaman emitted the opinion that after a verdict of atrocious partiality 'the bloomin' beaks go an' drink at the skipper's expense.' Others assented. It was clear, of course. Donkin said:— 'Well, six weeks hain't much trouble. You sleep hall night in, reg'lar, in chokey. Do it hon my 'ead.' 'You are used to it ainch'ee, Donkin?' asked somebody. Jimmy condescended to laugh. It cheered up every one wonderfully. Knowles, with surprising mental agility, shifted his ground. 'If we all went sick what would become of the ship? eh?' He posed the problem and grinned all round.—'Let 'er go to 'ell,' sneered Donkin. 'Damn'er. She ain't yourn.'—'What? Just let her drift?' insisted Knowles in a tone of unbelief.—'Aye! Drift, an' be blowed,' affirmed Donkin with fine recklessness. The other did not see it—meditated.—'The stores

would run out,' he muttered, 'and .... never get any-
where .... and what about pay-day?' he added with greater assurance.—'Jack likes a good pay-day,' exclaimed a listener on the
doorstep. 'Aye, because then the girls put one arm round his neck
an' t'other in his pocket, an' call him ducky. Don't they, Jack?'—
'Jack, you're a terror with the gals.'—'He takes three of 'em in tow
to once, like one of 'em Watkinses two-funnel tugs waddling away
with three schooners behind.'—'Jack, you're a lame scamp.'—
'Jack, tell us about that one with a blue eye and a black eye. Do.'—
'There's plenty of girls with one black eye along the Highway
by ....'—'No, that's a speshul one—come Jack.' Donkin looked
severe and disgusted; Jimmy very bored; a grey-haired sea-dog
shook his head slightly, smiling at the bowl of his pipe, discreetly
amused. Knowles turned about bewildered; stammered first at one,
then at another.—'No! .... I never! .... can't talk sensible sense
midst you. .... Always on the kid.' He retired bashfully—muttering and pleased. They laughed hooting in the crude light, around
Jimmy's bed, where on a white pillow his hollowed black face
moved to and fro restlessly. A puff of wind came, made the flame of
the lamp leap, and outside, high up, the sails fluttered, while near
by the block of the foresheet struck a ringing blow on the iron
bulwark. A voice far off cried, 'Helm up!' another, more faint,
answered, 'Hard-up, sir!' They became silent—waited expectantly.
The grey-haired seaman knocked his pipe on the doorstep and
stood up. The ship leaned over gently and the sea seemed to wake
up, murmuring drowsily. 'Here's a little wind comin',' said some
one very low. Jimmy turned over slowly to face the breeze. The
voice in the night cried loud and commanding:—'Haul the spanker
out.' The group before the door vanished out of the light. They
could be heard tramping aft while they repeated with varied
intonations:—'Spanker out!' .... 'Out spanker, sir!' Donkin
remained alone with Jimmy. There was a silence. Jimmy opened
and shut his lips several times as if swallowing draughts of fresher
air; Donkin moved the toes of his bare feet and looked at them
thoughtfully.

'Ain't you going to give them a hand with the sail?' asked
Jimmy.

'No. Hif six ov 'em hain't 'nough beef to set that blamed, rotten spanker, they hain't fit to live,' answered Donkin in a bored, far-away voice, as though he had been talking from the bottom of a hole. Jimmy considered the conical, fowl-like profile with a queer kind of interest; he was leaning out of his bunk with the calculating, uncertain expression of a man who reflects how best to lay hold of some strange creature that looks as though it could sting or bite. But he said only:—'The mate will miss you—and there will be ructions.'

Donkin got up to go. 'I will do for 'im hon some dark night, see hif I don't,' he said over his shoulder.

Jimmy went on quickly:—'You're like a poll-parrot, like a screechin' poll-parrot.' Donkin stopped and cocked his head attentively on one side. His big ears stood out, transparent and veined, resembling the thin wings of a bat.

'Yuss?' he said, with his back towards Jimmy.

'Yes! Chatter out all you know—like .... like a dirty white cockatoo.'

Donkin waited. He could hear the other's breathing, long and slow; the breathing of a man with a hundredweight or so on the breast-bone. Then he asked calmly:—'What do I know?'

'What? .... What I tell you .... not much. What do you want .... to talk about my health so ....'

'Hit's a blooming himposyshun. A bloomin', stinkin', first-class himposyshun—but hit don't tyke me hin. Not hit.'

Jimmy kept still. Donkin put his hands in his pockets, and in one slouching stride came up to the bunk.

'I talk—what's the hodds. They hain't men here—sheep they hare. A driven lot of sheep. I 'old you hup .... Vy not? You're well hoff.'

'I am .... I don't say anything about that. ....'

'Well. Let 'em see hit. Let 'em larn what a man can do. I ham a man, I know hall about yer. ....' Jimmy threw himself further away on the pillow; the other stretched out his skinny neck, jerked his bird face down at him as though pecking at the eyes. 'I ham a man. I've seen the hinside of every chokey in the Colonies rather'n give hup my rights. ....'

'You are a jail-prop,' said Jimmy weakly.

'I ham .... an' proud of it too. You! You 'aven't the bloomin' nerve—so you hinventyd this 'ere dodge. . . . .' He paused; then with marked afterthought accentuated slowly:—'Yer ain't sick—hare yer?'

'No,' said Jimmy firmly. 'Been out of sorts now and again this year,' he mumbled with a sudden drop in his voice.

Donkin closed one eye, amicable and confidential. He whispered:—'Ye 'ave done hit afore—aven'tchee?' Jimmy smiled—then as if unable to hold back he let himself go:—'Last ship—yes. I was out of sorts on the passage. See? It was easy. They paid me off in Calcutta, and the skipper made no bones about it either. . . . . I got my money all right. Laid up fifty-eight days! The fools! O Lord! The fools! Paid right off.' He laughed spasmodically. Donkin chummed giggling. Then Jimmy coughed violently. 'I am as well as ever,' he said, as soon as he could draw breath.

Donkin made a derisive gesture. 'In course,' he said profoundly, 'hany one can see that.'—'They don't,' said Jimmy, gasping like a fish.—'They would swallow any yarn,' affirmed Donkin.—'Don't you let on too much,' admonished Jimmy in an exhausted voice.—'Your little gyme? Eh?' commented Donkin jovially. Then with sudden disgust: 'Yer hall for yerself, s'long has ye're right. . . . .'

So charged with egoism James Wait pulled the blanket up to his chin and lay still for awhile. His heavy lips protruded in an ever-lasting black pout. 'Why are you so hot on making trouble?' he asked without much interest.

''Cos hit's a bloomin' shayme. We hare put hon . . . . bad food, bad pay . . . . I want hus to kick up a bloomin' row; a blamed 'owling row that would make 'em remember! Knocking people habout . . . . brain hus . . . . hindeed! Ain't we men?' His altruistic indignation blazed. Then he said calmly:—'I've been a-hairing ov yer clothes.'—'All right,' said Jimmy languidly, 'bring them in.'—'Giv' us the key of your chest, I'll put 'em away for yer,' said Donkin with friendly eagerness.—'Bring 'em in, I will put them away myself,' answered James Wait with severity. Donkin looked down, muttering. . . . . 'What d'you say? What d'you say?' inquired Wait anxiously.—'Nothink. The night's dry, let 'em 'ang out till the morning,' said Donkin, in a strangely trembling voice, as though restraining laughter or rage. Jimmy seemed satisfied.—'Give me a little water for the night in my mug—there,' he said.

Donkin took a stride over the doorstep.—'Git it yerself,' he replied in a surly tone. 'You can do it, hunless you *hare* sick.'—'Of course I can do it,' said Wait, 'only . . . .'—'Well, then, do it,' said Donkin viciously, 'if yer can look hafter yer clothes, yer can look hafter yerself.' He went on deck without a look back.

Jimmy reached out for the mug. Not a drop. He put it back gently with a faint sigh—and closed his eyes. He thought:—That lunatic Belfast will bring me some water if I ask. Fool. I am very thirsty. . . . . It was very hot in the cabin, and it seemed to turn slowly round, detach itself from the ship, and swing out smoothly into a luminous, arid space where a black sun shone, spinning very fast. A place without any water! No water! A policeman with the face of Donkin drank a glass of beer by the side of an empty well, and flew away flapping vigorously. A ship whose mastheads protruded through the sky and could not be seen, was discharging grain, and the wind whirled the dry husks in spirals along the quay of a dock with no water in it. He whirled along with the husks—very tired and light. All his inside was gone. He felt lighter than the husks—and more dry. He expanded his hollow chest. The air streamed in carrying away in its rush a lot of strange things that resembled houses, trees, people, lamp-posts. . . . . No more! There was no more air—and he had not finished drawing his long breath. But he was in gaol! They were locking him up. A door slammed. They turned the key twice, flung a bucket of water over him—Phoo! What for?

He opened his eyes, thinking the fall had been very heavy for an empty man—empty—empty. He was in his cabin. Ah! All right! His face was streaming with perspiration, his arms heavier than lead. He saw the cook standing in the doorway, a brass key in one hand and a bright tin hook-pot in the other.

'I have been locking up for the night,' said the cook, beaming benevolently. 'Eight-bells just gone. I brought you a pot of cold tea for your night's drinking, Jimmy. I sweetened it with some white cabin sugar, too. Well—it won't break the ship.'

He came in, hung the pot on the edge of the bunk, asked perfunctorily, 'How goes it?' and sat down on the box.—'H'm,' grunted Wait inhospitably. The cook wiped his face with a dirty cotton rag, which, afterwards, he tied round his neck.—'That's how them firemen do in steamboats,' he said serenely, and much pleased with himself. 'My work is as heavy as theirs—I'm thinking—and longer hours. Did you ever see them down the stokehold? Like fiends they look—firing—firing—firing—down there.'

He pointed his forefinger at the deck. Some gloomy thought darkened his shining face, fleeting, like the shadow of a travelling cloud over the light of a peaceful sea. The relieved watch tramped noisily forward, passing in a body across the sheen of the doorway. Some one cried, 'Good night!' Belfast stopped for a moment and looked in at Jimmy, quivering and speechless as if with repressed emotion. He gave the cook a glance charged with dismal foreboding, and vanished. The cook cleared his throat. Jimmy stared upwards and kept as still as a man in hiding.

The night was clear, with a gentle breeze. The ship heeled over a little, slipping quietly over a sombre sea towards the inaccessible and festal splendour of a black horizon pierced by points of flickering fire. Above the mastheads the resplendent curve of the Milky Way spanned the sky like a triumphal arch of eternal light, thrown over the dark pathway of the earth. On the forecastle head a man whistled with loud precision a lively jig, while another could be heard faintly, shuffling and stamping in time. There came from forward a confused murmur of voices, laughter—snatches of song. The cook shook his head, glanced obliquely at Jimmy, and began to mutter. 'Aye. Dance and sing. That's all they think of. I am surprised the Providence don't get tired. . . . . They forget the day that's sure to come . . . . but you. . . . .'

Jimmy drank a gulp of tea, hurriedly, as though he had stolen it, and shrank under his blanket, edging away towards the bulkhead. The cook got up, closed the door, then sat down again and said distinctly:—

'Whenever I poke my galley fire I think of you chaps—swearing, stealing, lying, and worse—as if there was no such thing as another world. . . . . Not bad fellows, either, in a way,' he conceded slowly; then, after a pause of regretful musing, he went on in a resigned tone:—'Well, well. They will have a hot time of it. Hot! Did I say? The furnaces of one of them White Star boats ain't nothing to it.'

He kept very quiet for a while. There was a great stir in his brain; an addled vision of bright outlines; an exciting row of rousing

84

songs and groans of pain. He suffered, enjoyed, admired, approved. He was delighted, frightened, exalted—like on that evening (the only time in his life—twenty-seven years ago; he loved to recall the number of years) when as a young man he had—through keeping bad company—become intoxicated in an East-end music-hall. A tide of sudden feeling swept him clean out of his body. He soared. He contemplated the secret of the hereafter. It commended itself to him. It was excellent; he loved it, himself, all hands, and Jimmy. His heart overflowed with tenderness, with comprehension, with the desire to meddle, with anxiety for the soul of that black man, with the pride of possessed eternity, with the feeling of might. Snatch him up in his arms and pitch him right into the middle of salvation . . . . the black soul—blacker—body—rot—Devil. No! Talk—strength—Samson. . . . . There was a great din as of cymbals in his ears; he flashed through an ecstatic jumble of shining faces, lilies, prayer-books, unearthly joy, white shirts, gold harps, black coats, wings. He saw flowing garments, clean shaved faces, a sea of light—a lake of pitch. There were sweet scents, a smell of sulphur—red tongues of flame licking a white mist. An awesome voice thundered! . . . . It lasted three seconds.

'Jimmy!' he cried in an inspired tone. Then he hesitated. A spark of human pity glimmered yet through the infernal fog of his supreme conceit.

'What?' said James Wait, unwillingly. There was a silence. He turned his head just the least bit, and stole a cautious glance. The cook's lips moved inaudibly; his face was rapt, his eyes turned up. He seemed to be mentally imploring deck beams, the brass hook of the lamp, two cockroaches.

'Look here,' said Wait, 'I want to go to sleep. I think I could.'

'This is no time for sleep!' exclaimed the cook, very loud. He had prayerfully divested himself of the last vestige of his humanity. He was a voice—a fleshless and sublime thing, as on that memorable night—the night when he went over the sea to make coffee for perishing sinners. 'This is no time for sleeping,' he repeated with exaltation. 'I can't sleep.'

'Don't care damn,' said Wait, with factitious energy. 'I can. Go an' turn in.'

'Swear . . . . in the very jaws! . . . . In the very jaws! Don't you

85

see the fire . . . . don't you feel it? Blind, chock-full of sin! I can see it for you. I can't bear it. I hear the call to save you. Night and day. Jimmy let me save you!' The words of entreaty and menace broke out of him in a roaring torrent. The cockroaches ran away. Jimmy perspired, wriggling stealthily under his blanket. The cook yelled. . . . . 'Your days are numbered! . . . .'—'Get out of this,' boomed Wait, courageously.—'Pray with me! . . . .'—'I won't! . . . .' The little cabin was as hot as an oven. It contained an immensity of fear and pain; an atmosphere of shrieks and moans; prayers vociferated like blasphemies and whispered curses. Outside, the men called by Charley, who informed them in tones of delight that there was a row going on in Jimmy's place, pushed before the closed door, too startled to open it. All hands were there. The watch below had jumped out on deck in their shirts, as after a collision. Men running up, asked:—'What is it?' Others said:— 'Listen!' The muffled screaming went on:—'On your knees! On your knees!'—'Shut up!'—'Never! You are delivered into my hands. . . . . Your life has been saved. . . . . Purpose . . . . . Mercy . . . . . Repent.'—'You are a crazy fool! . . . .'—'Account of you . . . . you . . . . Never sleep in this world, if I . . . .'— 'Leave off.'—'No! . . . . stokehold . . . . only think! . . . .' Then an impassioned screeching babble where words pattered like hail.— 'No!' shouted Jim.—'Yes. You are! . . . . No help. . . . . Everybody says so.'—'You lie!'—'I see you dying this minnyt . . . . before my eyes . . . . as good as dead now.'—'Help!' shouted Jimmy, piercingly.—'Not in this valley. . . . . look upwards,' howled the other.— 'Go away! Murder! Help!' clamoured Jimmy. His voice broke. There were moanings, low mutters, a few sobs.

'What's the matter now?' said a seldom-heard voice.—'Fall back, men! Fall back, there!' repeated Mr. Creighton sternly, pushing through.—'Here's the old man,' whispered some.—'The cook's in there, sir,' exclaimed several, backing away. The door clattered open; a broad stream of light darted out on wondering faces; a warm whiff of vitiated air passed. The two mates towered head and shoulders above the spare, grey-headed man who stood revealed between them, in shabby clothes, stiff and angular, like a small carved figure, and with a thin, composed face. The cook got up from his knees. Jimmy sat high in the bunk, clasping his drawn-up legs. The tassel of the blue nightcap almost imperceptibly trembled over his knees. They gazed astonished at his long, curved back, while the white corner of one eye gleamed blindly at them. He was afraid to turn his head, he shrank within himself; and there was an aspect astounding and animal-like in the perfection of his expectant immobility. A thing of instinct—the unthinking stillness of a scared brute.

'What are you doing here?' asked Mr. Baker, sharply.—'My duty,' said the cook, with ardour.—'Your . . . . what?' began the mate. Captain Allistoun touched his arm lightly.—'I know his caper,' he said, in a low voice. 'Come out of that, Podmore,' he ordered, aloud.

The cook wrung his hands, shook his fists above his head, and his arms dropped as if too heavy. For a moment he stood distracted and speechless.—'Never,' he stammered, 'I . . . . he . . . . I.'—'What—do—you—say?' pronounced Captain Allistoun. 'Come out at once—or . . . .'—'I am going,' said the cook, with a hasty and sombre resignation. He strode over the doorstep firmly—hesitated—made a few steps. They looked at him in silence.—'I make you responsible!' he cried desperately, turning half round. 'That man is dying. I make you . . . .'—'You there yet?' called the master in a threatening tone.—'No, sir,' he exclaimed hurriedly in a startled voice. The boatswain led him away by the arm; some one laughed; Jimmy lifted his head for a stealthy glance, and in one unexpected leap sprang out of his bunk; Mr. Baker made a clever catch and felt him very limp in his arms; the group at the door grunted with surprise.—'He lies,' gasped Wait, 'he talked about black devils—he is a devil—a white devil—I am all right.' He stiffened himself, and Mr. Baker, experimentally, let him go. He staggered a pace or two; Captain Allistoun watched him with a quiet and penetrating gaze; Belfast ran to his support. He did not appear to be aware of any one near him; he stood silent for a moment, battling single-handed with a legion of nameless terrors, amidst the eager looks of excited men who watched him far off, utterly alone in the impenetrable solitude of his fear. Heavy breathings stirred the darkness. The sea gurgled through the scuppers as the ship heeled over to a short puff of wind.

'Keep him away from me,' said James Wait at last in his fine baritone voice, and leaning with all his weight on Belfast's neck. 'I've been better this last week . . . . I am well . . . . I was going back to duty . . . . to-morrow—now if you like—Captain.' Belfast hitched his shoulders to keep him upright.

'No,' said the master, looking at him fixedly.

Under Jimmy's armpit Belfast's red face moved uneasily. A row of eyes gleaming stared on the edge of light. They pushed one another with elbows, turned their heads, whispered. Wait let his chin fall on his breast and, with lowered eyelids, looked round in a suspicious manner.

'Why not?' cried a voice from the shadows, 'the man's all right, sir.'

'I am all right,' said Wait with eagerness. 'Been sick . . . . better . . . . turn-to now.' He sighed.—'Howly Mother!' exclaimed Belfast with a heave of the shoulders, 'stand up, Jimmy.'—'Keep away from me then,' said Wait, giving Belfast a petulant push, and reeling fetched against the door-post. His cheek-bones glistened as though they had been varnished. He snatched off his night-cap, wiped his perspiring face with it, flung it on the deck. 'I am coming out,' he said without stirring.

'No. You don't,' said the master curtly. Bare feet shuffled, disapproving voices murmured all round; he went on as if he had not heard:—'You have been skulking nearly all the passage and now you want to come out. You think you are near enough to the pay-table now. Smell the shore, hey?'

'I've been sick . . . . now—better,' mumbled Wait glaring in the light.—'You have been shamming sick,' retorted Captain Allistoun with severity; 'Why . . . .' he hesitated for less than half a second. 'Why, anybody can see that. There's nothing the matter with you, but you choose to lie-up to please yourself—and now you shall lie-up to please me.⁴³ Mr. Baker, my orders are that this man is not to be allowed on deck to the end of the passage.'

There were exclamations of surprise, triumph, indignation. The dark group of men swung across the light. 'What for?' 'Told you so . . . .' 'Bloomin' shame . . . .'—'We've got to say something habout that,' screeched Donkin from the rear.—'Never mind, Jim— we will see you righted,' cried several together. An elderly seaman stepped to the front. 'D'ye mean to say, sir,' he asked ominously,

'that a sick chap ain't allowed to get well in this 'ere hooker?'
Behind him Donkin whispered excitedly amongst a staring crowd
where no one spared him a glance, but Captain Allistoun shook a
forefinger at the angry bronzed face of the speaker.—'You—you
hold your tongue,' he said warningly.—'This isn't the way,'
clamoured two or three younger men.—'Hare we bloomin'
masheens?' inquired Donkin in a piercing tone, and dived under
the elbows of the front rank.—'Soon show 'im we ain't boys . . . .'—
'The man's a man if he is black.'—'We ain't goin' to work this
bloomin' ship shorthanded if Snowball's all right . . . .'—'He says
he is.'—'Well then, strike, boys, strike!'—'That's the bloomin'
ticket.' Captain Allistoun said sharply to the second mate: 'Keep
quiet, Mr. Creighton,' and stood composed in the tumult, listening
with profound attention to mixed growls and screeches, to every
exclamation and every curse of the sudden outbreak. Somebody
slammed the cabin door to with a kick; the darkness full of
menacing mutters leaped with a short clatter over the streak of
light, and the men became gesticulating shadows that growled,
hissed, laughed excitedly. Mr. Baker whispered:—'Get away from
them, sir.' The big shape of Mr. Creighton hovered silently about
the slight figure of the master.—'We have been hymposed upon all
this voyage,' said a gruff voice, 'but this 'ere fancy takes the cake.'—
'That man is a shipmate.'—'Are we bloomin' kids?'—'The port
watch will refuse duty.' Charley carried away by his feelings
whistled shrilly, then yelped:—'Giv'us our Jimmy!' This seemed to
cause a variation in the disturbance. There was a fresh burst of
squabbling uproar. A lot of quarrels were set going at once.—
'Yes'—'No.'—'Never been sick.'—'Go for them to once.'—'Shut
yer mouth, youngster—this is men's work.'—'Is it?' muttered
Captain Allistoun bitterly. Mr. Baker grunted: 'Ough! They're gone
silly. They've been simmering for the last month.'—'I did notice,'
said the master.—'They have started a row amongst themselves
now,' said Mr. Creighton with disdain, 'better get aft, sir. We will
soothe them.'—'Keep your temper, Creighton,' said the master.
And the three men began to move slowly towards the cabin door.

In the shadows of the fore rigging a dark mass stamped, eddied,
advanced, retreated. There were words of reproach, encouragement, unbelief, execration. The elder seamen, bewildered and

angry, growled their determination to go through with something
or other; but the younger school of advanced thought exposed
their and Jimmy's wrongs with confused shouts, arguing amongst
themselves. They clustered round that moribund carcass, the fit
emblem of their aspirations,⁴⁴ and encouraging one another they
swayed, they tramped on one spot, shouting that they would not
be 'put upon.' Inside the cabin, Belfast, helping Jimmy into his
bunk, twitched all over in his desire not to miss all the row, and
with difficulty restrained the tears of his facile emotion. James
Wait, flat on his back under the blanket, gasped complaints.—'We
will back you up, never fear,' assured Belfast, busy about his feet.—
'I'll come out to-morrow morning——take my chance——you
fellows must——' mumbled Wait, 'I come out to-morrow——
skipper or no skipper.' He lifted one arm with great difficulty,
passed the hand over his face; 'Don't you let that cook . . . .' he
breathed out.—'No, no,' said Belfast, turning his back on the bunk,
'I will put a head on him if he comes near you.'—'I will smash his
mug!' exclaimed faintly Wait, enraged and weak; 'I don't want to
kill a man, but . . . .' He panted fast like a dog after a run in
sunshine. Some one just outside the door shouted, 'He's as fit as
any ov us!' Belfast put his hand on the door-handle.—'Here!' called
James Wait hurriedly and in such a clear voice that the other spun
round with a start. James Wait, stretched out black and deathlike
in the dazzling light, turned his head on the pillow. His eyes stared
at Belfast, appealing and impudent. 'I am rather weak from lying-
up so long,' he said distinctly. Belfast nodded. 'Getting quite well
now,' insisted Wait.—'Yes. I noticed you getting better
this . . . . last month,' said Belfast looking down. 'Hallo! What's
this?' he shouted and ran out.

He was flattened directly against the side of the house by two
men who lurched against him. A lot of disputes seemed to be going
on all round. He got clear and saw three indistinct figures standing
alone in the fainter darkness under the arched foot of the mainsail,
that rose above their heads like a convex wall of a high edifice.
Donkin hissed:—'Go for them . . . . it's dark!' The crowd took a
short run aft in a body—then there was a check. Donkin, agile and
thin, flitted past with his right arm going like a windmill—and
then stood still suddenly with his arm pointing rigidly above his

head. The hurtling flight of some small heavy object was heard; it passed between the heads of the two mates, bounded heavily along the deck, struck the after hatch with a ponderous and deadened blow. The bulky shape of Mr. Baker grew distinct. 'Come to your senses, men!' he cried, advancing at the arrested crowd. 'Come back, Mr. Baker!' called the master's quiet voice. He obeyed unwillingly. There was a minute of silence, then a deafening hubbub arose. Above it Archie was heard energetically:—'If ye do oot ageen I wull tell!' There were shouts. 'Don't!' 'Drop it!'—'We ain't that kind!' The black cluster of human forms reeled against the bulwark, back again towards the house. Shadowy figures could be seen tottering, falling, leaping up. Ringbolts rang under stumbling feet.—'Drop it!' 'Let me!'—'No!'—'Curse you .... hah!' Then sounds as of some one's face being slapped; a piece of iron fell on the deck; a short scuffle, and some one's shadowy body scuttled rapidly across the main hatch before the shadow of a kick. A raging voice sobbed out a torrent of filthy language .... — 'Throwing things—good God!' grunted Mr. Baker in dismay.— 'That was meant for me,' said the master quietly; 'I felt the wind of that thing; what was it—an iron belaying-pin?'[45]—'By Jove!' muttered Mr. Creighton. The confused voices of men talking amidships mingled with the wash of the sea, ascended between the silent and distended sails—seemed to flow away into the night, further than the horizon, higher than the sky. The stars burned steadily over the inclined mastheads. Trails of light lay on the water, broke before the advancing hull, and, after she had passed, trembled for a long time as if in awe of the murmuring sea.

Meantime the helmsman, anxious to know what the row was about, had let go the wheel, and, bent double, ran with long stealthy footsteps to the break of the poop. The *Narcissus*, left to herself, came up gently to the wind without any one being aware of it. She gave a slight roll, and the sleeping sails woke suddenly, coming all together with a mighty flap against the masts, then filled again one after another in a quick succession of loud reports that ran down the lofty spars, till the collapsed mainsail flew out last with a violent jerk. The ship trembled from trucks to keel; the sails kept on rattling like a discharge of musketry; the chain sheets and loose shackles jingled aloft in a thin peal; the gin blocks groaned. It was as if an invisible hand had given the ship an angry shake to recall the men that peopled her decks to the sense of reality, vigilance, and duty.—'Helm up!' cried the master sharply. 'Run aft, Mr. Creighton, and see what that fool there is up to.'— 'Flatten in the head sheets. Stand by the weather fore-braces,' growled Mr. Baker. Startled men ran swiftly repeating the orders. The watch below, abandoned all at once by the watch on deck, drifted towards the forecastle in twos and threes, arguing noisily as they went.—'We shall see to-morrow!' cried a loud voice, as if to cover with a menacing hint an inglorious retreat. And then only orders were heard, the falling of heavy coils of rope, the rattling of blocks. Singleton's white head flitted here and there in the night, high above the deck, like the ghost of a bird.—'Going off, sir!' shouted Mr. Creighton from aft.—'Full again.'—'All right . . . .'— 'Ease off the head sheets. That will do the braces. Coil the ropes,' grunted Mr. Baker, bustling about.

Gradually the tramping noises, the confused sound of voices, died out, and the officers, coming together on the poop, discussed the events. Mr. Baker was bewildered and grunted; Mr. Creighton was calmly furious; but Captain Allistoun was composed and thoughtful. He listened to Mr. Baker's growling argumentation, to Creighton's interjected and severe remarks, while looking down on the deck he weighed in his hand the iron belaying-pin—that a moment ago had just missed his head—as if it had been the only tangible fact of the whole transaction. He was one of those commanders who speak little, seem to hear nothing, look at no one—and know everything, hear every whisper, see every fleeting shadow of their ship's life. His two big officers towered above his lean, short figure; they talked over his head; they were dismayed, surprised, and angry, while between them the little quiet man seemed to have found his taciturn serenity in the profound depths of a larger experience. Lights were burning in the forecastle; now and then a loud gust of babbling chatter came from forward, swept over the decks, and became faint, as if the unconscious ship, gliding gently through the great peace of the sea, had left behind and for ever the foolish noise of turbulent mankind. But it was renewed again and again. Gesticulating arms, profiles of heads with open mouths appeared for a moment in the illuminated squares of doorways; black fists darted—withdrew..... 'Yes. It was most damnable to have such an unprovoked row sprung on one,' assented the master..... A tumult of yells rose in the light, abruptly ceased..... He didn't think there would be any further trouble just then..... A bell was struck aft, another, forward, answered in a deeper tone, and the clamour of ringing metal spread round the ship in a circle of wide vibrations that ebbed away into the immeasurable night of an empty sea..... Didn't he know them! Didn't he! In past years. Better men, too. Real men to stand by one in a tight place. Worse than devils too sometimes— downright, horned devils. Pah! This—nothing. A miss as good as a mile..... The wheel was being relieved in the usual way.—'Full and by,' said, very loud, the man going off.—'Full and by,' repeated the other, catching hold of the spokes.—'This head wind is my trouble,' exclaimed the master, stamping his foot in sudden anger; 'head wind! all the rest is nothing.' He was calm again in a moment. 'Keep them on the move to-night, gentlemen; just to let them feel we've got hold all the time—quietly, you know. Mind you keep your hands off them, Creighton. To-morrow I will talk to them like a Dutch Uncle. A crazy crowd of tinkers! Yes, tinkers! I could count the real sailors amongst them on the fingers of one hand. Nothing will do but a row—if—you—please.' He paused. 'Did you think I had gone wrong there, Mr. Baker?' He tapped his forehead, laughed short. 'When I saw him standing there, three parts dead and so scared—black amongst that gaping lot—no grit to face what's coming to us all—the notion came to me all at once, before I could think. Sorry for him—like you would be for a sick brute. If ever creature was in a mortal funk to die!.... I thought I would let him go out in his own way. Kind of impulse. It never came into my head, those fools..... H'm! Stand to it now—of course.' He stuck the belaying-pin in his pocket, seemed ashamed of himself, then sharply:—'If you see Podmore at his tricks again tell him I will have him put under the pump. Had to do it once before. The fellow breaks out like that now and then. Good cook tho'.' He walked away quickly, came back to the companion. The two mates followed him through the starlight with amazed eyes. He went down three steps, and changing his tone, spoke with his head near the deck:—'I shan't turn in to-night, in case of anything; just call out if . . . . Did you see the eyes of that sick nigger, Mr. Baker? I fancied he begged me for something. What? Past all help. One lone black beggar amongst the lot of us, and he seemed to look through me into the very hell. Fancy, this wretched Podmore! Well, let him die in peace. I am master here after all. Say what I like. Let him be. He might have been half a man once . . . . Keep a good look-out.' He disappeared down below, leaving his mates facing one another, and more impressed than if they had seen a stone image shed a miraculous tear of compassion over the incertitudes of life and death. . . . .

In the blue mist spreading from twisted threads that stood upright in the bowls of pipes, the forecastle appeared as vast as a hall. Between the beams a heavy cloud stagnated; and the lamps surrounded by halos burned each at the core of a purple glow in two lifeless flames without rays. Wreaths drifted in denser wisps. Men sprawled about on the deck, sat in negligent poses, or, bending a knee, drooped with one shoulder against a bulkhead. Lips moved, eyes flashed, waving arms made sudden eddies in the smoke. The murmur of voices seemed to pile itself higher and higher as if unable to run out quick enough through the narrow doors. The watch below in their shirts, and striding on long white legs, resembled raving somnambulists; while now and then one of the watch on deck would rush in, looking strangely over-dressed, listen a moment, fling a rapid sentence into the noise and run out again; but a few remained near the door, fascinated, and with one ear turned to the deck.—'Stick together, boys,' roared Davis. Belfast tried to make himself heard. Knowles grinned in a slow, dazed way. A short fellow with a thick clipped beard kept on yelling periodically:—'Who's afeard? Who's afeard?' Another one jumped up, excited, with blazing eyes, sent out a string of unattached curses and sat down quietly. Two men discussed familiarly, striking one another's breast in turn, to clinch arguments. Three others, with their heads in a bunch, spoke all together with a confidential air, and at the top of their voices. It was a stormy chaos of speech where intelligible fragments tossing, struck the ear. One could hear:—'In the last ship'—'Who cares? Try it on any one of us if——.' 'Knock under'—'Not a hand's turn'—'He says he is all right'—'I always thought'—'Never mind. . . . .' Donkin, crouching all in a heap against the bowsprit, hunched his shoulder-blades as high as his ears, and hanging a peaked nose, resembled a sick vulture with ruffled plumes. Belfast, straddling his legs, had a face red with yelling, and with arms thrown up, figured a Maltese cross. The two Scandinavians, in a corner, had the dumbfounded and distracted aspect of men gazing at a cataclysm. And, beyond the light, Singleton stood in the smoke, monumental, indistinct, with his head touching the beam; like a statue of heroic size in the gloom of a crypt.

He stepped forward, impassive and big. The noise subsided like a broken wave: but Belfast cried once more with uplifted arms:—'The man is dying I tell ye!' then sat down suddenly on the hatch and took his head between his hands. All looked at Singleton, gazing upwards from the deck, staring out of dark corners, or turning their heads with curious glances. They were expectant and appeased as if that old man, who looked at no one, had possessed the secret of their uneasy indignations and desires, a sharper vision, a clearer knowledge. And indeed standing there amongst them, he had the uninterested appearance of one who had seen multitudes of ships, had listened many times to voices such as theirs, had already seen all that could happen on the wide seas. They heard his voice rumble in his broad chest as though the words had been rolling towards them out of a rugged past. 'What do you want to do?' he asked. No one answered. Only Knowles muttered—'Aye, aye,' and somebody said low:—'It's a bloomin' shame.' He waited, made a contemptuous gesture.—'I have seen rows aboard ship before some of you were born,' he said slowly, 'for something or nothing; but never for such a thing.'—'The man is dying, I tell ye,' repeated Belfast woefully, sitting at Singleton's feet.—'And a black fellow, too,' went on the old seaman, 'I have seen them die like flies.' He stopped, thoughtful, as if trying to recollect gruesome things, details of horrors, hecatombs of niggers. They looked at him fascinated. He was old enough to remember slavers, bloody mutinies, pirates perhaps; who could tell through what violences and terrors he had lived! What would he say? He said:—'You can't help him; die he must.' He made another pause. His moustache and beard stirred. He chewed words, mumbled behind tangled white hairs; incomprehensible and exciting, like an

oracle behind a veil. . . . . —'Stop ashore——sick.——Instead——
bringing all this head wind. Afraid. The sea will have her own.——
Die in sight of land.[46] Always so. They know it——long passage——more days, more dollars.——You keep quiet.——What
do you want? Can't help him.' He seemed to wake up from a
dream. 'You can't help yourselves,' he said austerely, 'Skipper's no
fool. He has something in his mind. Look out—I say! I know 'em!'
With eyes fixed in front he turned his head from right to left, from
left to right, as if inspecting a long row of astute skippers.—'He
said 'e would brain me!' cried Donkin in a heartrending tone.
Singleton peered downwards with puzzled attention, as though he
couldn't find him.—'Damn you!' he said vaguely, giving it up. He
radiated unspeakable wisdom, hard unconcern, the chilling air of
resignation. Round him all the listeners felt themselves somehow
completely enlightened by their disappointment, and, mute, they
lolled about with the careless ease of men who can discern perfectly
the irremediable aspect of their existence. He, profound and unconscious, waved his arm once, and strode out on deck without
another word.

Belfast was lost in a round-eyed meditation. One or two vaulted
heavily into upper berths, and, once there, sighed; others dived
head first inside lower bunks—swift, and turning round instantly
upon themselves, like animals going into lairs. The grating of a
knife scraping burnt clay was heard. Knowles grinned no more.
Davies said, in a tone of ardent conviction:—'Then our skipper's
looney.' Archie muttered:—'My faith! we haven't heard the last of
it yet!' Four bells were struck.—'Half our watch below is gone!'
cried Knowles in alarm, then reflected. 'Well, two hours' sleep is
something towards a rest,' he observed consolingly. Some already
pretended to slumber; and Charley, sound asleep, suddenly said a
few slurred words in an arbitrary, blank voice.—'This blamed boy
has worrums!' commented Knowles from under a blanket, and in
a learned manner. Belfast got up and approached Archie's berth.—
'We pulled him out,' he whispered sadly.—'What?' said the other,
with sleepy discontent.—'And now we will have to chuck him
overboard,' went on Belfast, whose lower lip trembled.—'Chuck
what?' asked Archie.—'Poor Jimmy,' breathed out Belfast.—'He be
blowed!' said Archie with untruthful brutality, and sat up in his

bunk; 'It's all through him. If it hadn't been for me, there would have been murder on board this ship!'—"Tain't his fault, is it?' argued Belfast, in a murmur; 'I've put him to bed . . . . an' he ain't no heavier than an empty beef-cask,' he added, with tears in his eyes. Archie looked at him steadily, then turned his nose to the ship's side with determination. Belfast wandered about as though he had lost his way in the dim forecastle, and nearly fell over Donkin. He contemplated him from on high for awhile. 'Ain't ye going to turn in?' he asked. Donkin looked up hopelessly.—'That black-'earted Scotch son of a thief kicked me!' he whispered from the floor, in a tone of utter desolation.—'And a good job, too!' said Belfast, still very depressed; 'You were as near hanging as damn-it to-night, sonny. Don't you play any of your murthering games around my Jimmy! You haven't pulled him out. You just mind! 'Cos if I start to kick you'—he brightened up a bit—'if I start to kick you, it will be Yankee fashion—to break something!' He tapped lightly with his knuckles the top of the bowed head. 'You moind, me bhoy!' he concluded, cheerily. Donkin let it pass.—'Will they split on me?' he asked, with pained anxiety.—'Who—split?' hissed Belfast, coming back a step. 'I would split your nose this minyt if I hadn't Jimmy to look after! Who d'ye think we are?' Donkin rose and watched Belfast's back lurch through the doorway. On all sides invisible men slept, breathing calmly. He seemed to draw courage and fury from the peace around him. Venomous and thin-faced, he glared from the ample misfit of borrowed clothes as if looking for something he could smash. His heart leaped wildly in his narrow chest. They slept! He wanted to wring necks, gouge eyes, spit on faces. He shook a dirty pair of meagre fists at the smoking lights. 'Ye're no men!' he cried, in a deadened tone. No one moved. 'Yer 'aven't the pluck of a mouse!' His voice rose to a husky screech. Wamibo darted out a dishevelled head, and looked at him wildly. 'Ye're sweepings ov ships! I 'ope you will hall rot before you die!' Wamibo blinked, uncomprehending but interested. Donkin sat down heavily; he blew with force through quivering nostrils, he ground and snapped his teeth, and, with the chin pressed hard against the breast, he seemed busy gnawing his way through it, as if to get at the heart within. . . . .

In the morning the ship, beginning another day of her wandering life, had an aspect of sumptuous freshness, like the spring-time of the earth. The washed decks glistened in a long clear stretch; the oblique sunlight struck the yellow brasses in dazzling splashes, darted over the polished rods in lines of gold, and the single drops of salt water forgotten here and there along the rail were as limpid as drops of dew, and sparkled more than scattered diamonds. The sails slept, hushed by a gentle breeze. The sun, rising lonely and splendid in the blue sky, saw a solitary ship gliding close-hauled on the blue sea.

The men pressed three deep abreast of the mainmast and opposite the cabin-door. They shuffled, pushed, had an irresolute mien and stolid faces. At every slight movement Knowles lurched heavily on his short leg. Donkin glided behind backs, restless and anxious, like a man looking for an ambush. Captain Allistoun came out suddenly. He walked to and fro before the front. He was grey, slight, alert, shabby in the sunshine, and as hard as adamant. He had his right hand in the side-pocket of his jacket, and also something heavy in there that made folds all down that side. One of the seamen cleared his throat ominously.—'I haven't till now found fault with you men,' said the master, stopping short. He faced them with his worn, steely gaze, that by an universal illusion looked straight into every individual pair of the twenty pairs of eyes before his face. At his back Mr. Baker, gloomy and bull-necked, grunted low; Mr. Creighton, fresh as paint, had rosy cheeks and a ready, resolute bearing. 'And I don't now,' continued the master; 'but I am here to drive this ship and keep every man-jack aboard of her up to the mark. If you knew your work as well as I do mine, there would be no trouble. You've been braying in the dark about "See to-morrow morning!" Well, you see me now. What do you want?' He waited, stepping quickly to and fro, giving them searching glances. What did they want? They shifted from foot to foot, they balanced their bodies; some, pushing back their caps, scratched their heads. What did they want? Jimmy was forgotten; no one thought of him, alone forward in his cabin, fighting great shadows, clinging to brazen lies, chuckling painfully over his transparent deceptions. No, not Jimmy; he was more forgotten than if he had been dead. They wanted great things. And suddenly all the simple words they knew seemed to be lost for ever

98

in the immensity of their vague and burning desire. They knew what they wanted, but they could not find anything worth saying. They stirred on one spot, swinging, at the end of muscular arms, big tarry hands with crooked fingers. A murmur died out.—'What is it—food?' asked the master, 'you know the stores had been spoiled off the Cape.'—'We know that, sir,' said a bearded shell-back in the front rank.—'Work too hard—eh? Too much for your strength?' he asked again. There was an offended silence.—'We don't want to go shorthanded, sir,' began at last Davies in a wavering voice, 'and this 'ere black— . . . .'—'Enough!' cried the master. He stood scanning them for a moment, then walking a few steps this way and that began to storm at them coldly, in gusts violent and cutting like the gales of those icy seas that had known his youth.—'Tell you what's the matter? Too big for your boots. Think yourselves damn good men. Know half your work. Do half your duty. Think it too much. If you did ten times as much it wouldn't be enough.'—'We did our best by her, sir,' cried some one with shaky exasperation.—'Your best,' stormed on the master; 'You hear a lot on shore, don't you? They don't tell you there your best isn't much to boast of. I tell you—your best is no better than bad. You can do no more? No, I know, and say nothing. But you stop your caper or I will stop it for you. I am ready for you! Stop it!' He shook a finger at the crowd. 'As to that man,' he raised his voice very much; 'as to that man, if he puts his nose out on deck without my leave I will clap him in irons. There!' The cook heard him forward, ran out of the galley lifting his arms, horrified, unbelieving, amazed, and ran in again. There was a moment of profound silence during which a bow-legged seaman, stepping aside, expectorated decorously into the scupper. 'There is another thing,' said the master calmly. He made a quick stride and with a swing took an iron belaying-pin out of his pocket. 'This!' His movement was so unexpected and sudden that the crowd stepped back. He gazed fixedly at their faces, and some at once put on a surprised air as though they had never seen a belaying-pin before. He held it up. 'This is my affair. I don't ask you any questions, but you all know it; it has got to go where it came from.' His eyes became angry. The crowd stirred uneasily. They looked away from the piece of iron, they appeared shy, they were embarrassed and shocked as though it had been something horrid, scandalous, or indelicate, that in common decency should not have been flourished like this in broad daylight. The master watched them attentively. 'Donkin,' he called out in a short, sharp tone.

Donkin dodged behind one, then behind another, but they looked over their shoulders and moved aside. The ranks kept on opening before him, closing behind, till at last he appeared alone before the master as though he had come up through the deck. Captain Allistoun moved close to him. They were much of a size, and at short range the master exchanged a deadly glance with the beady eyes. They wavered.—'You know this,' asked the master.—'No, I don't,' answered the other with cheeky trepidation.—'You are a cur. Take it,' ordered the master. Donkin's arms seemed glued to his thighs; he stood, eyes front, as if drawn on parade. 'Take it,' repeated the master, and stepped closer; they breathed on one another. 'Take it,' said Captain Allistoun again, making a menacing gesture. Donkin tore away one arm from his side.—'Vy hare yer down hon me?' he mumbled with effort and as if his mouth had been full of dough.—'If you don't . . . .' began the master. Donkin snatched at the pin as though his intention had been to run away with it, and remained stock still holding it like a candle. 'Put it back where you took it from,' said Captain Allistoun, looking at him fiercely. Donkin stepped back opening wide eyes. 'Go, you blackguard, or I will make you,' cried the master, driving him slowly backwards by a menacing advance. He dodged, and with the dangerous iron tried to guard his head from a threatening fist. Mr. Baker ceased grunting for a moment.—'Good! By Jove,' murmured appreciatively Mr. Creighton in the tone of a connoisseur.—'Don't tech me,' snarled Donkin, backing away.—'Then go. Go faster.'—'Don't yer 'it me. . . . . I will pull yer hup afore the magistryt. . . . . I'll show yer hup.' Captain Allistoun made a long stride, and Donkin, turning his back fairly, ran off a little, then stopped and over his shoulder showed yellow teeth.—'Further on, fore-rigging,' urged the master, pointing with his arm.—'Hare yer goin' to stand by and see me bullied,' screamed Donkin at the silent crowd that watched him. Captain Allistoun walked at him smartly. He started off again with a leap, dashed at the fore-rigging, rammed the pin into its hole violently. 'I will be heven with yer yet,' he screamed at the ship at large and vanished beyond the foremast. Captain Allistoun spun round and walked back aft with a composed face, as though he had already forgotten the scene. Men moved out of his way. He looked at no one.—'That will do, Mr. Baker. Send the watch below,' he said quietly. 'And you men try to walk straight for the future,' he added in a calm voice. He looked pensively for a while at the backs of the impressed and retreating crowd. 'Breakfast, steward,' he called in a tone of relief through the cabin door.—'I didn't like to see you—Ough!—give that pin to that chap, sir,' observed Mr. Baker; 'he could have bust—Ough!—bust your head like an eggshell with it.'—'O! he!' muttered the master absently. 'Queer lot,' he went on in a low voice. 'I suppose it's all right now. Can never tell tho', nowadays, with such a . . . . Years ago; I was a young master then—one China voyage I had a mutiny; real mutiny, Baker. Different men tho'. I knew what they wanted: they wanted to broach cargo and get at the liquor. Very simple. . . . . We knocked them about for two days, and when they had enough—gentle as lambs. Good crew. And a smart trip I made.' He glanced aloft at the yards braced sharp up. 'Head wind day after day,' he exclaimed bitterly. 'Will we never get a decent slant this passage?'—'Ready, sir,' said the steward, appearing before them as if by magic and with a stained napkin in his hand.—'Ah! All right. Come along, Mr. Baker—it's late—with all this nonsense.'

Jimmy
Dies

V

A HEAVY atmosphere of oppressive quietude pervaded the ship. In the afternoon men went about washing clothes and hanging them out to dry in the unprosperous breeze with the meditative languor of disenchanted philosophers. Very little was said. The problem of life seemed too voluminous for the narrow limits of human speech, and by common consent it was abandoned to the great sea that had from the beginning enfolded it in its immense grip; to the sea that knew all, and would in time infallibly unveil to each the wisdom hidden in all the errors, the certitude that lurks in doubts, the realm of safety and peace beyond the frontiers of sorrow and fear. And in the confused current of impotent thoughts that set unceasingly this way and that through bodies of men, Jimmy bobbed up upon the surface, compelling attention, like a black buoy chained to the bottom of a muddy stream. Falsehood triumphed. It triumphed through doubt, through stupidity, through pity, through sentimentalism. We set ourselves to bolster it up, from compassion, from recklessness, from a sense of fun. Jimmy's steadfastness to his untruthful attitude in the face of the inevitable truth had the proportions of a colossal enigma—of a manifestation grand and incomprehensible that at times inspired a wondering awe; and there was also, to many, something exquisitely droll in fooling him thus to the top of his bent. The latent egoism of tenderness to suffering appeared in the developing anxiety not to see him die.⁴⁷ His obstinate non-recognition of the only certitude whose approach we could watch from day to day was as disquieting as the failure of some law of nature. He was so utterly wrong about himself that one could not but suspect him of having access to some source of supernatural knowledge. He was absurd to the point of inspiration. He was unique, and as fascinating as only something inhuman could be; he seemed to shout his denials already from beyond the awful border. He was becoming immaterial like an apparition; his cheekbones rose, the forehead slanted more; the face was all hollows, patches of shade; and the fleshless head resembled a disinterred black skull, fitted with two restless globes of silver in the sockets of eyes. He was demoralising. Through him we were becoming highly humanised, tender, complex, excessively decadent:⁴⁸ we understood the subtlety of his fear, sympathised with all his repulsions, shrinkings, evasions, delusions—as though we had been over-civilised, and rotten, and without any knowledge of the meaning of life. We had the air of being initiated in some infamous mysteries; we had the profound grimaces of conspirators, exchanged meaning glances, significant short words. We were inexpressibly vile and very much pleased with ourselves. We lied to him with gravity, with emotion, with unction, as if performing some moral trick with a view to an eternal reward. We made a chorus of affirmation to his wildest assertions, as though he had been a millionaire, a politician, or a reformer—and we a crowd of ambitious lubbers. When we ventured to question his statements we did it after the manner of obsequious sycophants, to the end that his glory should be augmented by the flattery of our dissent. He influenced the moral tone of our world as though he had it in his power to distribute honours, treasures, or pain; and he could give us nothing but his contempt. It was immense; it seemed to grow gradually larger, as his body day by day shrank a little more, while we looked. It was the only thing about him—of him—that gave the impression of durability and vigour. It lived within him with an unquenchable life. It spoke through the eternal pout of his black lips; it looked at us through the profound impertinence of his large eyes, that stood far out of his head like the eyes of crabs. We watched them intently. Nothing else of him stirred. He seemed unwilling to move, as if distrustful of his own solidity. The slightest gesture must have disclosed to him (it could not surely be otherwise) his bodily weakness, and caused a pang of mental suffering. He was chary of movements. He lay stretched out, chin on blanket, in a kind of sly, cautious immobility. Only his eyes roamed over faces: his eyes disdainful, penetrating and sad.

It was at that time that Belfast's devotion—and also his pugnacity—secured universal respect. He spent every moment of his spare time in Jimmy's cabin. He tended him, talked to him; was as gentle as a woman, as tenderly gay as an old philanthropist, as sentimentally careful of his nigger as a model slave-owner. But outside he was irritable, explosive as gunpowder, sombre, suspicious, and never more brutal than when most sorrowful. With him it was a tear and a blow: a tear for Jimmy, a blow for any one who did not seem to take a scrupulously orthodox view of Jimmy's case. We talked about nothing else. The two Scandinavians, even, discussed the situation—but it was imposible to know in what spirit, because they quarrelled in their own language. Belfast suspected one of them of irreverence, and in this incertitude thought that there was no option but to fight them both. They became very much terrified by his truculence, and henceforth lived amongst us, dejected, like a pair of mutes. Wamibo never spoke intelligibly, but he was as smileless as an animal—seemed to know much less about it all than the cat—and consequently was safe. Moreover he had belonged to the chosen band of Jimmy's rescuers, and was above suspicion. Archie was silent generally, but often spent an hour or so talking to Jimmy quietly with an air of proprietorship. At any time of the day and often through the night some man could be seen sitting on Jimmy's box. In the evening, between six and eight, the cabin was crowded, and there was an interested group at the door. Every one stared at the nigger.

He basked in the warmth of our interest. His eyes gleamed ironically, and in a weak voice he reproached us with our cowardice. He would say, 'If you fellows had stuck out for me I would be now on deck.' We hung our heads. 'Yes, but if you think I am going to let them put me in irons just to show you sport . . . . Well, no . . . . It ruins my health, this lying up, it does. You don't care.' We were as

THE NIGGER OF THE 'NARCISSUS'

abashed as if it had been true. His superb impudence carried all
before it. We would not have dared to revolt. We didn't want to
really. We wanted to keep him alive till home—to the end of the
voyage.

Singleton as usual held aloof, appearing to scorn the insignificant
events of an ended life. Once only he came along, and unexpectedly
stopped in the doorway. He peered at Jimmy in profound silence,
as if desirous to add that black image to the crowd of Shades that
peopled his old memory. We kept very quiet, and for a long time
Singleton stood there as though he had come by appointment to
call for some one, or to see some important event. James Wait lay
perfectly still, and apparently not aware of the gaze scrutinising
him with a steadiness full of expectation. There was a sense of
tussle in the air. We felt the inward strain of men watching a
wrestling bout. At last Jimmy with perceptible apprehension turned
his head on the pillow.—'Good evening,' he said in a conciliating
tone.—'H'm,' answered the old seaman, grumpily. For a moment
longer he looked at Jimmy with severe fixity, then suddenly went
away. It was a long time before any one spoke in the little cabin,
though we all breathed more freely as men do after an escape from
some dangerous situation. We all knew the old man's ideas about
Jimmy, and nobody dared to combat them. They were unsettling,
they caused pain; and, what was worse, they might have been
true for all we knew. Only once did he condescend to explain them
fully, but the impression was lasting. He said that Jimmy was the
cause of head winds. Mortally sick men—he maintained—linger
till the first sight of land, and then die; and Jimmy knew that the
land would draw his life from him. It is so in every ship. Didn't we
know it? He asked us with austere contempt: what did we know?
What would we doubt next? Jimmy's desire encouraged by us and
aided by Wamibo's (he was a Finn—wasn't he? Very well!) by
Wamibo's spells[49] delayed the ship in the open sea. Only lubberly
fools couldn't see it. Whoever heard of such a run of calms and
head winds? It wasn't natural . . . . We could not deny that it was
strange. We felt uneasy. The common saying, 'more days, more
dollars,' did not give the usual comfort because the stores were
running short. Much had been spoiled off the Cape, and we were
on half allowance of biscuit. Peas, sugar and tea had been finished

long ago. Salt meat was giving out. We had plenty of coffee but very little water to make it with. We took up another hole in our belts and went on scraping, polishing, painting the ship from morning to night. And soon she looked as though she had come out of a band-box; but hunger lived on board of her. Not dead starvation, but steady, living hunger that stalked about the decks, slept in the forecastle; the tormentor of waking moments, the disturber of dreams. We looked to windward for signs of change. Every few hours of night and day we put her round with the hope that she would come up on that tack at last! She didn't. She seemed to have forgotten the way home; she rushed to and fro, heading north-west, heading east; she ran backwards and forwards, distracted, like a timid creature at the foot of a wall. Sometimes, as if tired to death, she would wallow languidly for a day in the smooth swell of an unruffled sea. All up the swinging masts the sails thrashed furiously through the hot stillness of the calm. We were weary, hungry, thirsty; we commenced to believe Singleton, but with unshaken fidelity dissembled to Jimmy. We spoke to him with jocose allusiveness, like cheerful accomplices in a clever plot; but we looked to the westward over the rail with mournful eyes for a sign of hope, for a sign of fair wind; even if its first breath should bring death to our reluctant Jimmy. In vain! The universe conspired with James Wait. Light airs from the northward sprang up again; the sky remained clear; and round our weariness the glittering sea, touched by the breeze, basked voluptuously in the great sunshine, as though it had forgotten our life and trouble.

Donkin looked out for a fair wind along with the rest. No one knew the venom of his thoughts now. He was silent, and appeared thinner, as if consumed slowly by an inward rage at the injustice of men and of fate. He was ignored by all and spoke to no one, but his hate for every man looked out through his eyes. He talked with the cook only, having somehow persuaded the good man that he—Donkin—was a much calumniated and persecuted person. Together they bewailed the immorality of the ship's company. There could be no greater criminals than we, who by our lies conspired to send the soul of a poor ignorant black man to everlasting perdition. Podmore cooked what there was to cook, remorsefully, and felt all the time that by preparing the food of such sinners he imperilled his own salvation. As to the Captain—he had lived with him for seven years, he said, and would not have believed it possible that such a man . . . . 'Well. Well . . . . There it is . . . . Can't get out of it. Judgment capsized all in a minute . . . . Struck in all his pride . . . . More like a sudden visitation than anything else.' Donkin, perched sullenly on the coal-locker, swung his legs and concurred. He paid in the coin of spurious assent for the privilege to sit in the galley; he was disheartened and scandalised; he agreed with the cook; could find no words severe enough to criticise our conduct; and when in the heat of reprobation he swore at us, Podmore, who would have liked to swear also if it hadn't been for his principles, pretended not to hear. So Donkin, unrebuked, cursed enough for two, cadged for matches, borrowed tobacco, and loafed for hours, very much at home before the stove. From there he could hear us on the other side of the bulkhead, talking to Jimmy. The cook knocked the pots about, slammed the oven door, muttered prophecies of damnation for all the ship's company; and Donkin, who did not admit of any hereafter, except for purposes of blasphemy, listened, concentrated and angry, gloating fiercely over a called-up image of infinite torment—like men gloat over the accursed images of cruelty and revenge, of greed, and of power. . . . .

On clear evenings the silent ship, under the cold sheen of the dead moon, took on the false aspect of passionless repose resembling the winter of the earth. Under her a long band of gold barred the black disc of the sea. Footsteps echoed on her quiet decks. The moonlight clung to her like a frosted mist, and the white sails stood out in dazzling cones as of stainless snow. In the magnificence of the phantom rays the ship appeared pure like a vision of ideal beauty, illusive like a tender dream of serene peace. And nothing in her was real, nothing was distinct and solid but the heavy shadows that filled her decks with their unceasing and noiseless stir; the shadows blacker than the night and more restless than the thoughts of men.

Donkin prowled spiteful and alone amongst the shadows, thinking that Jimmy too long delayed to die. That evening, just before dark, land had been reported from aloft, and the master, while adjusting the tubes of the long glass, had observed with quiet bitterness to Mr. Baker that, after fighting our way inch by inch to the Western Islands, there was nothing to expect now but a spell of calm. The sky was clear and the barometer high. The light breeze dropped with the sun, and an enormous stillness, forerunner of a night without wind, descended upon the heated waters of the ocean. As long as daylight lasted, the hands collected on the forecastle-head watched on the eastern sky the island of Flores, that rose above the level expanse of the sea with irregular and broken outlines like a sombre ruin upon a vast and deserted plain. It was the first land seen for nearly four months. Charley was excited, and in the midst of general indulgence took liberties with his betters. Men strangely elated without knowing why, talked in groups, and pointed with bared arms. For the first time that voyage Jimmy's sham existence seemed for a moment forgotten in the face of a solid reality. We had got so far anyhow. Belfast discoursed, quoting imaginary examples of short homeward passages from the Islands. 'Them smart fruit schooners do it in five days,' he affirmed. 'What do you want?—only a good little breeze.' Archie maintained that seven days was the shortest passage, and they disputed amicably with insulting words. Knowles declared he could already smell home from there, and with a heavy list on his short leg laughed fit to split his sides. A group of grizzled sea-dogs looked out for a time in silence and with grim absorbed faces. One said suddenly—'Tain't far to London now.'—'My first night ashore, blamme if I haven't steak and onions for supper . . . . and a pint of bitter,' said another.—'A barrel ye mean,' shouted some one.—'Ham an' eggs three times a day. That's the way I live!' cried an excited voice. There was a stir, appreciative murmurs; eyes began to shine; jaws champed; short nervous laughs were heard. Archie smiled with reserve all to himself. Singleton came up, gave a negligent glance, and went down again without saying a word, indifferent, like a man who had seen Flores an incalculable number of times. The night travelling from the East blotted out of the limpid sky the purple stain of the high land. 'Dead calm,' said somebody quietly. The murmur of lively talk suddenly wavered, died out; the clusters broke up; men began to drift away one by one, descending the ladders slowly and with serious faces as if sobered by that reminder of their dependence upon the invisible. And when the big yellow moon ascended gently above the sharp rim of the clear horizon it found the ship wrapped up in a breathless silence; a fearless ship that seemed to sleep profoundly, dreamlessly, on the bosom of the sleeping and terrible sea.

Donkin chafed at the peace—at the ship—at the sea that stretching away on all sides merged into the illimitable silence of all creation. He felt himself pulled up sharp by unrecognised grievances. He had been physically cowed, but his injured dignity remained indomitable, and nothing could heal his lacerated feelings. Here was land already—home very soon—a bad pay-day— no clothes—more hard work. How offensive all this was. Land. The land that draws away life from sick sailors. That nigger there had money—clothes—easy times; and would not die. Land draws life away . . . . He felt tempted to go and see whether it did. Perhaps already . . . . It would be a bit of luck. There was money in the beggar's chest. He stepped briskly out of the shadows into the moonlight, and, instantly, his craving, hungry face from sallow became livid. He opened the door of the cabin and had a shock. Sure enough, Jimmy was dead! He moved no more than a recumbent figure with clasped hands, carved on the lid of a stone coffin. Donkin glared with avidity. Then Jimmy, without stirring, blinked his eyelids, and Donkin had another shock. Those eyes were rather startling. He shut the door behind his back with gentle care, looking intently the while at James Wait as though he had come in there at a great risk to tell some secret of startling importance. Jimmy did not move but glanced languidly out of the corners of his eyes.—'Calm?' he asked.—'Yuss,' said Donkin, very disappointed, and sat down on the box.

Jimmy breathed with composure. He was used to such visits at all times of night or day. Men succeeded one another. They spoke in clear voices, pronounced cheerful words, repeated old jokes, listened to him; and each, going out, seemed to leave behind a little of his own vitality, surrender some of his own strength, renew the assurance of life—the indestructible thing! He did not like to be alone in his cabin, because, when he was alone, it seemed to him as if he hadn't been there at all. There was nothing. No pain. Not now. Perfectly right—but he couldn't enjoy his healthful repose unless some one was by to see it. This man would do as well as anybody. Donkin watched him stealthily.—'Soon home now,' observed Wait.—'Why d'yer whisper?' asked Donkin with interest, 'can't yer speak hup?' Jimmy looked annoyed and said nothing for a while; then in a lifeless unringing voice:—'Why should I shout? You ain't deaf that I know.'—'Oh! I can 'ear right enough,' answered Donkin in a low tone, and looked down. He was thinking sadly of going out when Jimmy spoke again.—'Time we did get home . . . . to get something decent to eat . . . . I am always hungry.' Donkin felt angry all of a sudden.—'What habout me,' he hissed, 'I am 'ungry too an' got ter work. You, 'ungry!'—'Your work won't kill you,' commented Wait, feebly; 'there's a couple of biscuits in the lower bunk there—you may have one. I can't eat them.' Donkin dived in, groped in the corner, and when he came up again his mouth was full. He munched with ardour. Jimmy seemed to doze with open eyes. Donkin finished his hard bread and got up.—'You're not going?' asked Jimmy, staring at the ceiling.— 'No,' said Donkin impulsively, and instead of going out leaned his back against the closed door. He looked at James Wait, and saw him long, lean, dried up, as though all his flesh had shrivelled on his bones in the heat of a white furnace; the meagre fingers of one hand moved lightly upon the edge of the bunk playing an endless tune. To look at him was irritating and fatiguing; he could last like this for days; he was outrageous—belonging wholly neither to death nor life, and perfectly invulnerable in his apparent ignorance of both. Donkin felt tempted to enlighten him.—'What hare yer thinkin' of?' he asked surlily. James Wait had a grimacing smile that passed over the deathlike impassiveness of his bony face, incredible and frightful as would, in a dream, have been the sudden smile of a corpse.

'There is a girl,' whispered Wait . . . . 'Canton Street girl——She chucked a third engineer of a Rennie boat——for me. Cooks oysters just as I like . . . . She says——she would chuck——any toff—— for a coloured gentleman . . . . That's me. I am kind to wimmen,' he added a shade louder.

Donkin could hardly believe his ears. He was scandalised.— 'Would she? Yer wouldn't be hany good to 'er,' he said with un-restrained disgust. Wait was not there to hear him. He was swaggering up the East India Dock Road; saying kindly, 'Come along for a treat,' pushing glass swing-doors, posing with superb assurance in the gaslight above a mahogany counter.—'D'yer think yer will hever get ashore?' asked Donkin angrily. Wait came back with a start.—'Ten days,' he said promptly, and returned at once to the regions of memory that know nothing of time. He felt untired, calm, and as if safely withdrawn within himself beyond the reach of every grave incertitude. There was something of the immutable quality of eternity in the slow moments of his complete restfulness. He was very quiet and easy amongst his vivid reminiscences which he mistook joyfully for images of an undoubted future. He cared for no one. Donkin felt this vaguely like a blind man may feel in his darkness the fatal antagonism of all the surrounding existences, that to him shall for ever remain irrealisable, unseen and enviable. He had a desire to assert his importance, to break, to crush; to be even with everybody for everything; to tear the veil, unmask, expose, leave no refuge—a perfidious desire of truthfulness! He laughed in a mocking splutter and said:

'Ten days. Strike me blind if I hever! . . . . You will be dead by this time to-morrow p'r'aps. Ten days!' He waited for a while. 'D'ye 'ear me? Blamme if yer don't look dead halready.'

Jimmy must have been collecting his strength for he said almost aloud—'You're a stinking, cadging liar. Every one knows you.' And sitting up, against all probability, startled his visitor horribly. But very soon Donkin recovered himself. He blustered, 'What? What? Who's a liar? You hare—the crowd hare—the skipper—heverybody. I haint! Putting on hairs! Who's yer?' He nearly choked himself with indignation. 'Who's yer to put on hairs,' he repeated trembling. ''Ave one—'ave one, says 'ee—an' cawn't heat 'em 'isself. Now I'll 'ave both. By Gawd—I will! Yer nobody!'

He plunged into the lower bunk, rooted in there and brought to light another dusty biscuit. He held it up before Jimmy—then took a bite defiantly.

'What now?' he asked with feverish impudence. 'Yer may take one—says yer. Why not giv' me both? No. I'm a mangy dorg. One fur a mangy dorg. I'll tyke both. Can yer stop me? Try. Come on. Try.'

Jimmy was clasping his legs and hiding his face on the knees.

His shirt clung to him. Every rib was visible. His emaciated back was shaken in repeated jerks by the panting catches of his breath.

'Yer won't? Yer can't! What did I say?' went on Donkin fiercely. He swallowed another dry mouthful with a hasty effort. The other's silent helplessness, his weakness, his shrinking attitude exasperated him. 'Ye're done!' he cried. 'Who's yer to be lied to; to be waited on 'and an' foot like a bloomin' hymperor. Yer nobody. Yer no one at all!' he spluttered with such a strength of unerring conviction that it shook him from head to foot in coming out, and left him vibrating like a released string.

Jimmy rallied again. He lifted his head and turned bravely at Donkin, who saw a strange face, an unknown face, a fantastic and grimacing mask of despair and fury. Its lips moved rapidly; and hollow, moaning, whistling sounds filled the cabin with a vague mutter full of menace, complaint and desolation, like the far-off murmur of a rising wind. Wait shook his head; rolled his eyes; he denied, cursed, menaced—and not a word had the strength to pass beyond the sorrowful pout of those black lips. It was incomprehensible and disturbing; a gibberish of emotions, a frantic dumb show of speech pleading for impossible things, threatening a shadowy vengeance. It sobered Donkin into a scrutinising watchfulness.

'Yer can't holler. See? What did I tell yer?' he said slowly after a moment of attentive examination. The other kept on headlong and unheard, nodding passionately, grinning with grotesque and appalling flashes of big white teeth. Donkin, as if fascinated by the dumb eloquence and anger of that black phantom, approached, stretching his neck out with distrustful curiosity; and it seemed to him suddenly that he was looking only at the shadow of a man crouching high in the bunk on the level with his eyes.—'What? What?' he said. He seemed to catch the shape of some words in the continuous panting hiss. 'Yer will tell Belfast! Will yer? Hare yer a bloomin' kid?' He trembled with alarm and rage. 'Tell yer gran'mother! Yer afeard! Who's yer ter be afeard more'n hanyone?' His passionate sense of his own importance ran away with a last remnant of caution. 'Tell an' be damned! Tell, if yer can!' he cried. 'I've been treated worser'n a dorg by your blooming back-lickers. They 'as set me on, honly to turn aginst me. I ham the honly man 'ere. They clouted me, kicked me—an' yer laffed—yer black, rotten hincumbrance, you! You will pay fur it. They giv' yer their grub, their water—yer will pay fur hit to me, by Gawd! Who haxed me ter 'ave a drink of water? They put their bloomin' rags on yer that night, an' what did they giv' ter me—a clout on the bloomin' mouth—blast their . . . . S'elp me! . . . . Yer will pay fur hit with yer money. Hi'm goin' ter 'ave it in a minyte; has soon has ye're dead, yer bloomin' useless fraud. That's the man I ham. An' ye're a thing—a bloody thing. Yah—you corpse!'

He flung at Jimmy's head the biscuit he had been all the time clutching hard, but it only grazed, and striking with a loud crack the bulkhead beyond burst like a hand-grenade into flying pieces. James Wait, as though wounded mortally, fell back on the pillow. His lips ceased to move and the rolling eyes became quiet and stared upwards with an intense and steady persistence. Donkin was surprised; he sat suddenly on the chest, and looked down, exhausted and gloomy. After a moment he began to mutter to himself, 'Die, you beggar—die. Somebody'll come in . . . . I wish I was drunk . . . . Ten days . . . . Hoysters . . . .' He looked up and spoke louder. 'No . . . . No more for yer . . . . no more bloomin' gals that cook hoysters . . . . Who's yer? Hit's my turn now . . . . I wish I was drunk; I would soon giv' you a leg up haloft. That's where yer will go. Feet fust, through a port . . . . Splash! Never see yer hany more. Hoverboard! Good 'nuff fur yer.'

Jimmy's head moved slightly and he turned his eyes to Donkin's face; a gaze unbelieving, desolated and appealing, of a child frightened by the menace of being shut up alone in the dark. Donkin observed him from the chest with hopeful eyes; then without rising he tried the lid. Locked. 'I wish I was drunk,' he muttered and getting up listened anxiously to the distant sound of footsteps on the deck. They approached—ceased. Some one yawned interminably just outside the door, and the footsteps went away shuffling lazily. Donkin's fluttering heart eased its pace, and when he looked towards the bunk again Jimmy was staring as before at the white beam.—"Ow d'yer feel now?' he asked.—'Bad,' breathed out Jimmy.

Donkin sat down patient and purposeful. Every half-hour the bells spoke to one another ringing along the whole length of the ship. Jimmy's respiration was so rapid that it couldn't be counted, so faint that it couldn't be heard.[50] His eyes were terrified as though he had been looking at unspeakable horrors; and by his face one could see that he was thinking of abominable things. Suddenly with an incredibly strong and heart-breaking voice he sobbed out:

'Overboard! . . . . I! . . . . My God!'[51]

Donkin writhed a little on the box. He looked unwillingly. Jimmy was mute. His two long bony hands smoothed the blanket upwards,[52] as though he had wished to gather it all up under his chin. A tear, a big solitary tear, escaped from the corner of his eye and, without touching the hollow cheek, fell on the pillow. His throat rattled faintly.

And Donkin, watching the end of that hateful nigger, felt the anguishing grasp of a great sorrow on his heart at the thought that he himself, some day, would have to go through it all—just like this—perhaps! His eyes became moist. 'Poor beggar,' he murmured. The night seemed to go by in a flash; it seemed to him he could hear the irremediable rush of precious minutes. How long would this blooming affair last? Too long surely. No luck. He could not restrain himself. He got up and approached the bunk. Wait did not stir. Only his eyes appeared alive and his hands continued their smoothing movement with a horrible and tireless industry. Donkin bent over.

'Jimmy,' he called low. There was no answer, but the rattle stopped. 'D'yer see me?' he asked trembling. Jimmy's chest heaved. Donkin, looking away, bent his ear to Jimmy's lips, and heard a sound like the rustle of a single dry leaf driven along the smooth sand of a beach. It shaped itself.

'Light . . . . the lamp . . . . and . . . . go,' breathed out Wait.

Donkin, instinctively, glanced over his shoulder at the blazing flame; then, still looking away, felt under the pillow for a key. He got it at once and for the next few minutes was shakily but swiftly busy about the box. When he got up, his face—for the first time in his life—had a pink flush—perhaps of triumph.

He slipped the key under the pillow again, avoiding to glance at Jimmy,[53] who had not moved. He turned his back squarely from the bunk, and started to the door as though he were going to walk a mile. At his second stride he had his nose against it. He clutched the handle cautiously, but at that moment he received the irresistible impression of something happening behind his back. He spun round as though he had been tapped on the shoulder. He was just in time to see Jimmy's eyes blaze up and go out at once, like two lamps overturned together by a sweeping blow. Something resembling a scarlet thread hung down his chin out of the corner of his lips—and he had ceased to breathe.[54]

Donkin closed the door behind him gently but firmly. Sleeping men, huddled under jackets, made on the lighted deck shapeless dark mounds that had the appearance of neglected graves. Nothing had been done all through the night and he hadn't been missed. He stood motionless and perfectly astounded to find the world outside as he had left it; there was the sea, the ship—sleeping men; and he wondered absurdly at it, as though he had expected to find the men dead, familiar things gone for ever: as though, like a wanderer returning after many years, he had expected to see bewildering changes. He shuddered a little in the penetrating freshness of the air, and hugged himself forlornly. The declining moon drooped sadly in the western board as if withered by the cold touch of a pale dawn. The ship slept. And the immortal sea stretched away, immense and hazy, like the image of life, with a glittering surface and lightless depths; promising, empty, inspiring—terrible. Donkin gave it a defiant glance and slunk off noiselessly as if judged and cast out by the august silence of its might. *emotional center is gone*

Jimmy's death, after all, came as a tremendous surprise. We did not know till then how much faith we had put in his delusions. We had taken his chances of life so much at his own valuation that his death, like the death of an old belief, shook the foundations of our society. A common bond was gone; the strong, effective and respectable bond of a sentimental lie. All that day we mooned at our work, with suspicious looks and a disabused air. In our hearts we thought that in the matter of his departure Jimmy had acted in a perverse and unfriendly manner. He didn't back us up, as a shipmate should. In going he took away with himself the gloomy and solemn shadow in which our folly had posed, with humane satisfaction, as a tender arbiter of fate. And now we saw it was no

lies of encouraging Jimmy

such thing. It was just common foolishness; a silly and ineffectual meddling with issues of majestic import—that is, if Podmore was right. Perhaps he was? Doubt survived Jimmy; and, like a community of banded criminals disintegrated by a touch of grace, we were profoundly scandalised with each other. Men spoke unkindly to their best chums. Others refused to speak at all. Singleton only was not surprised. 'Dead—is he? Of course,' he said, pointing at the island right abeam: for the calm still held the ship spell-bound within sight of Flores. Dead—of course. *He* wasn't surprised. Here was the land, and there, on the forehatch and waiting for the sailmaker—there was that corpse. Cause and effect. And for the first time that voyage, the old seaman became quite cheery and garrulous, explaining and illustrating from the stores of experience how, in sickness, the sight of an island (even a very small one) is generally more fatal than the view of a continent. But he couldn't explain why.

Jimmy was to be buried at five, and it was a long day till then—a day of mental disquiet and even of physical disturbance. We took no interest in our work and, very properly, were rebuked for it. This, in our constant state of hungry irritation, was exasperating. Donkin worked with his brow bound in a dirty rag, and looked so ghastly that Mr. Baker was touched with compassion at the sight of this plucky suffering.—'Ough! You, Donkin! Put down your work and go lay-up this watch. You look ill.'—'Hi ham, sir—in my 'ead,' he said in a subdued voice, and vanished speedily. This annoyed many, and they thought the mate 'bloomin' soft to-day.' Captain Allistoun could be seen on the poop watching the sky cloud over from the south-west, and it soon got to be known about the decks that the barometer had begun to fall in the night, and that a breeze might be expected before long. This, by a subtle association of ideas, led to violent quarrelling as to the exact moment of Jimmy's death. Was it before or after 'that 'ere glass started down'? It was impossible to know, and it caused much contemptuous growling at one another. All of a sudden there was a great tumult forward. Pacific Knowles and good-tempered Davies had come to blows over it. The watch below interfered with spirit, and for ten minutes there was a noisy scrimmage round the hatch, where, in the balancing shade of the sails, Jimmy's body, wrapped up in a white blanket, was watched over by the sorrowful Belfast, who, in his desolation, disdained the fray. When the noise had ceased, and the passions had calmed into surly silence, he stood up at the head of the swathed body, and lifting both arms on high, cried with pained indignation:—'You ought to be ashamed of yourselves! . . . .' We were.

Belfast took his bereavement very hard. He gave proofs of unextinguishable devotion. It was he, and no other man, who would help the sailmaker to prepare what was left of Jimmy for a solemn surrender to the insatiable sea. He arranged the weights carefully at the feet: two holystones, an old anchor-shackle without its pin, some broken links of a worn-out stream cable. He arranged them this way, then that. 'Bless my soul! you aren't afraid he will chafe his heel?' said the sailmaker, who hated the job. He pushed the needle, puffing furiously, with his head in a cloud of tobacco smoke; he turned the flaps over, pulled at the stitches, stretched at the canvas.—'Lift his shoulders . . . . Pull to you a bit . . . . So—o—o. Steady.' Belfast obeyed, pulled, lifted, overcome with sorrow, dropping tears on the tarred twine.—'Don't you drag the canvas too taut over his poor face, Sails,' he entreated tearfully.—'What are you fashing yourself for? He will be comfortable enough,' assured the sailmaker, cutting the thread after the last stitch, that came about the middle of Jimmy's forehead. He rolled up the remaining canvas, put away the needles. 'What makes you take on so?' he asked. Belfast looked down at the long package of grey sailcloth.—'I pulled him out,' he whispered, 'and he did not want to go. If I had sat up with him last night he would have kept alive for me . . . . but something made me tired.' The sailmaker took vigorous draws at his pipe and mumbled:—'When I . . . . West India Station . . . . In the *Blanche* frigate . . . . Yellow Jack . . . . sewed in twenty men a day . . . . Portsmouth—Devonport men— townies—knew their fathers, mothers—sisters—the whole boiling of 'em. Thought nothing of it. And these niggers like this one—you don't know where it comes from. Got nobody. No use to nobody. Who will miss him?'—'I do—I pulled him out,' mourned Belfast dismally.

On two planks nailed together, and apparently resigned and still under the folds of the Union Jack with a white border, James Wait, carried aft by four men, was deposited slowly, with his feet pointing at an open port. A swell had set in from the westward, and following on the roll of the ship, the red ensign, at half-mast, darted out and collapsed again on the grey sky, like a tongue of flickering fire; Charley tolled the bell; and at every swing to starboard the whole vast semi-circle of steely waters visible on that side seemed to come up with a rush to the edge of the port, as if impatient to get at our Jimmy. Every one was there but Donkin, who was too ill to come; the Captain and Mr. Creighton stood bareheaded on the break of the poop; Mr. Baker, directed by the master, who had said to him gravely:—'You know more about the prayer book than I do,' came out of the cabin door quickly and a little embarrassed. All the caps went off. He began to read in a low tone, and with his usual harmlessly menacing utterance, as though he had been for the last time reproving confidentially that dead seaman at his feet. The men listened in scattered groups; they leaned on the fife rail, gazing on the deck; they held their chins in their hands thoughtfully, or, with crossed arms and one knee slightly bent, hung their heads in an attitude of upright meditation. Wamibo dreamed. Mr. Baker read on, grunting reverently at the turn of every page. The words, missing the unsteady hearts of men, rolled out to wander without a home upon the heartless sea; and James Wait, silenced for ever, lay uncritical and passive under the hoarse murmur of despair and hopes.

Two men made ready and waited for those words that send so many of our brothers to their last plunge. Mr. Baker began the passage. 'Stand by,' muttered the boatswain. Mr. Baker read out: 'To the deep,'[55] and paused. The men lifted the inboard end of the planks, the boatswain snatched off the Union Jack, and James Wait did not move.—'Higher,' muttered the boatswain angrily. All the heads were raised; every man stirred uneasily, but James Wait gave no sign of going.[56] In death and swathed up for all eternity, he yet seemed to hang on to the ship with the grip of an undying fear. 'Higher! Lift!' whispered the boatswain fiercely.—'He won't go,' stammered one of the men shakily, and both appeared ready to drop everything. Mr. Baker waited, burying his face in the book, and shuffling his feet nervously. All the men looked profoundly disturbed; from their midst a faint humming noise spread out—

growing louder . . . . . 'Jimmy!' cried Belfast in a wailing tone, and
there was a second of shuddering dismay.

'Jimmy, be a man!' he shrieked passionately. Every mouth was
wide open, not an eyelid winked. He stared wildly, twitching all
over; he bent his body forward like a man peering at an horror.
'Go!' he shouted, and leaped off with his arm thrown out. 'Go,
Jimmy!—Jimmy, go! Go!' His fingers touched the head of the body,
and the grey package started reluctantly to, all at once, whizz off
the lifted planks with the suddenness of a flash of lightning. The
crowd stepped forward like one man; a deep Ah—h—h! came out
vibrating from the broad chests. The ship rolled as if relieved of an
unfair burden;[57] the sails flapped. Belfast, supported by Archie,
gasped hysterically; and Charley, who anxious to see Jimmy's last
dive, leaped headlong on the rail, was too late to see anything but
the faint circle of a vanishing ripple.

Mr. Baker, perspiring abundantly, read out the last prayer in a
deep rumour of excited men and fluttering sails. 'Amen!' he said in
an unsteady growl, and closed the book.

'Square the yards!' thundered a voice above his head. All hands
gave a jump; one or two dropped their caps; Mr. Baker looked up
surprised. The master, standing on the break of the poop, pointed
to the westward. 'Breeze coming,' he said, 'square the yards. Look
alive, men!' Mr. Baker crammed the book hurriedly into his
pocket.—'Forward, there—let go the foretack!' he hailed joyfully,
bareheaded and brisk; 'Square the foreyard, you port-watch!'—
'Fair wind—fair wind,' muttered the men going to the braces.—
'What did I tell you?' mumbled old Singleton, flinging down coil
after coil with hasty energy; 'I knowed it—he's gone, and here it
comes.'

It came with the sound of a lofty and powerful sigh. The sails
filled, the ship gathered way, and the waking sea began to murmur
sleepily of home to the ears of men.

That night, while the ship rushed foaming to the Northward
before a freshening gale, the boatswain unbosomed himself to the
petty officers' berth:—'The chap was nothing but trouble,' he said,
'from the moment he came aboard—d'ye remember—that night
in Bombay? Been bullying all that softy crowd—cheeked the old
man—we had to go fooling all over a half-drowned ship to save

him. Dam' nigh a mutiny all for him—and now the mate abused me like a pickpocket for forgetting to dab a lump of grease on them planks. So I did, but you ought to have known better, too, than to leave a nail sticking up—hey, Chips?' 'And you ought to have known better than to chuck all my tools overboard for 'im, like a skeary greenhorn,' retorted the morose carpenter. 'Well—he's gone after 'em now,' he added in an unforgiving tone. 'On the China Station, I remember once, the Admiral he says to me . . . .' began the sailmaker.

A week afterwards the *Narcissus* entered the chops of the Channel.

Under white wings she skimmed low over the blue sea like a great tired bird speeding to its nest. The clouds raced with her mastheads; they rose astern enormous and white, soared to the zenith, flew past, and falling down the wide curve of the sky seemed to dash headlong into the sea—the clouds swifter than the ship, more free, but without a home. The coast to welcome her stepped out of space into the sunshine. The lofty headlands trod masterfully into the sea; the wide bays smiled in the light; the shadows of homeless clouds ran along the sunny plains, leaped over valleys, without a check darted up the hills, rolled down the slopes; and the sunshine pursued them with patches of running brightness. On the brows of dark cliffs white lighthouses shone in pillars of light. The Channel glittered like a blue mantle shot with gold and starred by the silver of the capping seas. The *Narcissus* rushed past the headlands and the bays. Outward-bound vessels crossed her track, lying over, and with their masts stripped for a slogging fight with the hard sou'wester. And, inshore, a string of smoking steamboats waddled, hugging the coast, like migrating and amphibious monsters, distrustful of the restless waves.

At night the headlands retreated, the bays advanced into one unbroken line of gloom. The lights of the earth mingled with the lights of heaven; and above the tossing lanterns of a trawling fleet a great lighthouse shone steadily, such as an enormous riding light burning above a vessel of fabulous dimensions. Below its steady glow, the coast, stretching away straight and black, resembled the high side of an indestructible craft riding motionless upon the immortal and unresting sea. The dark land lay alone in the midst of waters, like a mighty ship bestarred with vigilant lights—a ship carrying the burden of millions of lives—a ship freighted with dross and with jewels, with gold and with steel. She towered up immense and strong, guarding priceless traditions and untold suffering, sheltering glorious memories and base forgetfulness, ignoble virtues and splendid transgressions. A great ship! For ages had the ocean battered in vain her enduring sides; she was there when the world was vaster and darker, when the sea was great and mysterious, and ready to surrender the prize of fame to audacious men. A ship mother of fleets and nations! The great flagship of the race; stronger than the storms! and anchored in the open sea.

The *Narcissus*, heeling over to off-shore gusts, rounded the South Foreland, passed through the Downs, and, in tow, entered the river. Shorn of the glory of her white wings, she wound obediently after the tug through the maze of invisible channels. As she passed them the red-painted light-vessels, swung at their moorings, seemed for an instant to sail with great speed in the rush of tide, and the next moment were left hopelessly behind. The big buoys on the tails of banks slipped past her sides very low, and, dropping in her wake, tugged at their chains like fierce watch-dogs. The reach narrowed; from both sides the land approached the ship. She went steadily up the river. On the riverside slopes the houses appeared in groups—seemed to stream down the declivities at a run to see her pass, and, checked by the mud of the foreshore, crowded on the banks. Further on, the tall factory chimneys appeared in insolent bands and watched her go by, like a straggling crowd of slim giants, swaggering and upright under the black plummets of smoke, cavalierly aslant. She swept round the bends; an impure breeze shrieked a welcome between her stripped spars; and the land, closing in, stepped between the ship and the sea.

A low cloud hung before her—a great opalescent and tremulous cloud, that seemed to rise from the steaming brows of millions of men. Long drifts of smoky vapours soiled it with livid trails; it throbbed to the beat of millions of hearts, and from it came an immense and lamentable murmur—the murmur of millions of lips praying, cursing, sighing, jeering—the undying murmur of folly, regret, and hope exhaled by the crowds of the anxious earth. The *Narcissus* entered the cloud; the shadows deepened; on all sides there was the clang of iron, the sound of mighty blows, shrieks, yells. Black barges drifted stealthily on the murky stream. A mad jumble of begrimed walls loomed up vaguely in the smoke, bewildering and mournful, like a vision of disaster. The tugs, panting furiously, backed and filled in the stream, to hold the ship steady at the dock-gates; from her bows two lines went through the air whistling, and struck at the land viciously, like a pair of snakes. A bridge broke in two before her, as if by enchantment; big hydraulic capstans began to turn all by themselves, as though animated by a mysterious and unholy spell. She moved through a narrow lane of water between two low walls of granite, and men with check-ropes in their hands kept pace with her, walking on the broad flagstones. A group waited impatiently on each side of the vanished bridge: rough heavy men in caps; sallow-faced men in high hats; two bareheaded women; ragged children, fascinated, and with wide eyes. A cart coming at a jerky trot pulled up sharply. One of the women screamed at the silent ship—'Hallo, Jack!' without looking at any one in particular, and all hands looked at her from the forecastle head.—'Stand clear! Stand clear of that rope!' cried the dockmen, bending over stone posts. The crowd murmured, stamped where they stood.—'Let go your quarter-checks! Let go!' sang out a ruddy-faced old man on the quay. The ropes splashed heavily falling in the water, and the *Narcissus* entered the dock.

The stony shores ran away right and left in straight lines, enclosing a sombre and rectangular pool. Brick walls rose high above the water[58]—soulless walls, staring through hundreds of windows as troubled and dull as the eyes of over-fed brutes. At their base monstrous iron cranes crouched, with chains hanging from their long necks, balancing cruel-looking hooks over the decks of lifeless ships. A noise of wheels rolling over stones, the thump of heavy things falling, the racket of feverish winches, the grinding of strained chains, floated on the air. Between high buildings the dust of all the continents soared in short flights; and a penetrating smell of perfumes and dirt, of spices and hides, of things costly and of things filthy, pervaded the space, made for it an atmosphere precious and disgusting. The *Narcissus* came gently into her berth; the shadows of soulless walls fell upon her, the dust of all the continents leaped upon her deck, and a swarm of strange men, clambering up her sides, took possession of her in the name of the sordid earth. She had ceased to live.

A toff in a black coat and high hat scrambled with agility, came up to the second mate, shook hands, and said:—'Hallo, Herbert.' It was his brother. A lady appeared suddenly. A real lady, in a black dress and with a parasol. She looked extremely elegant in the midst of us, and as strange as if she had fallen there from the sky. Mr. Baker touched his cap to her. It was the master's wife. And very soon the Captain, dressed very smartly and in a white shirt, went with her over the side. We didn't recognise him at all till, turning on the quay, he called to Mr. Baker:—'Remember to wind up the chronometers to-morrow morning.' An underhand lot of seedy-looking chaps with shifty eyes wandered in and out of the forecastle looking for a job—they said.—'More likely for something to steal,' commented Knowles cheerfully. Poor beggars. Who cared? Weren't we home! But Mr. Baker went for one of them who had given him some cheek, and we were delighted. Everything was delightful.—'I've finished aft, sir,' called out Mr. Creighton.— 'No water in the well, sir,' reported for the last time the carpenter, sounding-rod in hand. Mr. Baker glanced along the decks at the expectant groups of men, glanced aloft at the yards.—'Ough! That will do, men,' he grunted. The groups broke up. The voyage was ended.

Rolled-up beds went flying over the rail; lashed chests went sliding down the gangway—mighty few of both at that. 'The rest is having a cruise off the Cape,' explained Knowles enigmatically to a dock-loafer with whom he had struck a sudden friendship. Men ran, calling to one another, hailing utter strangers to 'lend a hand with the dunnage,' then with sudden decorum approached the mate to shake hands before going ashore.—'Good-bye, sir,' they repeated in various tones. Mr. Baker grasped hard palms, grunted in a friendly manner at every one, his eyes twinkled.— 'Take care of your money, Knowles. Ough! Soon get a nice wife if you do.' The lame man was delighted.—'Good-bye, sir,' said Belfast with emotion, wringing the mate's hand, and looked up with swimming eyes. 'I thought I would take 'im ashore with me,' he went on plaintively. Mr. Baker did not understand, but said kindly:—'Take care of yourself, Craik,' and the bereaved Belfast went over the rail mourning and alone.

Mr. Baker in the sudden peace of the ship moved about solitary and grunting, trying door handles, peering into dark places, never done—a model chief mate! No one waited for him ashore. Mother dead; father and two brothers, Yarmouth fishermen, drowned together on the Dogger Bank; sister married and unfriendly. Quite a lady. Married to the leading tailor of a little town, and its leading politician, who did not think his sailor brother-in-law quite respectable enough for him. Quite a lady, quite a lady, he thought, sitting down for a moment's rest on the quarter-hatch. Time enough to go ashore and get a bite, and sup, and a bed somewhere. He didn't like to part with a ship. No one to think about then. The darkness of a misty evening fell, cold and damp, upon the deserted deck; and Mr. Baker sat smoking, thinking of all the successive ships to whom through many long years he had given the best of a seaman's care. And never a command in sight. Not once!—'I haven't somehow the cut of a skipper about me,' he meditated placidly, while the shipkeeper (who had taken possession of the galley), a wizened old man with bleared eyes, cursed him in whispers for 'hanging about so.'—'Now, Creighton,' he pursued the unenvious train of thought, 'quite a gentleman . . . . swell friends . . . . will get on. Fine young fellow . . . . a little more experience.' He got up and shook himself. 'I'll be back first thing tomorrow morning for the hatches. Don't you let them touch anything before I come, shipkeeper,' he called out. Then, at last, he also went ashore—a model chief mate!

The men scattered by the dissolving contact of the land came together once more in the shipping office.—'The *Narcissus* pays off,' shouted outside a glazed door a brass-bound old fellow with a crown and the capitals B. T. on his cap. A lot trooped in at once but many were late. The room was large, white-washed, and bare; a counter surmounted by a brass-wire grating fenced off a third of the dusty space, and behind the grating a pasty-faced clerk, with his hair parted in the middle, had the quick, glittering eyes and the vivacious, jerky movements of a caged bird. Poor Captain Allistoun also in there, and sitting before a little table with piles of gold and notes on it, appeared subdued by his captivity. Another Board of

Trade bird was perching on a high stool near the door: an old bird that did not mind the chaff of elated sailors. The crew of the *Narcissus*, broken up into knots, pushed in the corners. They had new shore togs, smart jackets that looked as if they had been shaped with an axe, glossy trousers that seemed made of crumpled sheet-iron, collarless flannel shirts, shiny new boots. They tapped on shoulders, button-holed one another, asked:—'Where did you sleep last night?' whispered gaily, slapped their thighs, stamped, with bursts of subdued laughter. Most had clean radiant faces; only one or two were dishevelled and sad; the two young Norwegians looked tidy, meek, and altogether of a promising material for the kind ladies that patronise the Scandinavian Home. Wamibo, still in his working clothes, dreamed, upright and burly in the middle of the room, and, when Archie came in, woke up for a smile. But the wide-awake clerk called out a name, and the paying-off business began.

One by one they came up to the pay-table to get the wages of their glorious and obscure toil. They swept the money with care into broad palms, rammed it trustfully into trousers' pockets, or, turning their backs on the table, reckoned with difficulty in the hollow of their stiff hands.—'Money right? Sign the release. There—there,' repeated the clerk, impatiently. 'How stupid those sailors are!' he thought. Singleton came up, venerable—and uncertain as to daylight; brown drops of tobacco juice maculated his white beard; his hands, that never hesitated in the great light of the open sea, could hardly find the small pile of gold in the profound darkness of the shore. 'Can't write?' said the clerk, shocked. 'Make a mark, then.' Singleton painfully sketched in a heavy cross, blotted the page. 'What a disgusting old brute,' muttered the clerk. Somebody opened the door for him, and the partriarchal seaman passed through unsteadily, without as much as a glance at any of us.

Archie had a pocket-book. He was chaffed. Belfast, who looked wild, as though he had already luffed up through a public-house or two, gave signs of emotion and wanted to speak to the Captain privately. The master was surprised. They spoke through the wires, and we could hear the Captain saying:—'I've given it up to the Board of Trade.' 'I should 've liked to get something of his,' mumbled Belfast. 'But you can't, my man. It's given up, locked and sealed, to the Marine Office,' expostulated the master; and Belfast stood back, with drooping mouth and troubled eyes. In a pause of the business we heard the master and the clerk talking. We caught 'James Wait—deceased—found no papers of any kind— no relations—no trace—the Office must hold his wages then.' Donkin entered. He seemed out of breath, was grave, full of business. He went straight to the desk, talked with animation to the clerk, who thought him an intelligent man. They discussed the account, dropping h's against one another as if for a wager—very friendly. Captain Allistoun paid. 'I give you a bad discharge,' he said, quietly. Donkin raised his voice:—'I don't want your bloomin' discharge—keep it. I'm goin' ter 'ave a job hashore.' He turned to us. 'No more bloomin' sea fur me,' he said, aloud. All looked at him. He had better clothes, had an easy air, appeared more at home than any of us; he stared with assurance, enjoying the effect of his declaration. 'Yuss. I 'ave friends well hoff. That's more'n yer got. But I ham a man. Yer shipmates for all that. Who's comin' fur a drink?'

No one moved. There was a silence; a silence of blank faces and stony looks. He waited a moment, smiled bitterly, and went to the door. There he faced round once more. 'Yer won't? Yer bloomin' lot of 'ypocrites. No? What 'ave I done to yer? Did I bully yer? Did I hurt yer? Did I? . . . . Yer won't drink? . . . . No! . . . . Then may yer die of thirst, hevery mother's son of yer! Not one of yer 'as the sperrit of a bug. Ye'rr the scum of the world. Work and starve!'

He went out, and slammed the door with such violence that the old Board of Trade bird nearly fell off his perch.

'He's mad,' said Archie. 'No! No! He's drunk,' insisted Belfast, lurching about, and in a maudlin tone. Captain Allistoun sat smiling thoughtfully at the cleared pay-table.

Outside, on Tower Hill,[59] they blinked, hesitated clumsily, as if blinded by the strange quality of the hazy light, as if discomposed by the view of so many men; and they who could hear one another in the howl of gales seemed deafened and distracted by the dull roar of the busy earth.—'To the Black Horse! To the Black Horse!' cried some. 'Let us have a drink together before we part.' They crossed the road, clinging to one another. Only Charley and Belfast wandered off alone. As I came up I saw a red-faced, blowsy woman, in a grey shawl, and with dusty, fluffy hair, fall on Charley's neck. It was his mother. She slobbered over him:—'O, my boy! My boy!'— 'Leggo of me,' said Charley, 'Leggo, mother!' I was passing him at the time, and over the untidy head of the blubbering woman he gave me a humorous smile and a glance ironic, courageous, and profound, that seemed to put all my knowledge of life to shame. I nodded and passed on, but heard him say again, good-naturedly:— 'If you leggo of me this minyt—ye shall 'ave a bob for a drink out of my pay.' In the next few steps I came upon Belfast. He caught my arm with tremulous enthusiasm.—'I couldn't go wi' 'em,' he stammered, indicating by a nod our noisy crowd, that drifted slowly along the other sidewalk. 'When I think of Jimmy . . . . . Poor Jim! When I think of him I have no heart for drink. You were his chum, too . . . . but I pulled him out . . . . didn't I? Short wool he had . . . . . Yes. And I stole the blooming pie . . . . . He wouldn't go . . . . . He wouldn't go for nobody.' He burst into tears. 'I never touched him—never—never!' he sobbed. 'He went for me like . . . . like . . . . a lamb.'

I disengaged myself gently. Belfast's crying fits generally ended in a fight with some one, and I wasn't anxious to stand the brunt of his inconsolable sorrow. Moreover, two bulky policemen stood near by, looking at us with a disapproving and incorruptible gaze.— 'So long!' I said, and went off.

But at the corner I stopped to take my last look at the crew of the *Narcissus*. They were swaying irresolute and noisy on the broad flagstones before the Mint. They were bound for the Black Horse, where men, in fur caps, with brutal faces and in shirt sleeves, dispense out of varnished barrels the illusions of strength, mirth, happiness; the illusion of splendour and poetry of life, to the paid-off crews of southern-going ships. From afar I saw them discoursing, with jovial eyes and clumsy gestures, while the sea of life thundered into their ears ceaseless and unheeded. And swaying about there on the white stones, surrounded by the hurry and clamour of men, they appeared to be creatures of another kind— lost, alone, forgetful, and doomed; they were like castaways, like reckless and joyous castaways, like mad castaways making merry in the storm and upon an insecure ledge of a treacherous rock.

The roar of the town resembled the roar of topping breakers, merciless and strong, with a loud voice and cruel purpose; but overhead the clouds broke; a flood of sunshine streamed down the walls of grimy houses. The dark knot of seamen drifted in sunshine. To the left of them the trees in Tower Gardens sighed, the stones of the Tower gleaming, seemed to stir in the play of light, as if remembering suddenly all the great joys and sorrows of the past, the fighting prototypes of these men; press-gangs; mutinous cries; the wailing of women by the riverside, and the shouts of men welcoming victories. The sunshine of heaven fell like a gift of grace on the mud of the earth, on the remembering and mute stones, on greed, selfishness; on the anxious faces of forgetful men. And to the right of the dark group the stained front of the Mint, cleansed by the flood of light, stood out for a moment, dazzling and white, like a marble palace in a fairy tale. The crew of the *Narcissus* drifted out of sight.

I never saw them again. The sea took some, the steamers took others, the graveyards of the earth will account for the rest. Singleton has no doubt taken with him the long record of his faithful work into the peaceful depths of an hospitable sea. And Donkin, who never did a decent day's work in his life, no doubt earns his living by discoursing with filthy eloquence upon the right of labour to live. So be it! Let the earth and the sea each have its own.

A gone shipmate, like any other man, is gone for ever; and I never saw one of them again. But at times the spring-flood of memory sets with force up the dark River of the Nine Bends.[60] Then on the waters of the forlorn stream drifts a ship—a shadowy ship manned by a crew of Shades. They pass and make a sign, in a shadowy hail. Haven't we, together and upon the immortal sea, wrung out a meaning from our sinful lives? Good-bye, brothers! You were a good crowd. As good a crowd as ever fisted with wild cries the beating canvas of a heavy foresail; or tossing aloft, invisible in the night, gave back yell for yell to a westerly gale.

what happened to

Allistoun
Baker
creighton
Belfast
cook (podmore)
Charley
Archie

COMMENTARY

In this commentary, the following abbreviations are used:

B-A: Guy de Maupassant: *Bel-Ami* [1885] (Paris: Garnier, 1959).

CLJC: *The Collected Letters of Joseph Conrad*, Volume I, edited by Frederick R. Karl and Laurence Davies (Cambridge: Cambridge University Press, 1983).

LCG: *Joseph Conrad's Letters to R. B. Cunninghame Graham*, edited by Cedric Watts (London: Cambridge University Press, 1969).

LL: G. Jean-Aubry: *Joseph Conrad: Life and Letters* (London: Heinemann, 1927).

M: François VI de La Rochefoucauld: *Maximes* [1678], edited by Jacques Truchet (Paris: Garnier, 1967).

NLL: Joseph Conrad: *Notes on Life and Letters* [1921] (London: Dent, 1949).

PM: David Masters: *The Plimsoll Mark* (London: Cassell, 1955).

TA: Friedrich Nietzsche: *'Twilight of the Idols' and 'The Anti-Christ'*, translated by R. J. Hollingdale (Harmondsworth: Penguin, 1968).

TDT: Cedric Watts: *The Deceptive Text* (Brighton: Harvester, 1984).

TY: R. H. Dana: *Two Years before the Mast* [1840] (Harmondsworth: Penguin, 1981).

'TO MY READERS IN AMERICA'

1 (p. xlv): *He was in my watch*: Conrad told Jean-Aubry (LL I, pp. 77–8):

> I remember, as if it had occurred but yesterday, the last occasion
> I saw the Nigger. That morning I was quarter officer, and about five
> o'clock I entered the double-bedded cabin where he was lying full
> length..... I asked him how he felt, but he hardly made me any

answer. A little later a man brought him some coffee in a cup
provided with a hook to suspend it on the edge of the bunk. At
about six o'clock the officer-in-charge came to tell me that he was
dead. We had just experienced an awful gale in the vicinity of the
Needles, south of the cape, of which I have tried to give an impression in my book . . .

2 (p. xlvi): *W. E. Henley*: William Ernest Henley (1849–1903) was a
journalist, playwright and poet who edited the *National Observer* and
subsequently the *New Review*. A vigorous cripple with a wooden leg,
full of combative gusto in spite of his painful disability, he served as
the model for Long John Silver in Stevenson's *Treasure Island*. His
literary circle, the 'Henley Regatta', included Stevenson, Kipling,
Charles Whibley, J. M. Barrie and George Wyndham. Conrad was
introduced to him by William Heinemann, who owned the *New Review*
and was to publish the book of *The Nigger of the 'Narcissus'*. Conrad's
novel appears to echo not only Henley's muscular patriotism but also
his avowed hostility to socialists (particularly socialist demagogues),
sentimentalists, religious salvationists and philanthropic welfare-
schemes.

3 (p. xlvi): *its proper title*: The original American edition had been entitled
The Children of the Sea: A Tale of the Forecastle. (Its publishers believed
that prospective readers would not wish to purchase a book whose
title contained the word 'Nigger'.)

'PREFACE'

4 (p. xlvii): *It is otherwise with the artist*: Conrad's postulated contrast
between the modes of truth attainable by the artist and those attainable by 'the thinker or the scientist' extends a discussion which is at
least as old as the disagreement between Plato and Aristotle. Plato (in
Republic, Book X) argued that the artist takes us far from the truth, for
he offers only an imitation (the artefact) of an imitation (earthly
manifestations) of the eternal metaphysical Forms. Aristotle, on the
other hand, argued (in *Poetics*, Section 9) that the artist takes us
closer to the truth, for he reveals the general laws underlying particular appearances; hence 'poetry is something more philosophical
and more worthy of serious attention than history; for while poetry is
concerned with universal truths, history treats of particular facts'.
(*Classical Literary Criticism*, translated by T. S. Dorsch [Harmonds-
worth: Penguin, 1965], pp. 43–4.) In this respect, Conrad's view is
basically Aristotelian; but he also echoes the claim, so frequently

made by Romantic and post-Romantic writers in the nineteenth century (notably by Wordsworth, Shelley and George Eliot), that art enlarges our social sympathies by strengthening the 'conviction of solidarity' which 'knits together the loneliness of innumerable hearts'. Shelley, for example, had declared:

> What were Virtue, Love, Patriotism, Friendship &c. – what were the scenery of this beautiful Universe which we inhabit – what were our consolations on this side of the grave – and what were our aspirations beyond it – if Poetry did not ascend to bring light and fire from those eternal regions where the owl-winged faculty of calculation dare not ever soar?

('A Defence of Poetry' [1821] in *Shelley's Poetry and Prose* [New York: Norton, 1977], p. 503.)

Conrad may have been encouraged to write this preface by the example of Maupassant's defence of naturalism in the essay 'Le Roman', the preface to *Pierre et Jean* (1888); and some of the ideas probably derive from Schopenhauer's *Die Welt als Wille und Vorstellung* (1818) and Pater's *The Renaissance* (1873) and *Marius the Epicurean* (1885). What is distinctively Conradian is a voice which might be termed, in an appropriate oxymoron, that of Augustan Romanticism: he emphasizes both solidarity and isolation, both the value of moral affirmation and the difficulties of the conscientious devotion to the task.

5 (p. xlix): *music – which is the art of arts*: In 'The School of Giorgione' (1877), Walter Pater stated: '*All art constantly aspires towards the condition of music.*' This notion, deriving from Schopenhauer, had become an aesthetic commonplace by the 1890s; it was argued that music manifests that indivisibility of form and content to which the other arts aspire.

6 (p. xlix): *to make you see*: Conrad exploits the ambiguity of '*see*', which can mean both 'visualize' and (as in the exclamation 'I *see*!') 'comprehend' or 'gain insight'. Shelley's 'Defence of Poetry' had claimed that poetry 'purges from our inward sight the film of familiarity which obscures from us the wonder of our being. It compels us to feel that which we perceive, and to imagine that which we know.' (*Shelley's Poetry and Prose*, p. 505.) Schopenhauer had stated:

> The artist lets us see the world through his eyes. That he has these eyes, that he knows the inner nature of things apart from all their relations, is the gift of genius, is inborn; but that he is able to lend us this gift, to let us see with his eyes, is acquired, and is the technical side of art.

(The World as Will and Idea, translated by R. B. Haldane and J. Kemp, Vol. I [London: Routledge & Kegan Paul, 1883], p. 252.)

7 (p. xlix): *the core of each convincing moment*: The ideas in the first half of this paragraph may echo those in the famous 'Conclusion' of Walter Pater's *The Renaissance*; and Paul Kirschner has postulated a further debt to Schopenhauer's *The World as Will and Idea*, Vol. I, which, on p. 239, says:

> Art. . . . . plucks the object of its contemplation out of the stream of the world's course, and has it isolated before it. And this particular thing, which in that stream was a small perishing part, becomes to art the representative of the whole, an equivalent of the endless multitude in space and time.

8 (p. I): *Art for Art*: In 1804 Henry Crabb Robinson, explaining Kant's aesthetics to Benjamin Constant, coined the phrase 'Art for Art' or 'Art for Art's sake'. (Constant rendered his expression as 'l'art pour l'art, et sans but': see *Journaux intimes* [Paris: Gallimard, 1952], p. 58.) Echoed by Victor Cousin and Théophile Gautier, the phrase eventually became a slogan of the Aesthetic Movement of the late nineteenth century.

9 (p. I): *a labourer in a distant field*: This paragraph offers an urbanely modest and slyly ironic analogy between the labourer and the artist and between the condescending traveller and the patronizing (and forgetful) reader. To envisage the literary artist as a manual labourer is an apt strategy in an 'Author's Note' to a novel which often identifies the narrator with the toiling seamen.

10 (p. I): *Art is long and life is short*: translation of the Latin tag (deriving from Hippocrates), '*Ars longa vita brevis*'.

THE NIGGER OF THE 'NARCISSUS'

11 (p. liii): The epigraph: The punctuation of the epigraph on the title-page differs slightly from that of the sentence as it is given on p. 41 of *Diary and Correspondence of Samuel Pepys, F.R.S.*, Vol. I (London: Colburn, Hurst and Blackett, 1854): 'My Lord, in his discourse, discovered a great deal of love to this ship.' Pepys's 'Lord' was his cousin and employer, Sir Edward Montagu. The ship was the *Nazeby*, on which the exiled King Charles II was brought back to England at the restoration of the monarchy in 1660. Pepys himself was an industrious Secretary to the Admiralty during the reigns of Charles and James II.

The relevance of this epigraph to the novel may be obvious and

COMMENTARY

unsubtle. Montagu loved the *Nazeby*, and the novel's narrator records his affection for the *Narcissus*. But possibly there is a subtler connection. Pepys's *Diary* records the rejoicing when the monarch was brought home aboard the vessel, marking an end to the era of civil war, regicide and the Cromwellian Protectorate; so the epigraph may serve to emphasize the conservative implications of a text which describes the failure of an attempt to subvert the captain's authority and to foment mutiny aboard the *Narcissus*. As traditional rule was restored, after turmoil, to 'the ship of state', so traditional order is restored, after turmoil, to the ship *Narcissus*.

12 (p. lv): *Garnett*. Edward Garnett (1868–1939) was not only a shrewd and sensitive critic but also the most important British literary midwife in the period 1890–1920. As a 'publisher's reader' for Fisher Unwin, Duckworth and Heinemann, he helped into print the early work of numerous important and innovatory authors, among them Conrad, Cunninghame Graham, W. H. Hudson, Galsworthy, D. H. Lawrence and Dorothy Richardson. He gave detailed critical attention to manuscripts submitted to him, and particularly encouraged writers to strive for ironic, realistic and original effects. Since 1895 he had corresponded with Conrad, who told him: ' [T]he *Nigger* is *your* book'; and in changing the name of the character Sullivan to 'Singleton', Conrad may have been influenced by the fact that 'Singleton' was the maiden-name of Garnett's mother (who received a complimentary copy of the novel).

13 (p. 3): *'Pelham.'*: Edward George Bulwer-Lytton's novel *Pelham; or, The Adventures of a Gentleman* was first published in London in 1828; it describes the varied experiences of an aristocratic dandy, Henry Pelham, as he moves through high society. Bulwer-Lytton (1803–73) was a prolific author and, in the nineteenth century, a popular one. R. H. Dana, in *Two Years before the Mast* (1840), recalls the pleasure of finding one of Bulwer-Lytton's novels aboard the American sailing-ship *Pilgrim*:

> [O]ne of the men said he had a book which 'told all about a great highwayman,' at the bottom of his chest, and producing it, I found, to my surprise and joy, that it was nothing else than Bulwer's Paul Clifford. . . . . I shall never forget the enjoyment I derived from it. To come across anything with the slightest claims to literary merit, was so unusual, that this was a perfect feast to me. The brilliancy of the book, the succession of capital hits, lively and characteristic sketches, kept me in a constant state of pleasing sensations. It was far too good for a sailor.

(*TY*, pp. 249–50.)

14 (p. 4): *in the pose of a crouching chimera*: an echo of Maupassant's *Bel-Ami* (1885), Pt. I, Chapter 6 (*B-A*, p. 122): 'le chat dans la cheminée . . . . ., avec sa pose de Chimère accroupie' ('the cat by the fireplace . . . . ., in the pose of a crouching chimera').

15 (p. 5): *so I seez to him*: 'seez' (for 'says') is part of Conrad's attempt to suggest the accent of a seaman from Belfast in Northern Ireland. Conrad's strenuous endeavours, throughout this novel, to provide a range of vernacular dialogue are often successful but sometimes specious.

16 (p. 6): *an American ship*: American vessels were notorious for harsh conditions. Dana's *Two Years before the Mast* (Chapter 15) records the brutal floggings which the master of the brig *Pilgrim* administered to his crew; and in *Round the Horn before the Mast* (London: Murray, 1902), pp. 33–4, Basil Lubbock says:

> On some of the Yankee hell ships the things that go on are almost incredible, and the captains have to be skilled surgeons to cope with the work of destruction wrought by their mates.
>
> Legs and arms broken were considered nothing, ribs stamped in by heavy sea-boots had to mend as best they could, faces smashed like rotten apples by iron belaying pins had to get well or fear worse treatment, eyes closed up by a brawny mate's fist had to see. There have been many instances of men triced up in the rigging, stripped, and then literally skinned alive with deck-scrapers.
>
> Thus the reputation of American ships has got so bad that none but a real tough citizen . . . . . will ship on them.

Lubbock predictably claims that 'on board a British ship a sailor can get justice in port, and a captain or mate knows he will get heavy punishment for brutality' (p. 32).

17 (p. 7): *The pet of philanthropists and self-seeking landlubbers*: This statement anticipates the criticism (in Chapter IV) of Plimsoll and his supporters.

18 (p. 7): *Blamme if you don't look a blamed sight worse*: 'Blamme' and 'blamed' are Conrad's euphemisms for 'Damn me' and 'damned': the serial text gives '. . . . . dam sight worse'. Although Conrad made various euphemistic modifications, some early reviewers objected to the text's profanities.

19 (p. 8): *those weird visions that haunt the men of his race*: In *Two Years before the Mast*, Dana refers to the superstitious belief that Finns are 'wizards' with supernatural powers. (*TY*, p. 80.)

20 (p. 11): *got to call your name twice*: As the text has previously indicated, Wamibo is deaf; hence, in part, his 'dreamy' air.

21 (p. 11): 'Wait!': Wait is as ambiguous in his name (which is here mistaken for a command) as he will subsequently seem in his nature. The text will also exploit the homophonous association of 'Wait' and 'Weight'.

22 (p. 12): *the repulsive mask of a nigger's soul*: The racism of this passage can be mitigated by noting that it is the mask, rather than the soul, which is declared 'repulsive'; but the declaration remains irredeemably racist.

23 (p. 13): *'Is your cook a coloured gentleman?'*: One implication is that Wait hopes to gain preferential treatment when rations are issued or the galley's hospitality is sought. (Dana notes that seamen who are in the cook's favour 'can get their wet mittens and stockings dried, or light their pipes at the galley in the night watch' [*TY*, p. 51].)

24 (p. 13): *When on shore he took his family to church twice every Sunday*: Conrad's account of Podmore recalls Dana's description of the African cook in *Two Years before the Mast* (*TY*, p. 78), who

was rather seriously inclined, always going to church twice a day when on shore, and reading his Bible on a Sunday in the galley, talked to the crew about spending their Sabbaths badly, and told them that they might go as suddenly as George [a drowned shipmate] had, and be as little prepared.

25 (p. 16): *'We haven't kept pigs together'*: This is a translation of the Polish idiom, *'Razem żeśmy świń nie paśli'* (literally, 'We have not taken pigs to pasture together'): a rebuke to someone who has wrongly assumed social equality with the speaker. (See *Conradiana* XVII, 1985, pp. 143–4.)

26 (p. 17): *Well-meaning people . . . . . fear of their lives*: Samuel Plimsoll, M.P., had told the House of Commons in 1874 of seamen who, obliged to embark on unseaworthy vessels, had sadly foreseen that they would never return to their wives and children. (*PM*, pp. 196–7.)

27 (p. 17): *men who knew toil*: Carlyle's *Past and Present* [1843] (London: Chapman and Hall, 1904), pp. 168–9, says:

Think it not thy business, this of knowing thyself; thou art an unknowable individual: know what thou canst work at; and work at it, like a Hercules! . . . . . Consider how, even in the meanest sorts of Labour, the whole soul of a man is composed into a kind of real harmony, the instant he set himself to work!

28 (p. 18): *if they had learned how to speak they have also learned how to whine*: Shakespeare's Caliban says: 'You taught me language, and my profit on't / Is, I know how to curse' (*Tempest*, I.ii.363–4). In *Two Years before the Mast* (*TY*, p. 479), Dana concludes: 'I fully believe that

135

those efforts which have their end in the intellectual cultivation of the
sailor; . . . . . in giving him political information, and interesting him
in newspapers; . . . . . are all doing a harm which the labors of many
faithful men cannot undo.' In a letter to Cunninghame Graham (*LCG*,
pp. 53-4), Conrad declares that Singleton, as long as he lacks the
power to think, remains 'simple and great like an elemental force'.

29   (p. 23): *the characteristics of a gentleman*: This discussion may have
been prompted by Singleton's copy of *Pelham*. In Chapter 1 of that
novel, the hero remarks that gentlemen are distinguished by 'a calm,
imperturbable quiet', whereas 'low persons cannot take up either a
spoon or an affront without making such an amazing noise about it'.
The passage lends ironic force to the way in which, on the *Narcissus*,
the discussion becomes a noisy altercation. Incidentally, in the issue
of *The New Review* for July 1897 (p. 69), David Hannay claimed that
'the real conviction of the average Englishman. . . . . concerning what
makes the gentleman' was summed up by a steward who complained
of his naval employers, ' "They think themselves gentlemen, and there
ain't but very few of them 'oo has got anythink, but 'is pay" '.

30   (p. 26): *I dinna ken what's wrang wi' him*: Scots idiom for 'I don't
know what's wrong with him'.

31   (p. 37): *She. . . . . had a weakness*: subsequently explained as instability.

32   (p. 41): *The main-topsail had to be goose-winged*: The sail-area had to
be drastically reduced, most of the main-topsail being furled up to the
yard so that only a triangle of sail remained exposed to the wind.

33   (p. 43): *The masts! Cut! Cut!*: When a ship is thrown on her beam-
ends, one expedient is to cut away a mast or masts in the hope of
righting her. However, not all manuals of seamanship advocate this
course. *Captain Alston's Seamanship* (Portsmouth: Griffin, 1871), p.
207, certainly says:

> *Thrown on your Beam-ends.* – Let fly everything – when, if she
> does not right, or continues to go over, there is no resource left but
> to cut the lanyards of the weather rigging, if you have time, and let
> the masts go over the side . . . . .

And *Tait's New Seamanship* (Glasgow: Brown, 1907), p. 100, concurs:

> Up helm, let go the lee sheets, and try to get her off before the
> wind. If she does not right herself it may be advisable to cut away
> the mizzen mast.

On the other hand, R. H. Dana's *Seaman's Manual* (London: Moxon,
1863), pp. 68-9, says:

> *On Beam-Ends.* – A vessel is usually thrown upon her beam-
> ends by a sudden squall taking her, when under a press of sail, and
> shifting the ballast. She must be righted, if possible, without cutting

away her masts. For, besides sacrificing them, the object can seldom be accomplished in that way, if the ballast and cargo have shifted.

On the *Narcissus*, the master's decision not to cut is vindicated by the outcome.

34 (p. 56): *Vy donch 'ee 'it 'im*: 'Why don't you hit him?'

35 (p. 61): *we wondered*: In the previous paragraphs, the crew have been 'they'; now they are 'we'. The degree of objectivity associated with the third person plural had permitted the narrator to combine the account of the crew with a panoramic depiction of the ship amid nature ('the bestarred black dome of the sky revolved slowly above the ship, that drifted, bearing their patience and their suffering'); whereas the degree of subjectivity invoked by the first person plural has now licensed the narrator to share the uncertainties and limited knowledge of the crew ('He had done it somehow . . . . . For many days we wondered . . . . .').

36 (p. 62): '*Wear ship!*': The men now have to hoist sails and endeavour to turn the ship on to another tack, so that it may gain headway and then steerage. As the ship turns, increasingly the wind-direction is from astern; then the vessel struggles to right itself and eventually succeeds.

37 (p. 66): *sages, demanding bliss and an empty heaven*: This probably means: 'philosophers and theologians, who (although the heavens are empty) presumptuously claim heavenly felicity and eternal life'. The whole of this paragraph constitutes a sonorously august statement of hard anti-rational primitivism: the belief that a life of toil is better than a life of reflection.

38 (p. 71): 'Here, Taffy – take that, you thief!': an echo of the nursery rhyme which alleges 'Taffy was a Welshman, / Taffy was a thief'.

39 (p. 74): *a troubled stream from a poisoned source*: The depiction of Donkin brings to mind Nietzsche's words in *The Anti-Christ*:

Whom among today's rabble do I hate the most? The Socialist rabble, the Chandala apostles who undermine the worker's instinct, his pleasure, his feeling of contentment with his little state of being – who make him envious, who teach him revengefulness . . . . .

(*TA*, p. 179.)

40 (p. 75): *warning whisper*: In this sentence, Conrad offers a politicized version of the 'pathetic fallacy' (the attribution of human feelings to non-human nature): the wind and the sea regret and rebuke Donkin's anarchistic blandishments.

41 (p. 76): *a wealthy and well-fed crew of satisfied skippers*: Nietzsche (*TA*, p. 179) declares:

Injustice never lies in unequal rights, it lies in the claim to *'equal'* rights ... What is *bad?* But I have already answered that question: everything that proceeds from weakness, from envy, from *revengefulness.* – The anarchist and the Christian have a common origin.

In a letter commenting on Liberal successes in a general election, Conrad had said in 1885:

the International Socialist Association are triumphant, and every disreputable ragamuffin in Europe feels that the day of universal brotherhood, despoliation and disorder is coming apace, and nurses day-dreams of well-plenished pockets amongst the ruin of all that is respectable, venerable and holy.

(*CLJC*, p. 16.)

42   (p. 79): *that 'ere Plimsoll man*: A Plimsoll man is a follower of Samuel Plimsoll (1824–98), 'The Seaman's Friend', who campaigned in Parliament and throughout Britain on behalf of seamen imperilled by unseaworthy ships. Admittedly, Plimsoll's humanitarian zeal sometimes blinded him to the truth: David Masters (*PM*, p. 171) states:

Out of the first twenty-six ships he complained about, one was a hoax, one could not be found, one could not be held because she had left port on her voyage, one plied on a river and was too small to be legally subject to the jurisdiction of the Board of Trade. Of the rest, sixteen ships were found to be seaworthy and only three of those reported were in fact unseaworthy . . . . .

Plimsoll's writings and speeches made strongly emotive and sometimes sentimental appeals; and there is no doubt that he took much of the credit that should really have gone to James Hall, the initiator of various maritime reforms – including the adoption of the safety-mark which became known as the 'Plimsoll Line'.

The fact remains that Plimsoll's publicity ended numerous abuses and saved the lives of many seamen. Before those reforms, seamen who refused to serve on an unseaworthy vessel could be jailed, and often were. One of many examples is provided by the case of the ship *Wimbledon* which, in 1872, put into Cape Town overladen and leaking. The crew refused duty, were convicted of mutiny and given three months' hard labour. She was repaired and returned to Britain. At Cardiff a new crew, seeing her still-suspect condition, declined to sail, and in 1873 were jailed for ten weeks; while a further group of five recusants was sentenced to ten weeks' hard labour. (*PM*, p. 139.) The reforms which Plimsoll persuaded Parliament to enact in 1875 and 1876 made ships safer, improved the conditions of seamen, and

COMMENTARY

established Plimsoll himself as a national hero; and in 1877 he was appointed the first President of the National Amalgamated Sailors' and Firemen's Union.

Conrad's 'hard primitivism' and his nostalgic allegiance to maritime tradition have led him into defensive hostility against 'outsiders' who were concerned to humanize the tradition. Similarly, the narrative's thematic hostility to the sympathy which is really covert self-pity has here led the narrator to depict as ignorant sentimentality what in practice was often a knowledgeable concern for the exploited.

Fifteen years after writing *The Nigger*, however, Conrad paid due tribute to Plimsoll, remarking that overladen ships were sent to sea in the era 'before Samuel Plimsoll uplifted his voice' (*NLL*, p. 242).

43 (p. 88): *There's nothing the matter with you . . . . . and now you shall lie-up to please me*: Here the vice of 'tenderness' which is causing division in the crew has tainted the captain himself and will be a factor which helps to precipitate the near-mutiny. Allistoun has correctly perceived that Wait (who has suffered from tuberculosis throughout the voyage) had claimed to be too ill to work when he was actually fit for work, but is now claiming to be fit for work when actually he is mortally ill. However, instead of telling Wait the truth (that he should remain in his cabin because he is a dying man), Allistoun tells a compassionate lie by declaring that Wait is to be confined to his cabin as a punishment for malingering. Naturally, some members of the crew think that the captain is thus being unduly harsh, and their mutinous resentment increases. Allistoun himself subsequently recognizes the political error of his act of compassionate falsehood. 'Sorry for him. . . . . I thought I would let him go out in his own way. Kind of impulse. It never came into my head, those fools . . . . . H'm! Stand to it now – of course.' (P. 93.)

44 (p. 90): *fit emblem of their aspirations*: While the grotesque, vicious and thieving Donkin is presented as a spokesman for left-wing politics, here a 'moribund carcass' is presented as the 'emblem' of men who have acquired a rudimentary sense of trade-unionism.

45 (p. 91): *belaying-pin*: In throwing the belaying-pin, Donkin is taking appropriate revenge for the captain's threat (p. 63): 'I will brain you with this belaying-pin if you don't catch hold of the brace.'

46 (p. 96): *bringing all this head wind . . . . . Die in sight of land*: The supernatural 'covert plot' that is indicated here is subsequently endorsed by the text. When land is sighted, Wait dies; and, as soon as he is buried at sea, favourable winds at last start to blow. (See *TDT*, pp. 59–74.)

47 (pp. 102–3): *The latent egoism of tenderness to suffering appeared in the
developing anxiety not to see him die*: The *Maximes* of La Rochefoucauld
include the following remarks (*M*, pp. 67–8):

> La pitié . . . . . est une habile prévoyance des malheurs où nous
> pouvons tomber; nous donnons du secours aux autres pour les
> engager à nous en donner en de semblables occasions; et ces services
> que nous leur rendons sont à proprement parler des biens que nous
> nous faisons à nous-mêmes par avance. [Pity . . . . . is an astute
> precaution against the misfortunes into which we may fall; we give
> help to others in order to induce them to give it to us on comparable
> occasions; and these services which we render them are, properly
> speaking, benefits which we grant to ourselves in advance.]

In 'The Soul of Man under Socialism' (1891), Oscar Wilde declared:

> All sympathy is fine, but sympathy with suffering is the least fine
> mode. It is tainted with egotism. It is apt to become morbid. There is
> in it a certain element of terror for our own safety.

(*The Works of Oscar Wilde* [London: Spring Books, 1963], p. 934.)

48 (p. 103): *He was demoralising. Through him we were becoming highly
humanised, tender, complex, excessively decadent*: Some of the ideas in
this paragraph, and particularly the association of 'tenderness' with
'decadence', resemble those in Nietzsche's *Der Antichrist* (written in
1888, first published in 1895), section 7:

> Pity stands in antithesis to the tonic emotions which enhance
> the energy of the feeling of life: it has a depressive effect. One loses
> force when one pities. The loss of force which life has already
> sustained through suffering is increased and multiplied even further
> by pity. Suffering itself becomes contagious through pity; sometimes
> it can bring about a collective loss of life and life-energy. . . . . Pity
> on the whole thwarts the law of evolution, which is the law of
> *selection*. It preserves what is ripe for destruction; it defends life's
> disinherited and condemned. . . . . One has ventured to call pity a
> virtue (– in every *noble* morality it counts as weakness –). . . . . To
> say it again, this depressive and contagious instinct thwarts those
> instincts bent on preserving and enhancing the value of life: both as
> a *multiplier* of misery and as a *conservator* of everything miserable it
> is one of the chief instruments for the advancement of *décadence* –
> pity persuades to *nothingness*!

(*TA*, p. 118.)

49 (p. 105): *Wamibo's spells*: Dana's *Two Years before the Mast* (*TY*, pp.
80–81) offers a suitable gloss:

> [T]he cook . . . . . was fully possessed with the notion that Fins

[*sic*] are wizards, and especially have power over winds and storms. . . . . John, who was the oldest seaman aboard, ... sided with the cook, and said that he himself had been in a ship where they had a head wind for a fortnight, and the captain found out at last that one of the men, whom he had had some hard words with a short time before, was a Fin, and immediately told him if he didn't stop the head wind he would shut him down in the fore peak. . . . . The Fin held out for a day and a half, when he could not stand it any longer, and did something or other which brought the wind round again, and they let him up.

50 (p. 114): *Jimmy's respiration was so rapid that it couldn't be counted, so faint that it couldn't be heard*: In *Conrad: The Psychologist as Artist* (Edinburgh: Oliver and Boyd, 1968), pp. 200–205, Paul Kirschner has pointed out that various details in Conrad's description of Wait's death have been borrowed from the account of Charles Forestier's death in Maupassant's novel *Bel-Ami*. Here Conrad is recalling 'L'haleine de Forestier était . . . . . si pressée qu'on ne la pouvait point compter, et si faible qu'on l'entendait à peine'. ['Forestier's respiration was . . . . . so rapid that it couldn't be counted, and so weak that it could hardly be heard.'] (*B-A*, p. 175.)

51 (p. 114): *His eyes were terrified. . . . . 'Overboard! . . . I! . . . My God!'*: Compare Maupassant's *Bel-Ami* (*B-A*, p. 175):

Il regardait devant lui quelque chose d'invisible pour les autres et de hideux, dont ses yeux fixes reflétaient l'épouvante. . . . .

Soudain il tressaillit d'un frisson brusque qu'on vit courir d'un bout à l'autre de son corps et il balbutia: – Le cimetière . . . moi . . . mon Dieu!

[He gazed before him at something invisible to the others and so hideous that his staring eyes reflected the terror . . . . .

Suddenly an abrupt shudder convulsed his body from end to end, and he stammered: 'The cemetery! . . . I! . . . My God!']

52 (p. 114): *His two long bony hands smoothed the blanket upwards*: In *Bel-Ami*, the dying Forestier's hands move continuously over his bed, 'comme pour recueillir quelque chose sur les draps' ['as if to gather something from the sheets']. (*B-A*, p. 175.)

53 (p. 114): *avoiding to glance at Jimmy*: 'refraining from glancing at Jimmy' is the sense.

54 (p. 115): *. . . . Jimmy's eyes. . . . . like two lamps . . . . . a scarlet thread . . . . . he had ceased to breathe*: In *Bel-Ami*, Duroy observes thus Forestier's final moments:

Il ouvrit les yeux juste à temps pour voir Forestier fermer les siens comme deux lumières que s'éteignent . . . . ., et deux filets de sang apparurent aux coins de sa bouche. . . . . Il avait fini de respirer. [He opened his eyes just in time to see Forestier's eyes close like two lamps extinguished . . . . ., and, at the corners of Forestier's mouth, two threads of blood appeared. . . . . He had ceased to breathe.] (B-A, pp. 175-6.)

55 (p. 118): *'To the deep'*: The service for the burial of the dead at sea (in the Anglican *Book of Common Prayer*) includes the words: 'We therefore commit his body to the deep, to be turned into corruption.'

56 (p. 118): *Wait gave no sign of going*: Even in death, Jimmy will wait – true to his name.

57 (p. 119): *The ship rolled as if relieved of an unfair burden*: another play on the homophonic association of 'Wait' and 'weight'.

58 (p. 122): *Brick walls rose high above the water*: St Katharine's Dock, near Tower Bridge, boasted 'sturdy warehouses of yellow brickwork, six floors high, ... to house such commodities as tea, rubber, wool, marble, sugar, tallow, matches and live turtles. The warehouses were unusual in being built close to the water. . . . . The lock to the river was somewhat narrow and could not admit larger ships.' (*The London Encyclopaedia*, edited by B. Weinreb and C. Hibbert [London: Macmillan, 1983], p. 729).

59 (p. 126): *Tower Hill*: The subsequent description of this area near the Tower of London is echoed in the opening of Conrad's *Chance* (London: Methuen, 1914), p. 4:

At that time the Marine Board examinations took place at the St. Katharine's Dock House on Tower Hill, and he informed us that he had a special affection for the view of that historic locality, with the Gardens to the left, the front of the Mint to the right, the miserable tumble-down little houses farther away, a cabstand, boot-blacks squatting on the edge of the pavement and a pair of big policemen gazing with an air of superiority at the doors of the Black Horse public-house across the road.

60 (p. 128): *the spring-flood of memory sets with force up the dark River of the Nine Bends*: In classical mythology, the dark 'River of the Nine Bends' is the 'ninefold' (*novies*) River Styx, across which the shades of the dead are borne (Virgil: *Aeneid* VI, line 439); but the context here indicates that Conrad is thinking predominantly of another underworld river, Lethe, the stream of oblivion. The narrator's statement could therefore be paraphrased: 'Although those seamen are gone and generally forgotten, sometimes my memory rescues them from oblivion.'

GLOSSARY

abaft: behind; in or towards the rear half of a vessel. *Abaft the beam*: to the
rear of the widest part of the vessel.

accommodation-ladder: removable ladder suspended from the side of a ship.

adze: cutting tool with an arched blade at right-angles to the handle.

aft: towards the stern.

all-fired (slang): hell-fired, infernal.

anchor-shackle: U-shaped link closed by a bolt through its two ends, used for
joining lengths of anchor-chain.

anna: Indian coin.

'baccy (slang): tobacco.

balancing (p. 116): wavering, swaying. (A Gallicism.)

band-box: light box for hats, caps, millinery, etc.; originally for clerical
bands.

battens: wooden or metal slats which fit through staples to secure the
tarpaulins covering hatches.

beak (slang): judge or magistrate.

beam: maximum width. *Beam ends*: ends of the transverse beams (timbers)
of a ship. *On her beam ends*: on her side.

belaying-pin: baton of metal or wood which fits a pin-rail; the end of a rope
can then be belayed (secured) to it.

bells: the bell is struck once for each half hour that has passed during the
four-hour watch; so 'four bells' indicate that two hours have passed, and
'eight bells' indicate that that watch has ended.

bend: secure. *Bend canvas*: secure sails to spars. *Bend the down-haul clear*:
secure the sail-rope tidily.

berth: (i) sleeping-place; (ii) mooring-place.

bights (p. 2): curves or coils.

binnacle: compass-container fitted with a lamp and mounted on a *binnacle-stand*.

Black Horse: tavern which formerly faced the Board of Trade Office at Tower Hill.

block: pulley or pulleys set within a frame or case.

boatswain: foreman of the crew; immediate overseer of work on ship's boats, rigging, etc.

bob: shilling, a sum or coin worth one-twentieth of one pound sterling. *Three bob*: three shillings.

bolster (noun): long pillow or cushion. *Bolster it up*: support it as with a cushion.

bone (slang): steal.

bosun: see *boatswain*.

bows: forward part of a vessel, where it curves to the stem.

bowsprit: heavy spar, projecting forward from the vessel, to which the headsails are set.

brace: rope connected to a yard and used to turn it. *Braces were rove* (p. 69): ropes were passed through blocks or holes.

break of the poop: foremost part of the raised rear deck.

B.T.: Board of Trade.

bulkhead: vertical partition.

bulwark: ship's side above deck-level.

Byculla: a central district of the city of Bombay (to the west of Bombay Harbour).

Canton Street: street then frequented by prostitutes, near the East India Docks.

Cape of Good Hope: cape near the southern tip of Africa.

caper (slang): reprehensible conduct or scheme.

capstan: machine, by which ropes or chains are wound, consisting of a rotating barrel on a vertical pivot.

caryatides: statues of female figures, serving as columns to support an entablature.

chain compressor: iron device to check the outgoing anchor-chain.

chimera: fabulous monster with a lion's head and a goat's body.

China Station: China Sea as a region of naval duties.

Chips: nickname of ship's carpenter.

chokey (slang): jail.

chops of the Channel: expanse of water (between Cornwall and Brittany) where the Atlantic Ocean meets the English Channel.

chronometer: sea-going clock, fitted with gimbals to neutralize the swaying of the vessel.

chump: block, lump; head (slang); hence *off his chump*: out of his mind, mad.

cleet (usually *cleat*): piece of wood or metal with two horns around which ropes are fastened.

close-hauled: with sails set away from square so that the vessel points as much against the wind as is consistent with making progress.

Clyde: the River Clyde in Scotland, then famous for its shipbuilding yards.

companion: covering over the entrance to a vessel's stairway (companion-ladder).

contemn: despise.

coon (slang, from racoon): timid creature (p. 79; cf. *LCG*, p. 153).

costermonger: street-vendor, barrow-boy.

counter: the curving part of a vessel's hull towards the stern, and the underside of its overhang.

crank (adjective): unstable.

crosshead of the windlass: beam that supports the windlass (machine for hoisting the anchor).

Dago (slang): man of Spanish or Portuguese origin (from Spanish name Diego).

dandy (adjective): fine, smart.

deadeye: flat round block of wood with three holes (used for retaining the mainmast ropes). *Lower deadeyes*: similar blocks used to connect the mainmast ropes to the deck-railing.

Dervish: Muslim ascetic noted for wild dancing and chanting.

dhow: Arab vessel with triangular sail or sails.

doctor: nickname of ship's cook (who sometimes administered medicine).

Dogger Bank: submerged sand-bank, 170 miles long, in the North Sea.

dog-watches: periods of duty from 4 to 6 p.m. and 6 to 8 p.m.

Downs: part of the English Channel between the eastern coast of Kent and the Goodwin Sands.

dunnage (slang): baggage.

Dutch Uncle (proverbial): one who delivers a stern reprimand.

Dutchy (slang): person deemed to be Dutch; though the term was used very loosely, and Basil Lubbock (in *Round the Horn before the Mast*, 1902) remarks that '"Dutchmen" include Germans, Swedes, Danes, Russians, Russian Finns, and Norwegians'.

East-end (adjective): from the working-class areas of East London.

fall: rope connected to a block and used for hoisting and lowering.

fashing yourself (Scots idiom): distressing or vexing yourself.

fife rail: pin-rail set in a semi-circle round the mast.

fist (verb): handle promptly a rope or sail.

Flores: western island of the Azores archipelago.

fluke: barb of an anchor.

fo'c'sle (abbreviation of *forecastle*): raised foremost deck, and the crew's accommodation within that foremost area.

forebrace: rope attached to the fore yard-arm, for changing the position of the foresail.

fore-capstan: cylindrical winch, standing on the forecastle, for raising anchors, hoisting yards, etc.

forecastle: see *fo'c'sle*.

forepeak hatch: square opening (and its cover) between the forecastle and the hold beneath it.

fore rigging: rigging of the foremast and its yards.

foresail: lowest of the sails on the foremast.

foresheet cleat: metal bracket to which a rope of the foresail can be fastened.

foretack: rope attached to the lowest windward corner of the foresail.

fore-topmast staysail: triangular sail set from the fore topmast stay (supporting-rope).

fore-topsails: on the foremast, the second and third sails up.

foreyard: on the foremast, the yard (spar) from which the lowest sail is suspended.

forward: near the bow.

'Full and by': 'Steer the ship so that it points as much towards the wind as is compatible with preserving the retention of the wind by the sails and thereby maintaining progress.'

funk: fear.

gaff-topsail hat: top hat.

galley: ship's kitchen.

gantline: rope (passing through a block) used to hoist a sail.

gin block: pulley in a hooked frame, used for raising or lowering cargo.

goose-winged sail: sail partly furled so that only a triangular area is left exposed to the wind.

greenhorn: novice.

Hallelujah: nickname for Christian bigot or pietist.

halyards: ropes or tackles for hoisting sails and yards.

ha'penny (pronounced 'hape-nee'): halfpenny, a copper coin of low value.

hard bread: ship's biscuits.

'*Hard-up* . . . . .*!*': 'The wheel has been turned so that the rudder swings to leeward and the vessel accordingly turns away from the wind . . . . .!'

hatches: square openings (and their covers) in a ship's deck.

'*Haul out!*': 'Pull the sail-ropes to adjust the sails and thus change the ship's course!'

hawse-pipe: metal tube through which anchor-cable runs.

head-earring: small rope to fasten the upper edge of a sail to a yard, or to reef the sail.

head sheet: rope at the lower corner of a headsail (fore-and-aft sail in front of the foremast).

head wind: wind directly opposing the vessel's course.

'*Helm up!*': 'Turn the wheel so that the vessel's bows swing away from the wind!'

Highway: road running past the dock areas of Wapping and Shadwell on the Thames at London.

hintymate: intimate.

holystone: brick of sandstone used for cleaning decks.

hooker (slang): oldfashioned or clumsy vessel.

house (p. 91): deckhouse, building on deck.

inabordable (French): inaccessible, unapproachable. *More inabordable than a hedgehog*: more hostile to the grasp than a prickly hedgehog.

incult: wild, uncultivated.

Jack: (i) sailor (slang); (ii) flag or ensign; (iii) nickname of Knowles.

jib-boom: spar (projecting from the front of the ship) which bears the foot of the triangular jib-sail.

joker (slang): odd character.

kid: tub or pan in which forecastle rations are carried. *On the kid*: kidding, teasing, bantering.

landlubbers: landsmen ignorant of ships and maritime ways.

lanyard: rope that is threaded through deadeyes to secure the rigging. *Lanyard knot*: knot made in the end of a lanyard to prevent its slipping through a deadeye.

lee: on the sheltered or downwind side. *Leeward* (pronounced 'loo-erd'): downwind.

liberty-man: sailor with permission to go ashore.

light airs: air-currents just sufficient to propel a sailing-ship (force 1 on the Beaufort Scale).

'*Light-to!*': 'Haul the rope to provide enough slack for it to be eventually secured with several turns!'

lubbers: lazy or clumsy fellows (or possibly landsmen). *Lubberly*: land-lubberly, ignorant of ships.

luffed up through a public-house or two: made a halting and ungainly progress through some taverns.

main brace: long rope attached to the end of the mainyard.

main deck: plank platform extending the length and breadth of a vessel.

main-hatch: square opening (and its cover) in the deck before the mainmast.

main-topsail: on the mainmast, the second sail up.

'Make fast!' (p. 68): 'Secure the sail-ropes!'

marlinspike: pointed steel tool for separating the strands of a rope in splicing.

maul: heavy hammer.

meed: reward.

midship-stop: rope rising from the midpoint (bunt) of the foot-rope of a square sail, to prevent the sail from bulging outwards when it is being furled.

milch-cow: cow kept for her milk. *As smart about the deck as a milch-cow on her first voyage*: extremely clumsy.

Mint: Royal Mint on Tower Hill, where the coins of the realm were struck.

mizen rigging: ropes of the mizzenmast (rear mast).

mizen topsails: on the mizzenmast, the second and third sails up.

monsoon: seasonal wind of the Indian Ocean (and other tropical areas).

mooned at our work: worked aimlessly.

mug (slang): face.

nigger: then a widely-used familar (and frequently derogatory) term for a dark-skinned person of African origin.

night-watch: The 'first night-watch' is the period of duty from 8 p.m. until midnight.

North Britain: archaic or derogatory English name for Scotland.

oilskins: cotton garments waterproofed by impregnation with linseed oil.

ould: (supposedly Irish pronunciation of) old.

pannikin: small metal cup.

paregoric: soothing medicine which sometimes contained opium.

Pentland Firth: channel between the Orkney Islands and the northernmost mainland of Scotland.

Peterhead: fishing-port (then famed for its whalers) of north-east Scotland.

pice: Indian copper coin of low value.

pin: wooden or metal peg which fits into the pin-rail, for securing the rigging.

Plimsoll man: proponent of the reforms advocated and established by Samuel Plimsoll (1824–98) to prevent the overloading of ships.

poop: high deck at the stern of a vessel.

port: (i) left side of a vessel, as one faces forwards; (ii) opening in the side of a vessel; (iii) the door, gate or covering of such an opening.

public-house: tavern.

Puget Sound: waterway and anchorage extending northwards from Seattle in the State of Washington (and eventually connecting, via the Strait of Juan de Fuca, with the Pacific Ocean).

putting on airs: adopting an unwarranted attitude of superiority.

quarter: either side of the rear part of a vessel (between the beam and the stern).

quarter-checks: ropes extending from the poop or quarter-deck to the dock walls on each side in order to keep the stern centred and prevent a scrape.

quarter-deck: length of the main deck between the poop and the mainmast.

quarter-hatch: square opening (and its cover) in the quarter-deck.

rampin': raging.

ratlines: rope rungs.

reefed sails: sails furled or folded.

reeve: pass a rope through a block or hole.

relieving tackle: tackle set on either side of a tiller to reduce the strain put on the gear by heavy seas.

Rennie boat: naval steamship of the type designed and built by John T. Rennie and Son, Ltd., London.

riding-light: white light set in a ship's rigging when the vessel rides at anchor at night.

rovings: loosely twisted lengths of fibrous material.

ructions: disturbances, noisy recriminations.

rumour: murmur.

rupee: Indian silver coin.

saraband: slow Spanish dance.

savee enough: sufficient intelligence.

savoir vivre (French): knowledge of the ways of the world.

Scandinavian Home: Scandinavian Sailors' Temperance Home by the West India Dock.

scend: quick upward motion of a pitching vessel.

screw-brake: brake that checks a windlass-chain.

scupper (noun): hole in a vessel's side to drain the deck.

sea (as in *knocked down by a sea*): great wave.

shackle: U-shaped iron with a pin across its open ends; often used for connecting lengths of chain.

sheets: ropes used to control sails.

shellback: experienced seaman.

shore-going rig: smart outfit of clothing to wear ashore.

shrouds: wire ropes extending from the mast-head to the ship's sides, in order to support the mast.

skeary greenhorn (slang): frightened ('scary') novice.

sojer (slang): malingerer or shirker.

sounding-rod: iron rod used by the ship's carpenter to assess the depth of water in the bilges.

South Foreland: eastern headland of Kent, near Dover.

sou'wester: (i) waterproof hat extending over the back of the neck; (ii) wind from the south-west.

spanker: fore-and-aft sail set from the rear mast.

sparrer: (Cockney pronunciation of) sparrow.

spars: stout poles used as masts or sail-supports.

split on me (colloquial): betray me by giving information.

springbok: South African antelope.

spunger: sponger, parasite.

spunyarn rovings: small ropes in lengths of two- or three-stranded material loosely twisted together.

square mainsail coat: frock-coat.

square yards: sail-spars set at right-angles to the fore-and-aft line of a vessel.

stanchion: upright supporting-post.

starboard: right side, relative to a forward-facing position.

St. Kitt's: Saint Christopher's Island in the British West Indies.

stream cable: close-linked anchor-chain.

'Strook 'im!': 'Strike him!'

stunsail: auxiliary sail on either side of a square sail.

swell around: behave arrogantly (like a 'swell', an ostentatiously prosperous person).

sybarite: person devoted to luxury, like an inhabitant of ancient Sybaris in Italy.

Taffy (slang): Welshman.

'Tally on to that gantline.': 'Together seize the rope to haul the sail to the masthead.'

tap-room: tavern-room where beer is served from the cask.

taytottlers: (supposedly Irish pronunciation of) teetotallers: people pledged to total abstinence from alcohol.

tech: touch.

tide-rode: borne by the tide.

tinkers (derogatory): botchers or bunglers.

toff (slang): upper-class or upper-middle-class (or imposingly dressed) male.

togs (slang): clothes.

top-gallant rail: hand-rail of the forecastle.

topmast: section between the lower mast and the topgallant mast.

topmast stunsail: light sail set from an extension of the yard-arm on the topmast.

topped his boom (slang): fled, departed.

topsails: sails next beneath the uppermost (royal) sails. *Lower topsail*: second sail up.

Tower Hill: road and hill to the rear of the Tower of London, above St Katharine's Dock and near the Royal Mint.

trade (wind): *north-east trade*: regular wind which, in the northern hemisphere, blows from the north-east towards the equator; *south-east trade*: regular wind which, in the southern hemisphere, blows from the southeast towards the equator. *Sunshine of the trade*: sunshine of the tropical latitudes across which the trade winds blow.

trivet: tripod. *Right as a trivet*: steady as a tripod; sound and reliable.

truck: disc of wood which caps a mast.

two poun' ten: wage of two pounds and ten shillings.

vang: rope leading from the peak of a gaff (spar rising from the after side of a mast) to the rails.

washboard: (p. 36) board fastened to lower part of a door to prevent the ingress of water; (p. 44) board fastened to bulwarks to check the ingress of water.

watch: (i) period of duty; (ii) group of men allotted to a period of duty.

Watkinses: steam tugs of the kind owned by the firm of William Watkins.

'Wear ship!':'Turn the ship round so as to bring her on to another tack!'

weather (adjective): windward; thus *weather bow*: side of the ship's front against which the wind blows.

well: cylindrical chamber around the pump in the hold.

Western Islands: Azores, in the North Atlantic, far to the west of Portugal.

Western Ocean: North Atlantic.

Whitechapel: nickname of a cockney or lower-class Londoner (after the working-class district of Whitechapel in East London).

White Star boats: passenger steamships of the White Star line (which plied between Liverpool and New York).

GLOSSARY

whopped (slang): whipped, struck or thrashed.

windlass: machine for hoisting the anchor. *Barrel of the windlass*: horizontally mounted cylinder on which the anchor-chain is wound.

windward: side against which the wind blows.

worrums (vernacular): worms.

Yankee fashion: brutally, as on some American vessels.

yard: spar crossing a mast horizontally, from which a square sail is set. *Yard-arm*: port or starboard half of a spar.

Yellow Jack: (i) yellow fever, an acute tropical disease characterized by jaundice; (ii) yellow quarantine flag signalling the presence of contagious disease.